A Very Village Scandal

Where love can be found at every turn

Whittleston-on-the-Water is a quaint village on the banks of the Thames, now under the ownership of the new Lord Hockley. Far from the Mayfair ballrooms, life still bustles and buzzes with scandalous gossip, simmering passion and unexpected love...

Read Sophie and Rafe's story in
The Earl's Inconvenient Houseguest

And look for Isobel and Ned's story
Coming soon

Author Note

I live to the east of London in the ancient county of Essex, a stone's throw from the River Thames where it empties into the sea. It is an area rich in history, largely because it is peppered with the ports that serve the capital, and although technology has lessened the burden on the river, ships from all over the world still float past daily.

Essex is also the home of the quintessential English village. I might be only half an hour from one of the busiest cities on the planet, but I am also thirty minutes away from wonky thatched cottages, medieval churches, Tudor pubs and winding country lanes. It is these that have been the inspiration of my new A Very Village Scandal series.

For a change, I decided to bring the Regency out of the ballrooms of Mayfair and away from the lords and ladies of the *ton*. To explore the lives and loves of more common folk—the farmers, innkeepers, doctors, butchers, bakers and candlestick makers—I created Whittleston-on-the-Water. It's a quaint, ramshackle but thriving village on the banks of the Thames bustling with busybodies, where everybody knows everyone's business and there are shenanigans aplenty. I hope you enjoy it!

VIRGINIA HEATH

The Earl's Inconvenient Houseguest

HARLEQUIN®
HISTORICAL™

Recycling programs
for this product may
not exist in your area.

ISBN-13: 978-1-335-40768-9

The Earl's Inconvenient Houseguest

Copyright © 2022 by Susan Merritt

This edition published by arrangement with Harlequin Books S.A.

For questions and comments about the quality of this book, please contact us at CustomerService@Harlequin.com.

Harlequin Enterprises ULC
22 Adelaide St. West, 41st Floor
Toronto, Ontario M5H 4E3, Canada
www.Harlequin.com

Printed in U.S.A.

When **Virginia Heath** was a little girl, it took her ages to fall asleep, so she made up stories in her head to help pass the time while she was staring at the ceiling. As she got older, the stories became more complicated—sometimes taking weeks to get to their happy ending. One day she decided to embrace her insomnia and start writing them down. Virginia lives in Essex, UK, with her wonderful husband and two teenagers. It still takes her forever to fall asleep...

Books by Virginia Heath

Harlequin Historical

His Mistletoe Wager
Redeeming the Reclusive Earl
The Scoundrel's Bartered Bride
Christmas Cinderellas
"Invitation to the Duke's Ball"

A Very Village Scandal

The Earl's Inconvenient Houseguest

The Talk of the Beau Monde

The Viscount's Unconventional Lady
The Marquess Next Door
How Not to Chaperon a Lady

Secrets of a Victorian Household

Lilian and the Irresistible Duke

The King's Elite

The Mysterious Lord Millcroft
The Uncompromising Lord Flint
The Disgraceful Lord Gray
The Determined Lord Hadleigh

Visit the Author Profile page
at Harlequin.com for more titles.

This series is dedicated to my adopted home of Essex, unfairly maligned by the uninitiated, but a diamond of the first water when you scratch beneath the surface.

Chapter One

February 1818

'He is a former military man, apparently. Fought at Waterloo.'

Mrs Outhwaite leaned forward and lowered her voice to the circle of ladies unsubtly eyeing the latest arrival to Whittleston-on-the-Water with barely disguised interest. As openly staring didn't sit well with Sophie, she instead made a great show of inspecting some apples on a market stall while surreptitiously sneaking the odd peek at their handsome and well-proportioned new lord of the manor while he loitered outside the smithy.

'He's from the distant Somerset branch of the Peel family and is—or rather was—Lord Hockley's second cousin. Another only child, of course, because at best the Peels only ever seem to manage one heir at a time. They are a *very* unfertile family. Lady Hockley, God rest her, was as barren as a desert and I hear the new earl's mother turned up her toes less than a year after he was born so there is no spare on that branch of the rotten tree either. No money neither, by all accounts, so he's had quite the windfall.'

Mrs Outhwaite was a shameless gossip who said exactly what she wanted irrespective of whether it was appropriate. Not that any of those gathered would dare to pull her up in her lack of propriety, for aside from being the wife of the owner of the *South Essex Gazette* and therefore the single best source for any local gossip for miles around, she could turn against you on a sixpence and had a tongue far more acid than it was loose. Sophie had certainly felt the sting of it whenever she had to disagree over the years, which thanks to her own inability to keep quiet had been more often than she could count. However, since her over-dramatic aunt's health had genuinely deteriorated, she was trying very hard to pick her battles carefully and this one wasn't a worthy enough cause to don her armour and throw caution to the wind for. Besides, Sophie was as curious and concerned about the latest addition to the village as the rest of them were.

'However...' Mrs Outhwaite dropped her voice and, as one, all the gathered ladies leaned closer. 'Yesterday, when the butcher made his weekly delivery to the big house, he thinks he overheard the housekeeper tell the butler that she overheard the new Lord Hockley telling his solicitor that he has no interest in the estate and has no plans to ever live here. All he cares about is the money!'

'He said that?' Aunt Jemima was as appalled by his alleged attitude as all the other ladies, never mind that the tenuous allegations came from an apparently overheard conversation of an overheard conversation. 'How mercenary!' She flapped her hand in front of her face as if she was about to have one of her legendary attacks of the vapours and instinctively Sophie rummaged in her reticule for the smelling salts she always carried for just such an eventuality. Although this time she did not roll her eyes at the affectation as she passed them over, because her aunt was genuinely ill this time—and not just with her nerves—and all the stress of the current uncertainty wasn't good for her.

'Mark my words!' Mrs Outhwaite shook her finger heavenward like a fire and brimstone preacher at the pulpit. 'This is another Hinkwell-on-the-Hill and he is already plotting to sell the land from under us!'

All the ladies gasped in horrified unison as they contemplated the worst. Nobody wanted a Hinkwell-on-the-Hill to happen here, but the stark reality was they were all powerless to stop it if the wheels were put in motion. In addition to his large estate to the west of the village, Lord Hockley owned practically all the land which bordered it. Which meant he was the landlord of practically every acre within a five-mile radius, most of the buildings within them and the walls of every single shop on this market square.

That alone did not make their village unique by any stretch, as there were likely hundreds the length and breadth of the country in a similar boat, but all but three paltry acres of the Hockley estate were unentailed—which left them vulnerable. Especially with their proximity to the capital and the convenience of the River Thames literally on their doorstep, Whittleston-on-the-Water was a very tempting prospect for those with delusions of grandeur. Decent land around here was scarce and went for a premium. A fact the unfortunate residents of the nearby village of Hinkwell had found out the hard way only four summers ago when their local squire sold the lot to the wealthy owner of a shipping fleet for an eye-watering sum.

At the time, nobody had worried about the transaction because the huge swathes of land had changed hands many times since the *Domesday Book*—but then the eviction notices began to arrive. Within months, the shipping magnate had thrown every villager out and then razed poor Hinkwell-on-the-Hill to the ground. On that hill now stood the most ostentatious mansion anyone had ever seen, and instead of the centuries-old thriving farms and vibrant local industry which he had claimed spoiled his view, there now stood acre upon acre of artificial parkland filled with imported grouse and deer. All put there by the selfish new owner to occasionally hunt when he left the capital long enough to play lord of the manor or wanted to impress his business associates or court more high society friends on his way up the ladder.

As the eyes widened around her, Mrs Outhwaite stared horrified at the newcomer as if he were the Devil incarnate. 'Old Hockley's mean blood courses through his veins and *his* determined silence is deafening. Mark my words, if the new lord gets his wicked way, we shall all be homeless by Christmas!'

All eyes swivelled across the square to the man in question. Even Sophie's briefly left the apples to rake him up and down, and as if he sensed the intense scrutiny, their new landlord turned his back to them to stare at a wall. Worryingly aloof and detached from all the market day hubbub around him as if he cared not one jot for their little village or the people within it at all.

The self-appointed harbinger of doom gestured expansively around her, intent on terrifying her captive audience irrespective of whether the apparent villain of the piece was nearby. 'And all of this will be gone by next summer!'

While Sophie always tried to take most of what Mrs Outhwaite said with a large pinch of salt, there was no denying his standoffishness today when the square was full with yet another bad omen.

In the eight days the new lord had been in residence, he had done his utmost to keep himself very much to himself and seemed in no hurry to do anything to alter that state of affairs. Even to his closest neighbours, of which she was one, he had been noticeable by his absence. So far, he had received only a few of the gentleman callers—briefly—but kept his own counsel about his plans during those woefully short interactions, even when directly asked. The only person he did receive, and daily, was Mr Spiggot the solicitor and he was duty bound not to reveal any of those private discussions at the risk of being disbarred. However, she wasn't the only one to have noticed that the usually jovial local solicitor was now pale-faced and withdrawn whenever he visited the village. He could barely meet anyone's eye this morning as he scurried across the square and that was as out of character for him as it was for Sophie to bite her tongue.

All very worrying indeed.

Today, on his first venture into the village proper, the new Lord Hockley had tipped his hat good morning to every person he passed—albeit begrudgingly—then sailed on by unsmiling like a standoffish man on a mission. Perfectly content to remain an enigma and obviously desirous of being left well alone even though Mr Spiggot would have informed him in their first meeting that he held the entire fate of the village in his hands, and everyone who lived in it was on tenterhooks.

In truth, his determined silence was indeed ominous. That was why gossip was rife. In the absence of any concrete facts, the neighbourhood, like Mrs Outhwaite, was coming to its own apocalyptic and probably prophetic conclusions.

That didn't mean Sophie didn't wince a bit at the older woman's public venom.

While it was true none of his neighbours had had much affection for the recently deceased earl, largely because he had been a thoroughly horrid man for the entirety of his life, it felt wrong to tar his replacement with the same brush based on wild assumptions which were, as yet, wholly groundless. The new Earl of Hockley might well be a perfectly affable gentleman for all they knew, generous in both spirit and in deed, and a man who took his responsibilities seriously. Therefore, he surely deserved the benefit of the doubt until he proved otherwise? Especially if their family connection was as distant as it seemed to be. Somerset was a good hundred and fifty miles from this sleepy little enclave near the Thames and nobody had ever seen him before. With his rugged good looks, windswept sandy hair, piercing blue eyes and exceedingly broad shoulders, her wayward and wanton eyes would have certainly remembered him if she had.

'We are in grave danger of upsetting ourselves unduly with wild speculations and tenuous hearsay. I am not sure anybody could be as rotten as his predecessor.' Always the diplomat despite her tendency to turn every minor drama into a major crisis, Aunt Jemima risked Mrs Outhwaite's wrath. 'The Reverend Spears called upon him yesterday and said he was perfectly polite, and that although he hadn't been offered any tea…' a cardinal sin as far as this village was concerned '…they had quite a pleasant conversation and he got no sense that the new Lord Hockley intended to sell the ground from under us.'

Like Sophie, her aunt was desperate to find some good in their new landlord. They both had their fingers and toes crossed he would be a much more forgiving and reasonable one than his predecessor. If he wasn't, then not to put too fine a point on it, the pair of them were done for.

Their pitiful funds barely stretched as it was and there was nothing in reserve to finance a rent increase, let alone a move. That aside, after sixty-seven years of living in the same house, Aunt Jemima would find it awful to start all over again somewhere new. She was so petrified of being evicted she had had to be cautioned twice already in as many days not to seek him out and beg for his mercy. She had also been too agitated to play her beloved pianoforte and sat for hours staring into space instead. It was tragic to see and not good for her failing heart. Surely he wasn't cruel enough to forcibly wrench a sick old lady from the comforting bosom of the life she had always known?

Sophie risked peeking at him again out of the corner of her eye and winced as he finally decided to glare back. By the flattened disapproval of his lips, it was clear the new Lord Hockley wasn't the slightest bit fooled by her intense perusal of the apples and knew, without a shadow of a doubt, that the gaggle of assembled women all cackling together were in the grip of a furtive and unflattering conversation about him.

She smiled blandly at the ladies as if they were simply chatting about the weather. 'Seeing as the gentleman concerned is but a stone's throw away and staring, perhaps we should all continue with our shopping and discuss this later in the privacy of the sewing circle?'

Mrs Outhwaite frowned at Sophie's suggestion and carried on regardless. 'Did he inform the good reverend of any of his plans? Hint that he intended to stay? Make any mention of what he was going to do with all the farmland and property that isn't entailed or why Mr Spiggot looks ashen after each of their meetings?' She shook her head and jabbed the air again with her righteous finger. 'Of course he didn't! If my husband couldn't prise any answers out of him, nobody could and a man who remains so tight-lipped when all around him are in fear of their livelihoods is not one who can be trusted. His silence smacks of treachery. Of ulterior motives and pure, unadulterated greed.' The fire and brimstone finger jabbed the air again. 'Mark my words, ladies, our new earl is going to sell our homes and businesses to the highest bidder for his own selfish profit with nary a care in the world for anyone else.' Which, in a nutshell, was what everybody was so worried about.

Mrs Outhwaite leaned closer still and rapt, all the other ladies followed. 'I have it on the highest authority that he was once married and then widowed in dubious circumstances.' Everyone gasped again.

Sophie didn't because the statement was caveated with the words 'highest authority' which was always a sure sign Mrs Outhwaite was scaremongering and actually had no earthly idea if her accusations were true but wanted to appear as if she were the oracle of all things anyway. While she took the accusation with the hugest pinch of salt, the others all shuddered in horror as if he had strangled his poor, unfortunate wife with his bare hands while she begged for mercy and then buried her in the woods. 'No children either—although that is hardly surprising given his family history and probably just as well. The world could do without more Peels and their tainted blood.'

'That might well change if he decides to settle here, find a wife and raise a family.' Isobel Cartwright patted her perfect coiffure as she glanced his way, clearly already fancying herself for the role. 'Have any of you considered that? Because I can assure you I have.' She offered Lord Hockley one of her come-hither smiles to let him know that she was available.

'Stop trying to flirt with the enemy, girl!' Mrs Outhwaite practically spat in Isobel's face. 'Never mind that you are wasting your time. No earl is ever going to marry a shopkeeper's daughter!'

To be fair to her, several years Sophie's junior, well connected, fashionably attired, slimmer and significantly prettier than anyone else for miles around, shopkeeper's daughter or not, the flirty Isobel stood a much higher chance than any other single female in Whittleston-on-the-Water of snaring herself a title. Especially as she was shameless in her pursuit of marrying well. 'As a peer he is duty bound to produce heirs to continue their ancient lineage, and it goes without saying he will need some company in Hockley Hall. I have always thought it is too big a house for one solitary bachelor to rattle around in all alone. I wonder if anybody has invited him to the monthly assembly? If they haven't, somebody really should as it would be very poor form to exclude him.'

Being as bold as brass, Isobel then shot him another

beguiling smile across the square; however, her blatant attempt at seduction was foiled by the local butcher who chose that precise moment to emerge out of his shop and introduce himself to the new lord and then began to lecture him on something which appeared to have a great deal to do with his roof. It didn't stop Isobel from ogling him as she jabbed Sophie with her elbow.

'Who knew sour-faced old Hockley had a second cousin who is a golden-haired Adonis?'

'Looks can be deceiving, young lady,' said Mrs Outhwaite who seemed determined to think ill of him at all costs. 'But I dare say we'll all have his full measure soon enough, although if you want my opinion...' Which of course Sophie didn't but everyone else did. 'Any handsomeness on his face is spoiled by the cruelty in his eyes. The Peel family are famously malicious and those eyes are as frigid as winter.' She shivered for effect, which made poor Aunt Jemima blanch.

'Have you considered that he might simply be shy?' Even as she said the words, Sophie didn't believe them because if his fierce scowl at the butcher was anything to go by he was more likely to be a chip off the old block rather than a breath of fresh air, and therefore as curmudgeonly, humourless and standoffish as his un-mourned distant relative had been. 'Or overwhelmed? It must be daunting to arrive in such a close-knit community burdened with such great responsibility. Especially if one isn't used to it.'

The close-knit aspect had certainly taken Sophie a few years to get used to when she had first arrived here a decade ago in dire need of privacy, so she sympathised if he felt overwhelmed by all the nosiness. To have come from the rigid structure of the army where he would have been told what to do by the powers above, to suddenly becoming the all-powerful master entirely responsible for all he surveyed, must have come as quite a shock too. Enough that it would explain away his reluctance to engage with anyone as yet.

Hopefully.

Mrs Outhwaite cocked her head in the direction of the glaring Lord Hockley who was now stood looming over the butcher with insolently folded arms and a frown so fierce the poor baker beside them appeared to shrink several inches under the force of it. 'Does that man look overwhelmed or shy to you?'

He didn't.

If anything, the new Lord Hockley seemed to be in the highest of dudgeons and didn't seem to care one wit who knew it. But even from this distance she could see Mrs Outhwaite had got one thing very wrong. There was nothing frigid about the new earl's eyes. The unfathomable and intense heat in them burned like the sun.

As they all stared, Lord Hockley stalked away from the gentlemen and, to everyone's horror, straight across the square towards them. Almost as if he had had quite enough of all their nonsense and was determined to put a stop to it. Mrs Outhwaite was the first to flee and within seconds all the ladies had scattered like ants, leaving only Sophie still scrutinising the same apple as if her life depended upon it and Aunt Jemima who hovered anxiously by her side.

With no other choice other than to brazen it out, Sophie picked up two more apples and thrust them at the greengrocer. 'Can I have a pound of potatoes too please, Mr Lynch?' With any luck, the new earl would storm past in the middle of the transaction so that she and her aunt could pretend not to notice. 'And half a pound of onions.' With the cobblestones beneath her feet vibrating from the furious march of his boots, he would be gone in a matter of moments, and they could both breathe again.

'Good day to you, Lord Hockley.' At the sound of her aunt's tremulous voice, Sophie cringed a split second before the boots skidded to an abrupt stop. 'I have been meaning to introduce myself all week…seeing as we are your closest neighbours.'

This was neither the time nor the place for her aunt to beg for his charity and she prayed the poor thing would see it too. Negotiating with a furious man was never going to end well. 'I am Miss Jemima Gilbert, a spinster of this parish, and this is my niece…' Aunt Jemima groped for her sleeve, forcing Sophie to turn and be part of the humiliating mortification of what she feared was about to come.

Two narrowed blue eyes flicked to her as if greatly put upon by the intrusion. After a brief perusal, during which he undoubtedly came to the inescapable conclusion that she was also a dusty old spinster of this parish, he turned back to her aunt with undisguised impatience. 'We are long-term tenants of yours at…' The blue eyes rolled.

'Of course you are. Isn't everyone in this godforsaken place?'

And with that, he strode away without so much as a backwards glance.

Chapter Two

An hour later and finally on his way home, Rafe was still kicking himself for his ill-timed and ill-considered visit to the village when all he wanted was a quiet life as far away from *life* as was humanly possible.

After living in the blissful anonymity of Cheapside, he had forgotten that it was virtually impossible to do anything in an English village unnoticed. But like a blithering idiot and fed up with being cooped inside the depressing mausoleum he had inherited, he had inadvertently chosen market day of all the days to get his horse shod. In dire need of a change of scenery, and completely convinced he could slip in and straight out again before anyone was the wiser, he had blithely set out without a care in the world. A horrendous mistake he would make damn sure not to do again before he and Archie hightailed it to pastures new.

And the sooner they did that, the better! He already loathed whinging Whittleston on the blasted Water completely and couldn't wait to see the back of it.

Hardly a huge surprise really.

For as long as he could remember, Rafe had always

hated the cloying confines of village life. There were so many things about the quintessential and quaint English village to dislike. The herd mentality and inflated importance of the few they all followed like brainless sheep. The small-minded pettiness which always ran rife. The prejudice and ignorance which they spouted at every turn and did little to correct. The suffocating and insular society who typically thought themselves a cut above the rest of the nation simply because they lived in such a small enclave. The way everyone unashamedly knew everybody else's business and, because they were incapable of minding their own, all had strong opinions regarding what a man should do for the best irrespective of whether or not those opinions had been sought in the first place.

And then, of course, there was the inevitable village rumour mill, fuelled by the inane and mindless gossip which they all took such fevered delight in. As if the subject of it were both blind, deaf and so thick-skinned they would have no clue the cruel, fevered whispers behind hands were about them. All the very antithesis of the quiet life he craved with every fibre of his over-burdened being.

They were an unsubtle lot here, that was for certain, if the brazen coven of witches who had held court smack bang in the middle of the market square were any gauge. All openly staring at him and speculating. No doubt casting unfounded aspersions about his character despite not knowing him from Adam. So acidic he had literally felt his ears burning from their toxic vitriol from fifty feet away.

He had abhorred that most of all in his youth—largely because his family had always been at the heart of it all—and it never ceased to infuriate him. That was why today's had cut more deeply than he should have allowed. He had heard the words 'tainted blood' carried across the market square on the breeze and the bile had risen in his throat. He had spent a lifetime overhearing much the same. Yet the unsubtle stares and comments when they all thought he wasn't looking were a stark contrast to the fake smiles and insincere pleasantries when they did. All so typical and all so gallingly familiar.

And he still simultaneously cringed and raged at the way his former village had treated Archie from the moment he had been born. It would be a cold day in hell before he ever put him through any of that again.

A week in, and already this village felt as suffocating as the one he had once called home, the inhabitants all determined to pile on as much guilt as they could to bend them to their will in much the same way. Back then, of course, it had been his father's debts they had all swarmed around him to repay, as if he could magically conjure money out of thin air to give to them. Here, from what he could make out, the villagers believed he owed them all too, and thanks to his idiotic trip to the blacksmith this morning, he now felt overwhelmingly guilty despite having no earthly reason to feel that way.

Up until a fortnight ago when Mr Spiggot's letter had found him in Cheapside, Rafe had been blissfully unaware he had any cousins. Therefore, to discover that he had always had one and that sole, distant relative on his father's side was now as dead as a doornail had come as quite a shock. More shocking still had been the revelation that he had not only been left the mystery fellow's estate but his title too—which in turn had left him with the money he had always desperately needed alongside a glut of fresh and unwelcome responsibilities which he absolutely didn't and was still royally furious about.

He had more than done his time in the soul-destroying service of others. Too many years, man and boy, and none of that mountain of responsibilities which had always weighed down his shoulders, apart from Archie, had ever brought him any joy. He felt no sense of accomplishment at using his hard-earned salary to clear his kind but financially hopeless father's debts. No sense of pride in his military career and the men he had marched victorious into battle on another man's orders. How could he when half of those men who had blindly followed him into the fray never got to march back out again?

For the past year and a half, from the comfortable and cosy sanctuary of his suite of rented rooms in Cheapside, Rafe had lived from day to day on what was left of his savings. Scrimping and tightening his belt while dreaming of the future that he and his brother both deserved. It hadn't been an easy eighteen months because they had started in tragedy, but once Archie had settled he blossomed so it had been, for want of a better word, sheer, unadulterated paradise not having to answer to anyone.

Until this all happened completely out of the blue, part miracle and a bigger part a nightmare, and Rafe had been dragged kicking and screaming right back to where he had started. Trapped by circumstances that were not in the slightest of his making, but he was still expected to fix it all regardless.

Well, fate might well be having a laugh at his expense by dangling the means to the perfect end on a gilded rope with a million unwanted strings attached, but he was damned if he was going to be imprisoned by such guilt and responsibility ever again!

Rafe had very different dreams that did not involve people. An overriding ambition which he wouldn't ignore and a million unfulfilled plans that were a decade overdue. He fully intended to take the money and run off into the sunset with it. He had no affinity to this place. No history here. No relationship to anyone who lived anywhere close apart from the unfortunate link he had with a total stranger buried under the soil. No binding ties whatsoever as far as he was concerned, and he certainly didn't want any either. Binding ties and quiet lives did not go hand in hand and he and Archie had more than earned the peace.

The trials and tribulations of whinging Whittleston on the blasted Water were nothing to do with him no matter what his long-lost second cousin's will, Mr Spiggot his lecturing solicitor or his legions of new and needy tenants had to say on the subject, and it would be a cold day in hell before he engaged with any of it!

No indeed! The quicker he could offload the unwanted, unsavoury aspects of his unexpected inheritance, the better. Mr Spiggot had already, albeit begrudgingly, written to the necessary people to start the proceedings but had warned it might be many, many months before a sale went through for the right price. Being impatient and delighted enough by the huge new fortune already nestled in his bank account, Rafe had taken the unseemly decision to place a half-page advertisement in *The Times* this coming Saturday to expediate matters for a quick sale. That, combined with the rest of his miraculous windfall, would give him more than enough money to set himself up for life several times over and still have change.

He could finally buy a remote farm somewhere miles from anyone and raise horses with Archie to his heart's content. Read, ride, even learn to paint if the mood struck him…whatever he and Archie wanted, when they wanted it, unjudged, entirely self-sufficient and with no recourse to anyone else. Frankly, there wasn't enough money in the world to encourage him to stay here—no matter how much the inhabitants of this fetid backwater seemed to think he owed it to them to do so.

As the lane turned left towards the unkempt drive-away to the mausoleum, Atlas his belligerent stallion voted with his hooves and went right towards the rickety thatched cottage which stood next to a bubbling stream. Rafe couldn't blame him. He was in no hurry to go back to the house and its piles of paperwork and ledgers either, so he indulged the horse's whim and lowered his behind to the bank while the animal drank, enjoying the peace and tranquillity of the moment.

Unfortunately, but typically here, it didn't last long.

'Lord Hockley—a word if you please.'

He turned to see one of the witches from earlier bustling towards him from the cottage and inwardly he groaned. It was the one who had been pretending to be enthralled by an apple while she publicly rubbished him with the rest of them. The old spinster's niece. The one he had glared at when he'd caught her staring.

The one that his eyes had wanted to continue staring at before he'd given them a piece of his mind.

The one who currently had a face like thunder and a determined glint beneath her furrowed eyebrows.

Ingrained good manners dictated he stand, so he did,

reluctantly, while already plotting his exit. 'Good afternoon, Mrs...' What was her blasted name again?

'It's *Miss* Gilbert.'

Miss? That surprised him.

Firstly, because she seemed to be around his age and therefore well past the proper age to have been married, and secondly, because if one ignored the stern expression, she was a comely wench, so it was a wonder some fellow hadn't snapped her up. There were some nice curves that he couldn't help noticing under her drab clothes. A pretty face beneath her plain bonnet. Lovely chocolate brown eyes too. Very comely indeed all things considered, even though it annoyed him to have noticed something like that in this blasted village when he was trying to remain detached. 'Good afternoon, *Miss* Gilbert.'

'You were very rude to my aunt earlier and she is still upset about it. So upset she has taken to her bed this afternoon because she doesn't have the strength to even face the Friday Sewing Circle which she has never missed once in thirty years.' She wagged her finger at him and, just like that, the reasons for her distinct lack of husband became apparent. She was an outspoken and opinionated nag of the first order. 'What on earth gives you the right to be so rude to a gently bred woman of such advanced years?'

'The same right that allows you to slander me in public with the other fishwives this morning while pretending to peruse a fruit stand in case I noticed. Which I did, by the way. I'd have to have been blind and deaf not to.' She hadn't expected that response and blinked rapidly as she gaped like a fish.

'We weren't slandering you, my lord, we were all

merely vocalising our curiosity as people are prone to do when they know little about a person. Especially when the person has taken up residence in our midst but is reluctant to be known by his neighbours.'

'Why would I want to know them when they all seem to be of the opinion that the world could do without more Peels and their tainted blood?' He smiled sweetly as he parroted that spiteful comment even though it stuck in his throat. It was no easier saying than it was hearing it, and he had heard it so many times he had lost count. Almost always from the lips of women before they bade a hasty retreat.

Her expression altered to one of begrudging contriteness. 'Those were not my words, Lord Hockley. That does not excuse them, however, and if I am guilty of anything this morning, it is of not saying as much to all those gathered. Talking about someone behind their back is rude and inexcusable and I apologise for my perceived part in any offence caused.'

Perceived! The nerve of the woman. As if he had read their furtive stares and horrified expressions wrong. And it hadn't been done behind his back, it had been right in front of his face. Brazenly.

'However, two wrongs do not make a right, my lord, and my poor aunt was, at best, an innocent bystander this morning who took no part in that uncalled-for slander. Therefore, she did not deserve your callous treatment of her when she attempted to introduce herself to you. If you will allow me to be frank, my lord...'

'Do I have any choice in the matter, Miss Gilbert?'

Her dark eyes narrowed at his interruption as her brows kissed above her disdainful and currently wrinkled nose, but she tried to temper her tone despite failing to do the same to her words. 'It is very poor form that a good tenant of the Peel family for over sixty years has to seek you out in order to introduce themselves, when a decent landlord would have sought them out in the first instance, rather than leave them to flounder in limbo for over a week worrying as to your intentions. My aunt has a right to know who she pays her rent to.'

'As I understand it, all rent is paid to the steward, Mr Higgins, and has been for the last twenty years.'

Her lips pinched at the mention of the estate manager's name. 'He regularly collects it—and *diligently* to be sure—but as *I* understand it, it is then paid directly into your coffers. Therefore, surely good manners dictate...'

Rafe laughed. She was so sanctimonious and self-righteous he couldn't help it. 'Do not presume to lecture me on good manners, madam, when you have so few of them yourself. But please do apologise to your aunt on my behalf for my curtness this morning. It is not usually my habit to be rude to old ladies, but then I am not usually the subject of vicious village titillation either nowadays, so she caught me on an off day.' And because that was all Rafe was prepared to say on the subject for the sake of his quiet life, he inclined his head politely. He grabbed Atlas's reins, enjoying the woman's outrage perhaps a little too much than was gentlemanly because it did wonders for her bosom and made those attractive eyes sparkle. 'Good day to you, Miss Gilbert.'

He had walked a good ten feet away when she found the wherewithal to speak again. 'When I apologise to my aunt on your behalf, can I also reassure her that she will *continue* to be a good tenant of the Peel family going forward?' His feet paused as yet more guilt washed over him. 'She knows no other home, my lord, and her health is not good, so to lose the cottage she has spent a life-time in would likely be the death of her.'

'I have no immediate plans to evict her.' Which was a cowardly answer he wasn't proud of, but a version of the truth. As her current landlord he had absolutely no intentions of doing anything at all for as long as it took to be rid of the place. What happened after that was any-body's guess, but by then he intended to be miles away buying horseflesh and it would no longer be his concern. Not that he was going to indulge in any concern before he sold either. He had a perfectly good plan to remain detached, distant and guilt-free, and he would stick to it no matter what.

'It is not your immediate plans which worry me, my lord, it is your future plans. May I enquire as to those?'

Despite the voice screaming in his head to keep walking and avoid elaborating, Rafe was compelled to turn then really wished he hadn't. Those pretty brown eyes were filled with anguish now and that tugged on his heartstrings, pricked his conscience and churned the acid in his gut some more exactly as he had known it would. But he had to stand firm because he owed these strangers nothing. *Nothing!* Whereas he owed Archie the world.

He hardened his soft heart and smiled, trying to ig-nore the shocking state of the walls of the cottage he apparently owned behind her. Walls which looked as though the only thing holding them up were a wing and a prayer and the ancient, tangled vines of the barren wis-teria wrapped around them. 'Once I have some, I shall be sure to appraise you of them, Miss Gilbert.'

'An answer which avoids the question.'

Uncomfortable, Rafe fiddled with Atlas's bit rather

than look at her or the appalling state of the thatch which clearly hadn't been replaced this century. 'Perhaps...but the best I have today.'

They both knew that was a shocking lie and he winced because Miss Gilbert absorbed it like a body blow.

'Then I must assume from your reticence and inability to meet my gaze, sir, that all the rumours are true.' She regarded him now as if he were a monster rather than an annoyance or a disappointment. 'You *do* intend to sell Whittleston-on-the-Water from under us.'

He shrugged, forcing his eyes to meet hers, oddly ashamed of the truth even though he had no cause to be. 'It is for the best, I can assure you. I am not cut out to be a landlord nor ever had any desire to be one.' At least that was the truth. 'And there is every chance that whomever my successor is, he will be much better suited to the role and will do a much better job of it than I ever could.' He attempted a smile of reassurance which he feared fell wildly shy of its mark. 'And he'll probably do it better than my predecessor did too, if the ramshackle state of most of the village is any guide.'

His gaze instinctively flicked briefly to her cottage again and it took all his willpower not to wince because parts of the wattle and daub structure really did look ready to collapse. The spluttering chimney especially looked like a puff of wind would send it tumbling. His long-lost, dead as a doornail second cousin should have done something about that if he had the gall to charge an old lady rent for it.

'And there is every chance he will simply want the land, Lord Hockley. The opportunities to purchase an impressive, sprawling, largely unentailed estate this close to London are rarer than hen's teeth. His views of the Thames would be quite spectacular without the inconvenience of our *ramshackle* village in the way.'

Chapter Three

She hurried back down to the village in a blind panic, both livid and frightened in equal measure. She had no earthly idea how she was going to break the news to Aunt Jemima, or what was to become of them if the worst happened, but Sophie knew without a shadow of a doubt that she wouldn't accept this travesty without a fight.

She owed her aunt everything.

Aunt Jemima had been the only person in the world who had stood by when her family had disowned her. She had not only given her a home despite the scandal, but she had also been her rock when the absolute worst had happened and her salvation ever since. Aunt Jemima had saved her and never once expected any thanks for doing so. As the loss of her beloved home would undoubtedly be the worst thing that could happen to her at this late stage of her life, it went without saying that Sophie would do whatever it took to repay her debt to her. There had to be something they could do. Some way she could save her aunt from her absolute worst nightmare.

No matter what the law said, this was their village.

It had stood proud on the banks of the Thames for eight hundred years. Survived wars and plagues and more lords of the manor than anyone could count. Therefore, she prayed it would take more than one greedy earl who had been here less than five minutes to stop it from standing proud for the next eight hundred.

She picked up speed as she approached St Hildelith's, then picked up her skirts as she ran to the village hall behind it. She must have looked quite a state when she burst in on the sewing circle because several ladies yelped in shock as they dropped their embroidery.

'He's selling the lot!' There was no time to beat around the bush. 'I heard it directly from the horse's mouth not ten minutes ago!' Which wasn't strictly true because she had said the actual words—but he hadn't denied them. 'Apparently, Lord Hockley is not *cut out* to be a landlord!'

'Who is he selling it to?' The reverend's wife fired the first question. 'Do you have a name, Sophie? Or any idea of the purchaser's character? Or his intent?'

She shook her head. 'He rode off within seconds, refusing to elaborate, and didn't seem too pleased even to have admitted that much.' Which they all knew boded very ill indeed. 'Though I got the distinct impression he was still selling rather that it was already sold.'

'And for a king's ransom too, I'll wager! Didn't I tell you he was malicious and callous?' Mrs Outhwaite slapped the table with her palm. '*Mark my words*, I said not two hours ago and now this! Barely a week in residence and he has already sold us down the river.' Clearly shaken, Mrs Outhwaite tossed her embroidery hoop down as she stood. 'I must tell my husband the bad news…he will be devastated.'

'We should all go home and do the same.' The post-mistress reached for her twin daughters' hands with tears in her eyes. 'Come, my dears…let us seek comfort with your father. Even though we have all long feared this dreadful day would come, I confess, I never expected it would come so soon after Lord Hockley's demise. I had hoped, when they miraculously found an heir…' Her voice trailed off as she dabbed at her cheeks with her handkerchief.

'I had the guest bedrooms redecorated…what a dread-ful waste of money that was.' Even the usually feisty innkeeper's daughter was bereft with grief as if she had already received her eviction notice. The rest sat down-cast and stunned. All of them accepting that their dire fate was already sealed.

Sophie stepped in front of the door blocking their exit. She couldn't let this happen. Wouldn't. 'He hasn't sold the village yet so we might all be able to stop him!'

Mrs Outhwaite huffed out a resigned breath. 'And how do you suggest we do that when he owns all the land?'

'He might own it, but we all work it! Surely that af-fords us some power. A say, at least? If we plead our case properly he might listen.' Something he hadn't been too good at ten minutes hence. 'We could enlist the help of the magistrate and the constable. Some prominent gen-tlemen and merchants who use the wherry boats or the brickworks.' Sophie would not surrender to the grief of hopelessness. Could not bear to feel that emotion ever again. 'Perhaps we could also bend the ear of our mem-ber of parliament to align him to our cause. It might hold much sway if he takes the trouble to educate the new earl of the economic benefits of a thriving village this close to the capital…'

Several of the older women scoffed before Mrs Outhwaite spoke. 'Good heavens, girl! What world do you live in that you contemplate such nonsense? Nobody cares what we think about anything—least of all our member of parliament. It is not as if any of us can vote for him. Only those with land can vote, which by default would put him squarely in Lord Hockley's silk-lined pocket!'

A depressingly accurate summary which Sophie couldn't deny. 'Then if we cannot appeal to his better nature…' Not that she believed he had one now! 'We could pool our resources and raise a legal challenge.' Onwards and upwards.

Always onwards and upwards.

'On what grounds, Sophie?' The reverend's wife shook her head as she gazed at her in pity. 'Mrs Outhwaite is right, dear. His name is on the deeds, so the law is on his side. We have no legal recourse. Don't you remember what happened at Hinkwell? How the new landowner used the courts and then the bailiffs to enforce his will irrespective of the villagers' wishes to the contrary?'

'That was because those villagers only found out about the sale after it had happened when all the papers had been signed and money transferred. We know about Lord Hockley's intentions before he has carried them out, therefore there has to still be a chance we can stop him? Or at least have some influence on the process to ensure that even if he does end up selling the land, he sells it to someone who won't destroy our village.'

All eyes stared at the floor and her temper snapped at their ready defeat. 'I cannot believe you are going to accept this without challenge! That you have surrendered already and are not prepared to fight for our home!'

'He is the sole landowner, Sophie.' All the usual pith and fight in Mrs Outhwaite seemed to have gone, making her seem old and haggard. 'And as such, we are at the mercy of his decisions. All we can pray for now is that whoever buys us sees the value in the farms and businesses, although I dare say that is unlikely when the old earl let so many of his buildings go to rack and ruin and flatly refused to modernise anything. In its current state, Whittleston-on-the-Water is hardly a tempting prospect for an entrepreneur.'

Ramshackle.

That was what Lord Hockley had said and he was right. His predecessor had been a miserly old skinflint who always put profit over people. Only when he had to, he repaired what he could claim back as her aunt's ancient, leaking thatch and rickety, blocked chimney were testament to. They had been begging him for years to fix both but because they had no land to farm and no means to farm it even if they had, there was nothing in it for him to do so. Which left them every winter with little heat, a smoking fireplace and pots all over the floor to catch the rainwater in.

That didn't mean that the farms and shops he held the leases on had fared much better. At best, holes were patched and usually badly by whichever disreputable tradesmen who charged the least. Because those canny crooks insisted on payment upfront thanks to his habit of not paying his bills if he could avoid it, they were long gone by the time their work inevitably failed and the interminable cycle of complaints hitting deaf ears until the annual rent rises were due went around and around again.

'Then let's either force Lord Hockley to make it a more tempting prospect so we get the right purchaser or do everything in our power to make it the least tempting prospect that ever was!' Suddenly, there was a fire in her belly. 'He is the *sole* landowner, is he not? Which means there is just one of him to one hundred and fifty of us. If we collectively revolt we can make his life a misery.'

The vicar's wife was appalled by that idea. 'If by revolution you are suggesting violence, Sophie, like they did in France, I cannot and will not condone that.'

'I am not suggesting we guillotine Lord Hockley in the middle of the square—' However tempting that thought currently was. 'Merely that we make his life difficult enough that he has to listen. A peaceful protest—but a determined one. Using fair means or foul!'

'Fair means or foul… I do like the sound of that, young lady.' Mrs Fitzherbert, who was the oldest resident of the village at the ripe old age of ninety-four, had the light of battle in her eyes as she leaned heavily on her cane. 'Because you are absolutely right. How dare that man come here and think he can treat us so abominably without recourse! We will not take it lying down.' She looked to Sophie smiling and then so did everyone else. 'What is your plan, Sophie dear?'

'*My* plan?'

'You remind me of me in my prime and inciting a rebellion is exactly the sort of thing that I would do if only I was five years younger. But alas, age is a cruel mistress and a revolution needs a younger body than my shrivelled old thing, so I can think of nobody better to lead us into battle against our enemy than the only one of us who could prise the truth from the blighter.' Everyone bar Mrs Outhwaite, whose nose was clearly put out at being overlooked for such a poison chalice, nodded enthusiastically.

'You clearly have a way with him,' said the reverend's wife after a long pause during which Sophie could only blink in shock. 'And us. A moment ago, we were all ready to wave the white flag of surrender—until you raised the call to arms, Sophie, and gave us hope.'

'I think a man would be a better choice.' Several groaned at Mrs Outhwaite's suggestion although she pretended not to hear it. 'A respected gentleman of the village…like my husband perhaps? One who is used to dealing with other gentlemen of rank and stature.' She puffed out her chest with self-importance. 'Men, in my experience, always respond better to one of their own. It is so much easier for them to discount a woman—no matter how formidable or capable she might seem on the outside.' The look she slanted Sophie made it plain she thought her entirely incapable of anything.

'Didn't he deftly avoid all your husband's questions, Agatha?' Mrs Fitzherbert rolled her sunken eyes. 'Just as he avoided every single pertinent question posed by *every* respected gentleman who has outright asked him in the past week. Yet he couldn't bring himself to ignore Sophie's.' She whacked her cane hard on the floor as she pointed at her. 'She is his Achilles heel.'

'I wouldn't go that far…perhaps I simply asked the right question at the right time?'

'Just as you knew exactly what to say to us to rouse us out of our pit of self-pity and give us hope. That is a gift, girl!' She bashed the floor with her stick once more as if the decision was made. 'When one gets to be as old as I am, one learns that when the path ahead seems impassable, even though they might not seek the accolade, a natural, worthy leader always springs to the fore who can see a way around it. Today—in this moment, for this rutted pathway—it is you, Sophie Gilbert.' Two wily old eyes held hers in challenge. 'So put your money where your outspoken mouth is and lead us, young lady—and we shall follow.'

After an atrocious night's sleep on the best of the cheaply made and lumpy old mattresses in the mausoleum, Rafe awoke with a start to the sound of a bugle.

Thanks to a decade of strict military training and discipline, he jumped to his feet confused, then briefly scrambled about for his uniform and his weapons before he remembered he wasn't a soldier any more.

At least that was what he consoled himself with until he tugged on his drawers, looked out of the window and saw the mob of angry people on his driveaway carrying what seemed to be...

Good grief, were they placards?

They were. A veritable sea of them.

As it was barely light, he had to squint a bit to read them, his jaw hanging slacker with each and every one.

Whittleston Will Not Be Wronged!
Repair Our Square!
Long Live Whittleston-on-the-Water!
How dare you put your GREED over our NEED?

As he gaped in disbelief, he watched the comely Miss Gilbert march to the front of the crowd alongside a wizened old lady with a walking stick who looked to be about a hundred years old. Miss Gilbert stared up at him in defiance with an expression of complete and utter contempt, before she and the wizened woman unfurled the long banner she had personally carried to his doorstep. The scarlet painted letters were so big they required no squinting whatsoever.

SHAME ON YOU, LORD HOCKLEY!

'My lord, we are under siege!' His unflappable new butler was as white as Miss Gilbert's damning sheet as he burst through the door, clearly in the flap to end all flaps. 'What should we do?' He began to pace and twitch like a headless chicken. 'I've already instructed the staff to batten down the hatches, but if they attack…'

Rafe grabbed the butler's shoulders. 'Calm down, Walpole! They are unarmed.'

Although by the fierce glint in her eyes, the strange old lady might well do some damage to his person with her cane if she got the chance. So too might Miss Gilbert and with her bare hands. He glanced back at her, stood tall and proud. Front and centre like Joan of Arc at Orléans as she raised her chin and skewered him with her glare.

'I'll go and talk to them.' But as he stalked towards the door and felt the early morning chill on his shrivelled nipples, he altered course to put some clothes on first. He was already at a disadvantage as far as numbers were concerned, and there was no doubt they thought they had the moral advantage already if they were here for what he suspected they were, and he didn't need to be naked and shivering as well when he faced them. 'Have a maid take Archie to his room and keep him there. A calm maid who won't frighten the life out of him.'

'Yes, my lord.' The butler nodded, wringing his hands as Rafe wriggled into his breeches. 'Once I have done that, shall I fetch the pistols, my lord? Or the Blunderbuss?'

Was everyone in this godforsaken village stark staring mad?

'We are not at war, Walpole!' At least not yet. Although judging by this palaver, it might become a distinct possibility if he didn't handle things delicately.

'But I have never seen the like, my lord, in my five years here! The villagers are friendly folk and not prone to rabble-rousing, so something is amiss. Perhaps I should I summon the constable instead? Have him read the Riot Act?' Because that would surely pour oil on troubled waters!

'No, Walpole. Let us not overreact.' There was enough of that going on outside without adding fuel to the fire. Rafe was famously diplomatic and a natural leader of men, or so the top brass said when they pinned that worthless medal to his chest. 'Have some tea brought to the dining room with plenty of cups and instruct cook to prepare a huge breakfast.' People shouted less when they were occupied and what better way to preoccupy them than with food. 'I shall invite the ringleaders in for a civilised discussion myself where hopefully we can find an amicable solution to calm their grievances.' One which did not involve him having to stay in whinging Whittleston on the blasted Water a single second longer than he had planned.

Chapter Four

Despite his very proper shirt and coat, Sophie's wayward, wanton mind kept remembering what had been under it as he approached the crowd with a confident smile. She had nearly choked on her own tongue when he had pulled open his curtains and filled the window with his splendid nakedness from the waist up. As much as she disliked him personally, it really had been splendid. Certainly enough to know that the broad shoulders which filled that burgundy coat so well were all real and not the least bit padded. And certainly enough to give her wayward, lustful body the sorts of ideas she had been trying to wean it off of for years with little success.

'Ladies and gentlemen, I presume that you are aggrieved by my plans to sell?'

Several of the villagers around her murmured their disgust. A few, including the rabble-rousing old woman beside her, booed. If any of that bothered him, he covered it well.

'I would welcome the opportunity to discuss it with you all this instant—but fear that such a discussion will be futile when I am but one voice and you are many, and tempers are clearly frayed. It is also freezing out here.'

He smiled and spread his palms, the very picture of reasonableness. 'Therefore, in the spirit of conciliation, I am prepared to invite a smaller delegation into this house who can speak for all of you in the hope that together we can reach an amicable compromise while the rest of you await the news in the warmth of your own homes.' He stared at Sophie directly. 'Would that be agreeable, Miss Gilbert?'

She nodded warily, wondering why on earth her silly pulse had quickened the moment their eyes had locked when she disliked him so. 'How small a delegation?' Because if it was just her and him, that was a big, fat, resounding no.

'My dining room is currently set up for twelve and I would only need the one seat.' He smiled his most charming smile, which, dash it, was about as disarming as any she had ever seen.

'Then we shall gladly take the other eleven, my lord, so long as we can choose who that eleven are.'

'You have carte blanche to fill those chairs with whomever you see fit, Miss Gilbert...' His eyes drifted to the sea of placards and furious faces. 'So long as the rest of your number have the good grace to retreat from my property and desist intimidating and frightening my innocent staff.' Then he inclined his head politely. 'If you will excuse me, I think it also prudent that I too retreat while you choose your seconds. I shall patiently and respectfully await them, and you, inside.' And with that, he disappeared back through his imposing front door which closed behind him.

Because it seemed the best way to do it, she decided to trust democracy again and organised the crowd into distinct groups to vote for their spokesperson. After an eternity, they were whittled down to ten who all fell into step behind her as Sophie led them to the door. Even Mrs Outhwaite seemed to accept that she was in charge—even if she did so with exceedingly pursed lips.

To her surprise, it was Lord Hockley himself who answered her knock and invited them inside with another dazzling smile. One which she was convinced he used with ruthless intent specifically to disarm as he certainly hadn't deployed it yesterday when she had tried to talk to him. 'Ladies and gentlemen—welcome to the cluttered mausoleum that is Hockley Hall.' He gestured to the ad hoc and eclectic mix of antiquities lining every foot of the panelled hallway with a self-deprecating shrug. 'Please do not judge me on my predecessor's peculiar, dust-collecting décor as I had no hand in it.' His blue eyes settled on the threadbare stuffed head of an ancient wild boar glaring down at them from above the door-frame and pulled an expression of comic disgust that made some of their number smile. 'There are refreshments awaiting you in the dining room.'

Sophie recognised a determined charm offensive when she saw one and the new Lord Hockley bent over backwards to come across as agreeable. He shook every hand heartily as he stood by while servants gathered their coats, making quips and friendly comments which were clearly designed to disarm them all. He even managed to make the sour-faced Mrs Outhwaite smile, which was no mean feat as Sophie had never managed it. Once that was concluded he then ushered them to follow his butler towards the delicious aromas emanating from down the hall as if they were all invited and eagerly anticipated guests rather than an angry mob who wanted his head on a spike. Before she followed, he caught her arm, the heat from his fingers radiating through the heavy fabric of her thickest winter coat to sear and stir her flesh in a most improper way.

'Miss Gilbert, before we begin, I feel I owe you a very personal apology.' He smiled his most dazzling smile just for her. 'You caught me at a bad time yesterday and I lashed out. I was rude and obnoxious, and I am heartily ashamed of myself for it.'

'I dare say you are, Lord Hockley—a crowd of angry protestors at the crack of dawn will doubtless do that.' She wasn't the slightest bit fooled by his sudden affability which had been sadly lacking yesterday. She snatched away her arm, annoyed that the touch of this man—this horrid, selfish, ridiculously attractive man—was playing such havoc with her long-dormant senses. 'It must be quite galling too, to realise that the ill-mannered fishwife you attempted to fob off, deceive and outright lie to not a day ago now finds herself the duly elected leader of this *godforsaken* and *ramshackle* village.' She smiled sweetly back as his melted, and continued to smile as she sailed regally after the others.

'I really am trying to be reasonable.' With ten angry people all shouting at once now that the bacon was gone, and their waspish leader sat in smug silence enjoying the spectacle, Rafe's patience was stretched way beyond its limits. 'We are here to find a compromise after all.'

'A compromise, according to Mr Johnson's dictionary, can only occur when both parties give a little, my lord. So far, and do please correct me if I am wrong…' Miss Gilbert offered him the insincere smile of a strict schoolmistress admonishing a wayward pupil. 'All we have ascertained is that you intend to sell come hell or high water and there is nothing we can do about it beyond accept your assertion that you will try your best to find the right buyer.' She had him there, he supposed, because that, in a convoluted nutshell, was all he had allowed himself to commit to in the last hour despite all their increasingly heated protestations. 'There is an ocean of difference between *try* and *will*, my lord, and we have no reason to trust you when we do not know you.'

'You have my word as an officer and a gentleman that I will try my best to find you the right buyer, Miss Gilbert. At this early stage in the proceedings, I cannot promise any more than that.' He offered his best placating expression to the other ten scowling faces, all but one were male. 'This has come as a bolt out of the blue for all of us, and while your concerns here this morning are understandable, it is still a little soon to expect me to make concrete promises when I have barely had any time to make any concrete plans.'

Stay calm. Appear reasonable. Stay measured. Remain in control at all costs. The sage advice of his favourite colonel during his military training had been his mantra ever since when he encountered insubordination in the ranks. It had never failed him yet.

'Why don't we let the dust settle and reconvene this meeting when we all have a clearer understanding of the situation? Nothing good ever comes from a hasty overreaction spewed in anger without full possession of all the facts.' *Assume the unswerving gravitas of command and they will follow.* 'Facts which I do not yet have myself even.' Rafe made sure to catch every eye as he scanned the table, another tip gleaned from his colonel at the start of his career as a young officer, relieved to see them all dip their heads as they contemplated the common sense in his cautionary words.

Except the final pair of fine brown eyes did not dip. They held his with the same unswerving gravitas. 'But what if the *right* buyer offers considerably less money than the *wrong* buyer?'

'I am not a greedy chap, Miss Gilbert.' Just one in a hurry to be shot of all this. 'And as Mr Spiggot will be the one brokering the sale on my behalf, I am sure he will do all the due diligence necessary to ensure whoever purchases this land will treat it with the respect it deserves.' Which sounded eminently reasonable even though Rafe felt a sharp pang of guilt for stretching the truth. Mr Spiggot would certainly liaise with the initial interested parties to vet and weed out the charlatans, and his solicitor would draw up the paperwork needed for the deed of sale so he would ultimately do the lion's share of the work. 'He was born and bred here, wasn't he? A local who you all trust.'

Several heads bobbed, their owners relieved the task would be handled by one of their own.

Cool as a cucumber, Miss Gilbert smiled tightly again. 'If I did not have your word that you are indeed an officer and a gentleman, my lord, I would swear that you are a politician. For you possess a politician's ease of saying absolutely nothing of any substance with the utmost conviction. You sidestep and deflect with such effortless, seamless and convincing fluidity, I dare say you would do well in parliament should you ever feel inclined to serve your country again.'

It was Rafe's turn to smile without humour at her blatant insult. 'Alas, my political ambitions are as lacklustre as my landowning ambitions, Miss Gilbert, and

I have done my service and some. All I want after too many years on the campaign trail is a quiet life. It has long been my dream to raise some horses in peaceful solitude.' And that was the whole and unvarnished truth.

'You have land aplenty to raise horses here, my lord.' She had him there too, damn it.

'When would I find the time to, Miss Gilbert, with such a large estate to run?'

If his charm wasn't working, perhaps his military background would find some sympathy from the nine men and one other woman she had brought in with her. Some of them must have experience of his particular sacrifices for king and country. 'After I was wounded at Waterloo...' He rubbed his ribs as if the shrapnel scar still pained him. 'I promised myself that I would chase my dreams for a change rather than dedicate every waking moment to the service of others. After ten years fighting for my country, I had more than earned it and was in the process of purchasing some land in the middle of nowhere when I learned of my inheritance.' The partial truth again and his toes curled inside his boots at the shocking number of white lies tripping off his tongue to get them off his back. He was certainly in the process of working out how the hell he was going to pay for some land when a veritable fortune and the solution had dropped out of the sky from nowhere and landed in his lap. 'I am eager to complete the purchase and live the quiet life that I am due.'

'So, from that we must conclude that your mind is made up and no matter what sound arguments or concerns we put forward, the sale of this estate is inevitable.'

He offered her a curt nod. 'My mind is quite made up on that score.' This wasn't about them, or even him—

not that he would admit that. It was about Archie and what was best for him.

'In less than a week?' She quirked one dark eyebrow before she raised them both in fake surprise, not caring one whit that she was admonishing someone who was technically—according to his unexpected new title—far above her station. 'Now who is overreacting in a hasty manner, my lord? When Whittleston-on-the-Water might be the perfect place for you to fulfil all your dreams, if only you would give it a chance once the *dust has settled*.' Sarcasm dripped from her tone.

'As I have repeatedly said, I am not cut out to be a landlord, have no experience of being one and know, without a shadow of a doubt, that my destiny lies elsewhere.' Which at this current moment was anywhere but here. 'Believe me, I'd be so hopeless at it, my selling up will be a blessing in disguise in the long run.'

Once again she used her eyebrows as weapons, arching them with such reasonable, heartfelt and tragic expectation they instantly triggered some misplaced guilt in him. 'As an officer and a gentleman, will you at least grant us the courtesy of vetting the candidates before you agree to any sale?'

'Why, Miss Gilbert? So that you can dismiss them all and delay my plans in perpetuity?' His own frustrated sarcasm slipped out before he had the wherewithal to stop it but awarded him the pleasure of seeing those manipulative raven's wings which graced her forehead flatten at being thwarted.

'We should all have a say in our own destinies, my lord.' The steely glare didn't fully mask her fear for her future, and much to his complete disgust that got to him more than any reasonable argument ever could have.

Rafe knew how it felt to be powerless and at the mercy of others. It was soul destroying.

Flustered, he raked a hand through his hair. 'I have assured you all that I will endeavour to sell to the right buyer. Unfortunately, at this early stage in the proceedings, I cannot do any more than that no matter how much both sides might wish it, especially if only one buyer ever comes forward.' Rafe never should have let them in. He certainly should have never uttered the word 'compromise' no matter what the provocation. He should have allowed his butler to call the constable and never stared a single scared, powerless villager in the eye because ignorance was indeed bliss. 'However, if I am fortunate enough to have a choice in the matter, rest assured that I will consult with you all again before I proceed. I cannot say fairer than that.' He stood to signal that their impromptu, dawn meeting was at a close.

As the others went to stand, Miss Gilbert motioned for them to stay seated as she stared straight into his lying soul. 'Can you at least clarify what your definition of *consult* means, my lord?'

She wanted to nail him to something, and for the sake of peace he had to let her or she would never leave. 'It means the same as Mr Johnson's dictionary definition, Miss Gilbert. If I can give you all a choice, you have my solemn pledge that I will.'

All eyes swivelled to Miss Gilbert to see what she thought of that answer, and damn her she took her time with her verdict. As the ugly gold mantel clock ticked loud and slow like a death knell, she held his gaze unwaveringly until she finally spoke. 'Can we have that solemn pledge in writing, Lord Hockley?'

And once again she had him, and by her sugary, butter-would-not-melt-in-her-mouth smile and smugly relaxed eyebrows she knew it.

'Who should I address the letter to, Miss Gilbert?' Through gritted teeth, he smiled back. 'And would normal ink suffice on the document—or do you require it to be written in my blood?'

Chapter Five

Sophie stared at the two-day-old copy of *The Times* and felt her blood boil. It hadn't been a week since Lord Hockley had asked them to temper their outrage and allow the dust to settle before they reconvened their discussions, and already the sale of every unentailed acre of his estate was advertised in the most influential newspaper in the land!

And by the wording of this article and price he was selling it at, he had every intention of selling it fast. Fifty thousand pounds was a veritable steal when he could probably get half as much again if he weren't in such a blatant hurry to be rid of them.

But as it stated on page four of this crumpled newspaper in bold black and white, open viewings would commence on the fifteenth of February—only two days hence—and all bids should be sent in writing care his solicitor no later than the twenty-ninth of February. A paltry time frame which gave the villagers less than two and a half weeks to save their village from potential oblivion.

And all this when she was still smarting from the

downright selfish treachery of the solemn pledge he had sent them in writing. A pledge which indeed gave them the final choice—but only out of the two choices he deigned to send to them. Both of which they would have no say in whatsoever, and with the very legal-sounding caveat that, as the landowner, he reserved the right to withdraw their choice if their decision was not forthcoming in a timely manner. In case there was any ambiguity of what a timely manner was, he had even ensured that Mr Spiggot clarify that a 'timely manner' consisted of no more than seven days. Therefore, it did not take a genius to work out that far from allowing the dust to settle, their fate could be all done and dusted and the entire village given their marching orders by Easter.

If he expected them to take this latest, low blow without a hasty overreaction spewed in anger, then he had another think coming! The inhabitants of Whittleston-on-the-Water weren't gullible idiots! To get an advertisement in *The Times* so fast, he had to have submitted the dratted thing before he had met with them all, yet for all his placating talk of 'early days' and 'bolts out of the blue,' the duplicitous scoundrel had neglected to mention that pertinent little detail of his apparently hazy plan!

Therefore, not only was an overreaction deserved, the oh-so-charming but two-faced slippery snake had it coming. The battle lines were drawn and the gauntlet thrown. When they retaliated it would be swift and aimed at both of his faces!

Incensed, Sophie snatched up the damning newspaper in case her aunt awoke from her afternoon nap and saw it, knowing it would come better from her once she had a clear plan of action to fight it. She rolled it up like a weapon and marched out of her front door ready to rally the troops to prepare for all-out war, then stopped dead in her tracks at the sight of a stranger apparently in some distress right outside her back gate.

Her temper already diluted by concern, she rushed towards him. 'Is everything all right, sir?'

With his head in his hands, the man turned his back to her and hastened to the middle of the lane to frantically glance up and down it, but not before she heard the unmistakable sounds of panic.

'Sir...can I help?' He shook his blond head while hiding his face, trying and failing to disappear into his collar, then flinched as she touched his shoulder as if he feared her. 'Has something happened? Has someone hurt you?' He kept edging away despite the panic he was in. 'Are you lost?' He was a stranger to the area of that she was certain.

He nodded, his breathing laboured as he fought for control. 'I didn't mean to...to wander off.' Even in his panicked state, there was something unusual about his voice. It was slow, a tad nasal with an over-pronounced lisp. 'Now I can't find Rafe.'

'Perhaps I can help you find him?'

The man shook his covered head again. Vehemently. 'Rafe says I'm not supposed to talk to strangers. No matter what.' His voice was choked. Childlike irrespective of its deepness. His hunched shoulders rising and falling rapidly. 'I mustn't speak to people I don't know.'

'Rafe sounds very sensible.' Sophie racked her brains for any memory of a Rafe ever venturing into Whittleston or hereabouts and drew a blank. 'Who is he to you?'

'My brother.'

'And where did you last see your brother?'

'In the dining room…but he had to work before we could go for our ride…so I went to see the horses…but there was a pretty deer and then…and then…' All attempts at covering his upset dissolved in an instant and he wept noisily into his hands. 'I'm not supposed to wander off without Rafe.'

'There, there.' He didn't flinch when she touched him again and allowed her to wrap a comforting arm about his shoulders. She passed him her handkerchief and, as he took it, she saw her first glimpse of his face and his distress all made perfect sense. His features were small and flat. The bright blue upward slanted eyes were filled with tragic tears and his wide, round jaw quivered with confused emotion. She smiled kindly and smoothed his hair. 'We'll find Rafe together, don't worry. I am sure he is not far away.'

He leaned his head on her shoulder for a moment then pulled away, blinking and ashamed as if he had just committed a cardinal sin. 'I'm not supposed to talk to strangers unless Rafe says it is all right.'

'That is very sensible advice—but Rafe isn't here for you to check with, is he? And you are lost and I would really like to help you find him so that you are not lost and scared any more.' She stroked his arm, trying to reassure him with her fingers that she was more friend than foe. 'But I think I have a solution which will make it all right for you to talk to me. If we introduce ourselves we won't be strangers any more—we shall be friends. I am sure Rafe lets you talk to friends, doesn't he?'

He nodded warily and she couldn't blame him or his brother for such a reluctance to trust. The world could be a cruel place for people who were different, especially if they were vulnerable. She beamed, dipped into an exaggerated curtsy then stuck out her hand. 'I am Miss Sophie Gilbert and I am very pleased to meet you.' He stared at her outstretched fingers uncertain. 'Now you tell me your name.'

He thought about it for several seconds as he stared at her outstretched palm. Finally, his eyes lifted shyly to hers. 'It's Archie.'

'How do you do, Archie.' She closed the distance to take his big hand and shook it. 'Now that we have shaken hands—and just as soon as you say "how do you do" back—we won't be strangers any more.'

The faintest hint of a smile tugged at the corners of his mouth as he nodded. 'How do you do…' Then he floundered so she helped him out.

'Sophie. I am Sophie Gilbert and I live here in Willow Cottage…' she gestured behind her to the house '…with my Aunt Jemima and a grumpy old cat called Socrates. Do you like cats, Archie?'

He nodded. 'I like horses the best. And dogs too.' Forgetting the handkerchief he had balled in his fist, he used the sleeve of his coat to wipe his face, oblivious of the fine fabric it was made from or the unmistakable quality of the cut. Clothes which screamed this young man was well cared for. And he was young. By her best estimation he couldn't be much more than twenty—on the outside at least. 'Rafe says he's going to get me a puppy soon. I've always wanted a puppy, but they made Papa sneeze. But now that Papa is gone Rafe says that we can have a dog and it can sleep on my bed every night.'

'Puppies are lovely and your brother sounds lovely too.' Beyond lovely if he had kept Archie by his side when most would have had him locked away. 'Why are you and your brother here in this village today, Archie? Are you visiting someone?' If they were, she was confident she knew absolutely everyone and all their business. It was nigh on impossible to keep a secret in Whittleston-on-the-Water—although she had bucked the odds to manage it.

He shook his sandy head again, his previous distress now lessened because he no longer felt alone. 'We have to live in the m…m…' His nose wrinkled as his tongue tripped over the words. 'Mossy-leem till Rafe can sell it.'

'Mossy-leem?' *Mausoleum?* Not a noun one heard every day yet Sophie had now heard it twice in one week. 'Is your surname Peel by any chance, Archie?' He nodded and she sighed, annoyed that it appeared she might have to re-evaluate a man she had already decided she disliked intensely. 'Then follow me because I think I know exactly where Rafe is.'

It was less than a ten-minute walk up the lane to Hockley Hall, and now that they were official friends, Archie never stopped talking. He took such delight in everything, from the gnarly oak tree which he said looked like it had a face to the drift of early snowdrops which were almost blooming on the side of the road. Nothing was mundane or taken for granted because he seemed to appreciate the beauty in all he saw and that was infectious. It certainly made Sophie pause and take stock again. She must have walked this exact route at least a thousand times in the decade she had lived here with her aunt, knew it like the back of her hand and could probably navigate it blindfold, yet with Archie beside her she saw it with fresh eyes.

'My horse is called Alan and he is five. He's a Welsh pony.'

'Alan is a funny name for a horse.'

Archie laughed. 'That's what Rafe says but I like the name. I can even spell it.' He held up his hand and counted the letters on his fingers. 'A-L-A-N.'

'Very clever.'

'I like words with four letters.'

As much as she adored it, she couldn't think of a response to that comment. 'What colour is Alan?'

'Grey and he stands thirteen hands.' Sophie had no idea how tall that was, or even what made a Welsh pony different from any other horse, but nodded as if she did. 'But Atlas is a thoroughbred, and he stands over sixteen hands and can jump over a whole hedge. He's Rafe's horse and he can be a bit grumpy like your cat. I am not allowed to ride Atlas under any circumstances, but I can groom him and feed him apples.'

'Do the apples make him less grumpy?'

Archie shrugged. 'Rafe says Atlas is a law unto himself and chooses what mood he will be in depending on the weather. Sometimes the apples make him happy and other times he just spits them back at you, so Rafe says you never really know where you stand with him so it's best to always be on your guard.'

Which pretty much summed up exactly how she currently felt about Rafe. The previously solid ground wasn't quite as steady as it had been less than an hour ago now that she had met Archie, and the more his brother waxed lyrical about his biggest hero, the more unsteady that became. Saint Rafe had apparently left the army solely to care for Archie after their father had died. They spent hours together every day doing all the sorts of idyllic things which most brothers only dreamed of doing with each other if only they had the time, like riding and fishing. He was in the process of teaching

Archie to read—something he apparently hadn't been able to do before the paragon became his guardian—and had taught his younger brother how to care for horses in preparation for the stud farm he planned to create.

'How old were you when you learned to ride, Archie?' She already knew it would have been Rafe who had taken the time and patience to teach him at some point. But before he could answer and as they turned the bend towards the imposing wrought iron gates of the hall, a shout went up.

'Found him!'

Then several men spilled out of the gates all pointing in their direction and obviously all on a quest to retrieve their master's missing sibling. Hot on their heels was the new master of Hockley Hall himself, except this time all the easy charm and arrogance had been replaced by the twin emotions of frantic concern and relief.

'Archie!' He dashed towards his brother, his breathing clearly laboured as if he too had been in a mad panic. 'Where the hell have you been?' It was more a rhetorical question than one he expected an answer to because the second he came within arm's length he grabbed Archie and hauled him into his arms to check him over. 'Are you all right? Are you hurt? I've been worried sick!' Then he cupped his cheeks to admonish him gently. 'How many times do I have to tell you not to wander off without telling me? Especially here when you haven't yet found your bearings!'

The younger man burrowed against him as the elder Peel hugged his brother tight again, the intense affection between them as clear as the striking bright cobalt-coloured irises they also shared. 'I'm sorry, Rafe. I didn't mean to get lost.'

'I know you didn't—and I am sorry for shouting—but you scared the life out of me.' Still holding his brother tight, Lord Hockley's blue eyes searched hers, but it wasn't just gratitude swirling in their stormy depths. There was an unease which unsettled her although she couldn't quite ascertain why.

'I found Archie in the lane outside my house.' Without thinking she used the rolled-up newspaper she still carried to point the direction and his expression altered as he saw it. Instinctively he gathered his brother closer as if he feared she was about to attack him with it—because they both plainly knew what he had done behind their backs to put in it.

'I was lost.' Archie's voice was muffled by the broad expanse of his significantly taller brother's chest. 'But Sophie knew the way home, so she helped me find you.'

He released his brother but tucked Archie behind him, ruffling his hair with obvious affection before he turned back around. 'Thank you for returning him safely, Soph... I mean, Miss Gilbert.' The thanks were tempered by a stiffening of his shoulders, almost as if he were bracing himself for an outraged onslaught.

She acknowledged it with a curt nod, not ready to lower her own guard even though the soft part of her heart clearly wanted to despite his inconsiderate attitude towards the village. 'It was no trouble at all—*my lord.*' It was also best to keep things as formal as possible. In fact, if her silly soft heart was so inclined to waver on the back of one tender moment between the duplicitous new earl and his delightful younger brother, it was probably best to keep things clipped and formal at all costs, so she held her cold stare for a few moments to make sure he knew she still despised him and all he stood for.

Only then did she offer a genuine smile to Archie while the damning newspaper seemed to vibrate in her clenched fist. He glanced at it again during yet another awkward, pregnant pause, and to vex him Sophie tucked it behind her back while she bobbed an insincere curtsy at the enemy before smiling again at her new friend. 'I shall bid you a good day, gentlemen.' Sophie couldn't help but take pleasure in the flicker of confusion in Lord Hockley's eyes before he smothered it. It would do him good to be left unsettled. As much as the elder Peel deserved a good thwack around the head with *The Times* for his underhand behaviour, now was neither the time nor the place because it would upset his brother and she still hadn't formulated a plan of attack to thwart the lord of the manor. 'Enjoy your afternoon ride, Archie, and I hope you get your puppy soon.'

Then she spun on her heel and marched back down the lane towards the village, trying and failing not to feel some sympathy for the selfish wretch who held the entire fate of the village in his blatantly responsible and disconcertingly caring, big hands.

Chapter Six

Despite the unmistakable copy of his advertisement that she must have seen—because it had been too coincidental that she had returned his brother in one hand while symbolically wielding a copy of *The Times* like a sword in the other—Miss Gilbert had still failed to mention it. Nor, apparently, had anyone else. Either that had been a coincidence, or the minx had let Rafe stew for two days to lull him into a false sense of security before her next ambush. Whatever her motives, and he did not doubt for one second the woman had something up her sleeve, there was no denying she had made quite the impression on Archie. His brother was so bewitched by his 'new friend' he hadn't stopped talking about her and had nagged Rafe narrow on the hour, every hour, to take him to visit her and her blasted cat Socrates.

He might have known the witch would have a cat.

And a kind way with troublesome, inquisitive siblings. Or at least he hoped she did. His worst nightmare would be her using her unique knowledge of Archie's existence against him in some way. The small staff on the estate payroll all lived on the grounds and had taken the king's shilling. *Mention my brother to anyone and it will be the last day you work here, and you will be tossed from the grounds without references. Stay silent on the subject and I'll double your salary immediately.* The classic carrot and stick incentive which every branch of the British military relied on for compliance, except Rafe had always preferred carrots to sticks and earned respect rather than threats.

However, with Archie's safety his main concern while in this toxic, cloying, judgemental village, he could not afford the risk of anyone stepping out of line. That was why the frankly ridiculous pay rise had come with such a severe stipulation attached. He hoped the money made the stick redundant, but so help him, if anyone—*anyone*—threw Archie to the wolves, he'd use the stick to bludgeon the traitor to a sticky pulp.

Unfortunately, the irksome Miss Gilbert or her judgemental eyebrows were not on his payroll, and neither were her assorted motley crew of villagers who seemed to hang on her every word. She was a loose cannon and, blast her, a natural and clever leader who was impervious to his charm and apparently read him like a book. Which now made her another damn good reason to offload this godforsaken estate as soon as possible. A task he was optimistic might begin in earnest this morning when the first eager buyers came to view it all.

So far, twenty-two wealthy gentlemen had expressed an interest, and while Rafe was happy to allow them all access to the mausoleum and grounds today and tomorrow, he had instructed Mr Spiggot to do some serious delving into their backgrounds too. Because, frankly, if they did not actually have the necessary funds in the bank now to buy it off him today, they weren't serious candidates. He wasn't interested in the protracted dance of negotiation—just the swift transfer of the deeds of ownership so he could get back on with his quiet life.

'Boiled eggs again?' He ruffled his brother's hair as he strode into the breakfast room, determined to snatch a few minutes with him before the estate was swarming with potential buyers. Or at least he hoped it would be swarming with them as Rafe had directed all his attention as well as pinned all his hopes on the success of these next two days. Opening the house and grounds to all without the need for an appointment was unconventional. Vulgar and unseemly too in the eyes of aristocracy because he was publicly selling off the family silver, but he was hopeful that made things more intriguing to the new money with deep pockets and a desire to rise within the ranks by the acquisition of a bona fide country estate. 'Aren't you a bit bored of them by now?'

Archie shook his head. 'The hens here lay the best eggs and they laid these for me this morning.' Usually a creature of habit, his brother had surprised Rafe at how quickly he had adapted to his routine here at Hockley Hall without too much rebellion. But then Archie had always adored animals of all sorts, so fetching the eggs every morning before he visited the horses, sheep and cows which lived in the closest barns and pastures wasn't something the most stubborn Peel would dig his heels in against. And as both the cook and the stablemaster had taken a shine to his brother and did not seem to mind him tagging along as they went about their work, the new morning routine had freed Rafe up some to get on with everything else the unwelcome portion of his unexpected inheritance now meant he had to do.

To get a rise out of Archie, Rafe snatched the yolk-soaked bread soldier his brother had just dipped into one of his perfectly soft-boiled eggs and playfully wrestled his grasping hand out of the way as he devoured it.

'Get your own eggs, thief!'

'Elder brother privileges, I'm afraid.' He ruffled Archie's hair again before he began to help himself to a huge plate of food from the sideboard. 'It's the law that all older siblings get first dibs on the youngest's food.'

'No, it isn't.' Archie wrapped one protective arm around his plate in case Rafe tried to steal any more then scowled. 'You're making that up.'

'Are you calling me a liar as well as a thief?'

'If the cap fits.' Archie dunked a fresh soldier in his egg then paused to pin Rafe with manipulative imploring eyes. 'Why can't we go riding today? Alan needs some exercise.'

He sighed before pasting a smile on his face. 'You know I have to work today—and tomorrow, and you know I'll more than make it up to you and Alan the day after. Several people are visiting today, all with pots of money and delusions of grandeur, and if we are lucky one of them will buy this horrid mausoleum. Which means that very soon we'll be able to buy our own place to raise all those horses we both keep talking about. Won't that be wonderful?' Distraction always worked better than arguments. As much as he hated confining Archie to his room for the day with a maid, he had no choice. A house filled with strangers and a brother whose feelings were bruised too easily were not a good combination.

'And then we can get my puppy.'

'We can indeed.'

'I was thinking I might call it Mary.'

'That's a splendid name—if the puppy we get happens to be a girl. A boy pup might not be so happy with it, though.' Rafe sat opposite his brother even though he really didn't have the time. It was almost nine o'clock and the first viewer who had requested a private appointment was due on the dot and another three on each consecutive half hour straight after that. All desirous of not just nosing around his unwanted house but clearly of talking business too. All well aware that opportunities to buy land this close to London came but once in a blue moon and therefore eager to make him a personal offer if they liked what they saw.

But as the gold clock on the mantel chimed nine and ticked away the next half an hour without interruption, and then the next hour, and still no carriages trundled up the drive, alarm bells began to ring.

By eleven, and with Archie long ensconced in safety with his drawings and a patient, friendly maid, Rafe knew without a shadow of a doubt something was afoot, so he saddled Atlas and decided to investigate.

He encountered nobody on the short ride down to the village, which he did not consider that strange as the locals had no reason to use the long, winding lane to Hockley Hall unless they had business there. But the village too was deserted, which was very peculiar for a market day, yet there was no getting away from the fact that every shop appeared to be closed. Even the smithy had been abandoned and on purpose because as he wandered into the unlocked forge, the furnace was barely warm from the residual heat of what he presumed were yesterday's embers.

Bewildered, yet conscious that he was a stranger around these parts and not familiar with the daily routines of this close-knit hellhole, Rafe knocked on the blacksmith's cottage door behind to see why everything was so quiet. When he received no answer from the silent dwelling, he called on three more before he heard signs of life coming from within. However, when he knocked, and the butcher's wife appeared at the window jiggling a squalling newborn baby, her eyes widened.

'My husband isn't here!' The shout came from behind the door as the bolt screeched home. 'But he will be back later.'

As she had battened down the hatches, Rafe had no choice but to speak to the peeling painted wooden door instead. 'Where is everyone?'

'You'd best ask my husband when he returns,' came the inhospitable answer, 'or take your grievances up with Miss Gilbert and the parish council. As you can plainly see, it has nought to do with me.'

An odd answer and one that raised all his soldier's hackles. 'Can you at least tell me where I might find Miss Gilbert?' Because she hadn't been in her ramshackle little cottage when he had ridden past, of that he was quite certain. The usual billowing black smoke hadn't been coughing out of her lopsided chimney and he had seen no movement behind the lead lights when he had slowed Atlas on purpose to try and get a glimpse of her.

Apart from the crying baby, his question was met with silence, so he hammered on the wood again with impatience, not caring if he came off as brash and rude when she hadn't considered her manners as she had locked her door. 'Madam—I am not leaving until you tell me where she is!'

Another long pause and then a muffled huff came

too close to the rickety woodwork for the butcher's wife not to have her ear pressed against the door. 'She's at the barricade.'

Barricade?

Barricade!

What the blazes was the witch up to now?

Fearing his imagination had already worked out the answer, Rafe sprinted back to Atlas, and then rode at pace across the empty market square towards the London Road.

He did not have to go far down the only lane to freedom from the growing nightmare that was Whittleston on the blasted Water to discover why none of his eager potential buyers had turned up. Not only was the entire width of the rutted road to nowhere completely blocked with placards, but the villagers had built a haphazard blockade out of everything from hay carts to milk churns. To one side, in case Rafe was left in any doubt that the lunatic villagers intended to sabotage the viewings for the duration, someone had erected a substantial makeshift tent out of planks and oilcloth where a cheery bonfire burned. Above that was a spit upon which some meat was roasting and even from a distance he could also see several kettles were suspended on metal hooks spouting steam.

In the thick of the melee, like Wellington at his battlefield command headquarters, Miss Gilbert stood giving orders. It was then that somebody spotted him and at least fifty smug faces turned towards him—hers included. Even from this distance he could tell her eyebrows meant business, causing him to experience a moment of unease as he warily stared back.

As he neared, her disciples parted like the Red Sea

to allow her through, then gathered behind her scowling with their homemade signs held aloft to intimidate him.

The comely witch had the gall to feed his mount an apple as she stared up at Rafe smarting in his saddle.

'Good morning, Lord Hockley. I trust you are having a pleasant day.'

'It is against the law to block the road.' He had no idea if it was or if it wasn't, but as she had the upper hand as well as the reinforcements, the only weapon he had in his ill-equipped arsenal was bravado. 'Remove yourselves immediately or I shall have the constable arrest you all.'

'Go on then.' She wiped the last remnants of the demolished apple from her palms and shrugged. 'Go fetch the constable, and the magistrate too while you are about it, because we are not moving unless someone in the high *official* office tells us to.'

She was calling his bluff, damn her, and in front of a baying audience who all hated his guts. And by the defiant glint in her lovely eyes and saucy angle of one arched brow that amused her.

Instead of grabbing the nearest placard and snapping it in half as he wanted, Rafe forced himself to breathe slowly and remember his favourite colonel's words of wisdom.

Stay calm.

Appear reasonable.

Stay measured.

Remain in control at all costs.

'Miss Gilbert, I am not sure what you hope to achieve beyond a stint in gaol, but this is ridiculous.' Rafe mirrored her amused expression as he swept his hand in the direction of the protestors as if he wasn't the least bit shaken by the sight of them and his poor heart wasn't hammering like a woodpecker in his chest. 'We are not at war.'

'What is ridiculous, Lord Hockley, is that you thought you could sneak a full-page advertisement in *The Times* past us. One that announces your intention to sell our village out from under us for a song.' Her hands went to her hips—her rather distracting and womanly hips—while she waited for him to explain himself.

'I take issue with the word *sneak*, Miss Gilbert, for it suggests I have been disingenuous when I absolutely have not. In fact, I have been nothing but honest with you. I have made it plain that I intend to sell, and during my last—and to my mind—cordial meeting with the village's representatives, I even went as far as granting you the final say in the sale. *In writing*, Miss Gilbert, as was requested. I have not rescinded on that promise, nor has anything changed in the short week since, so I do not understand this at all.' He pointed to the enormous red and white *SHAME ON YOU, LORD HOCKLEY!* banner which had been strung across the lane like a ship's sail from the branches of two tall trees. 'This is hardly in the spirit of reasonable compromise which I remain convinced we had agreed upon.'

'The same meeting where we all agreed to let the dust settle until we were all in full possession of the facts before we did anything rash?' He could tell by her innocent expression she was about to hoist him with his petard. 'Are we to assume that you clean forgot the pertinent and significant *fact* that you had already placed an advertisement in the most influential newspaper in the land? Or are you just a bare-faced liar, Lord Hockley, who we cannot trust as far as we can throw?'

'I take exception to that accusation as I have never lied

to you.' He forced himself to hold her gaze even though the suppressed need to wince was painful. For a man who prided himself in his abilities as a good leader of men and a born diplomat, he had made a total pig's ear of this. For some inexplicable reason, from the moment he had set foot in Whittleston, all those abilities had deserted him, or he had ignored them in his blinkered haste to be shot of the place, and he had handled everything wrong.

'You omitted to tell us the whole truth then? Which in my book is just as bad.'

'I should have mentioned it and I apologise whole-heartedly for that slip.'

Her vexing brows arched in mock surprise. 'Oh, it was a slip, was it? Well, I suppose that combined with your insincere apology makes all your cloak and dagger skulduggery perfectly acceptable.' The brows now flattened in disgust as the damning full-page advertisement materialised from behind her back. 'You've had a week to appraise us of this.'

Rafe sighed then tried a different tack. 'How on earth do you expect me to sell the estate without informing people that it is available for sale?'

Miss Gilbert read the advertisement aloud. *'"Society is but a stone's throw away."'* She rolled her eyes at his choice of headline. *'"Nestled in five hundred acres on the picturesque and fertile banks of the River Thames and only twenty-five miles from the excitement of London, Hockley Hall presents the rare opportunity to reside in the heart of the picturesque countryside yet still be conveniently situated close enough to the capital to feel its pulse."'*

Her eyes snapped back to his.

'You have a poetic and evocative way with words,

my lord, and a canny knack for romantic descriptions. This alluring advertisement waxes lyrical about watching the sun rise over the sublime river views, galloping through the rolling parkland and benefiting from the economic virtues of the rolling pasture which surrounds it. It even extolls the many health benefits of the fresh air and space which eludes them in London. In just five hundred and two words...' Of course the witch had counted them. 'You reiterate the *infinite potential* of the land thrice and for such a bargain price too—but nowhere in this flowery promise of paradise do you mention that our ramshackle village happens to lie smack in the middle of those five hundred acres. Why is that?'

She paused only long enough to blink.

'A cynic would say that the omission was deliberate because you know that the responsibility of being a landlord with all its myriad responsibilities rather ruins the idyllic, blissful, relaxing dream that you are selling. That inconvenient truth might put a potential buyer off, so you appear to have whitewashed us from the equation.'

'Again, Miss Gilbert, you seem to be suggesting that my motives were dishonest when I can hardly hide the existence of Whittleston-on-the-Water from the viewers.' He pointed to the vista behind them which encompassed not only the house, the rolling parkland and the river but also the village in all its ramshackle glory. Although from here, the cheerful patchwork of thatched and tiled roofs looked rather pretty against the backdrop of the water and the frigid winter sky. 'When, in fact, the village is one of the first things that they see.'

She shook her head. 'They will only see the *"infinite potential so close to the capital"*, Lord Hockley, exactly as you intend them to.' She wafted one imperious hand in the direction of the road. 'The ten carriages we turned away this morning were certainly surprised to discover that more than just you lived on this land.'

'You turned away *ten* carriages.' He made no attempt to hide his anger at that. Ten eager, potential buyers lost. Perhaps for ever.

'So far, yes.' Miss Gilbert folded her arms, a triumphant gleam in her eye. 'And it's barely midday.'

'You had no right to do that.' Almost half his first open day was done and the clock was ticking. 'And no right to do this!' Rafe jabbed his finger at the barricade, his anger obliterating all thoughts of his mantra and his favourite colonel. 'This is my land, Miss Gilbert. My land and my road so you will remove yourself from it now!' A couple of burly farmers stepped up behind her at his slightly raised voice like two glaring bodyguards. One of them, a dark and bearded brute, was the size of a tree.

'You shall have to take that up with the constable for we shall only move if the law tells us to.'

In case Rafe argued with that, the tree took two steps forward and clenched his meaty fists.

'As you wish.' Rafe shook his head, at his wit's end, and was about to turn around and do just that when his frustrations leaked out and he threw up his hands in exasperation. 'Why do you seem determined to make this as painful as possible, Miss Gilbert, when I can assure you it will make no difference to the end result?'

Granite hard indifference. Not a single hair in her dratted eyebrows so much as quivered in sympathy.

'You know my circumstances.' Rafe stared into her eyes beseechingly, hoping she would understand now that she knew about Archie. 'I never knew about this inheritance or expected it and I have no interest in your village or this land. No desire to live here and no compunction whatsoever to change the longed-for plans which have sustained me for years simply because a distant relation I never knew had nobody else to leave it to.' Something shimmered in her dark eyes and he spoke directly to that. 'All I have ever wanted, Miss Gilbert, is a quiet life. Finally unburdened and unbeholden to ignorance and prejudice and free to live in peace without judgement, rejection, fear or apology.' He swept his arm to encompass the bearded tree man, the baying villagers with their angry placards and the barricade blocking the road. 'If anything, this unreasonable display of belligerence only reinforces my determination to sell up as fast as I can as this is as far from a quiet life as it is possible to be, and frankly, I cannot wait to be shot of it!'

Indecision and something intangible briefly skittered across her features before she lifted her chin in defiance and Rafe realised that even with brutal honesty he was on the back foot. He was outnumbered and, for now, outmanoeuvred so had no choice other than turn Atlas back the way he had come.

But if Miss Gilbert wanted a war, he would give her one, and as God was his witness, he would win! Whatever it took, he was determined to wave goodbye to wretched Whittleston on the blasted Water before the month was out!

Chapter Seven

'Our sovereign lord the King chargeth and commandeth all persons, being assembled, immediately disperse themselves, and peaceably to depart to their habitations, or to their lawful business…' The justice of the peace's voice droned loud as the sun began to set. Flanking him to his left were six statue-still soldiers and to the right a not so local constable who had been drafted in from further up the river.

Next to him stood a silent and seething Lord Hockley, who was no doubt furious that Mr Truitt, the local constable, had chosen today to visit his mother in Chelmsford and was not due back until tomorrow night after his advertised open days were done. He knew that could not have been a coincidence and had lost an entire day of viewings on the back of it. As his unusual bright blue eyes lifted and locked defiantly with hers, Sophie could see he blamed her entirely for that. He was right to blame her, because it had indeed been her who had convinced their local constable to make himself scarce, just as it had been her who had suggested this barricade in the first place too. Both things had proved to be highly effective in thwarting the new lord of the manor's plans to sell and even with the benefit of hindsight, and for the sake of the fate of all the worried people who lived on his land, she wouldn't have done things any differently even if she could turn back time.

That did not mean that her conscience hadn't niggled all afternoon on the back of it as countless potential buyers were turned away from the barricade.

It had been his unusual blue eyes again earlier that had made her feel bad.

The obvious pain within them had got to her as he had raked a frustrated hand through his hair and stared straight into her soul as if he were begging her, and her alone, to understand that he had not taken his decision lightly. That he had reasons. Good reasons for wanting that quiet life. Noble and unselfish reasons. And she had, drat him, sympathised completely because she had realised in that oddly loaded and poignant moment that his desire for a quiet life wasn't born out of greed or a callous disregard for the feelings of others as they had all suspected. It came from his overwhelming need to protect the brother he loved from ignorance, judgement, prejudice, rejection and fear. Five awful things both he and Archie must have experienced first-hand for the pain in his unusual blue eyes to have been so visceral.

There was no evidence of that in them this evening though. The earlier pain had now been replaced by a steely determination, the strength of which unnerved her far more than the amassed forces of the law currently did.

Beside her, oblivious of Sophie's internal dilemma, the ancient and incorrigible Mrs Fitzherbert chuckled with glee.

'Who knew I'd ever have the Riot Act read to me

and at my age too?' She nudged Sophie with her elbow, winking before she booed, and thumped her cane on the ground, which encouraged some of the others gathered to boo too as he came to the end of his proclamation.

'Shame on you, Lord Hockley!' came a shout from the barricade. 'Shame on you!'

'Shame on you! Shame on you!'

Sixty incensed fingers jabbed the air in unison as they chanted the three words which seemed to have become the village's battle cry thanks to Sophie's outraged red daub on a pair of Aunt Jemima's well-darned bedsheets. Words which she could not deny she felt a tad ashamed of now that she understood the predicament of the man being jeered at a little bit more.

She risked glancing at him and wished that she hadn't as she saw more pain in his stormy blue irises. Pain which proved he wasn't immune to the feelings of others or from being cut to the quick by the accusing fingers. As if he sensed her looking, he flicked his gaze curtly her way and instantly his jaw hardened, and his shoulders stiffened before he stared back at the baying crowd defiantly.

'Move along now!' The justice of the peace spoke to them all like children. 'You have all had the warning read aloud as the law requires. Further insurrection will be met with force and arrests will be made.'

'A peaceful protest isn't an insurrection.' For good measure, Mrs Fitzherbert waved her stick at the line of soldiers. 'And the law is an ass if it allows our callous landlord to sell our homes from under us! It makes all who uphold it asses too, sir! I was a friend to your mother, George Rutland! Knew her like a sister for over sixty years. She was a principled, God-fearing woman who cared about this community. She'll be spinning in her grave to learn her only son has sunk so low as to become the unquestioning henchman of a duplicitous peer!'

The justice bristled at the insult, but because he could not quite bring himself to threaten an unruly nonagenarian who had been a dear friend of his dead mother, he jabbed his finger at Sophie instead. 'You are in breach of the law with this protest, madam, and be in no doubt that I will see to it personally that the ringleaders are charged if you do not comply with all haste or if they dare to blockade any road hereabouts in the future!' He turned to the so far silent constable who clearly did not want to be any part of this and issued a terse order. 'I want this road clear in ten minutes and woe betide anyone still lingering beyond that.' Then he wagged his gloved finger at Sophie again. 'This is not the way we do things in Essex!'

'Clearly you've never heard of the Peasants' Revolt of 1381 then!' The light of battle was lit in Mrs Fitzherbert's expression as she jabbed her cane at him. 'For that started in Fobbing just across the way.' But she was already talking to the justice's back as he stomped away, and the soldiers and the constable hurried to do his bidding.

Only Lord Hockley remained rooted to the spot, but far from looking smug at his triumph, his posture was uncomfortable. His stormy eyes mortified.

'I hope you are proud of yourself, young man.' Mrs Fitzherbert jabbed her stick at him this time. 'For this is a disgrace, sir! An absolute disgrace!'

'It is—one that could have easily been avoided!' He huffed his frustration at Sophie too rather than the old lady who had just taken issue with him, then stalked away as well, his broad shoulders stiffening as Mrs Fitzherbert took great delight in his retreat.

Mrs Outhwaite bustled towards them grinning with her henpecked husband in tow. 'It took him much longer to summon the law than we expected.' She pointed to the setting sun. 'I sincerely doubt anyone else will be arriving today. There hasn't been a carriage in two hours.'

'Well done, everyone.' Hooking his thumbs into his lapels as if he were in charge, Mr Outhwaite addressed nobody in particular. 'If the stars are aligned, the keenest buyers came today and won't dare come back tomorrow because we've scared them off so well.'

They had but Sophie did not take that for granted for a second. 'Still, we shall proceed with the second part of our plan tomorrow. So go home and decorate your houses and businesses in readiness.'

Having sympathy for Lord Hockley's plight did not overrule the greater empathy she had with the villagers or the love she had for her aunt. Unconsciously, she glanced over to the tent where Aunt Jemima stood impotently and lost while the menfolk dismantled the shelter around her, and wished she knew how to erase the abject fear in her expression. Despite insisting on coming here to protest with her neighbours, her usually theatrical and attention-seeking relative was not herself. The poor thing had been inconsolable all week. She was so scared she wouldn't eat. Hadn't slept. Looked so pale and fragile it scared her niece witless as none of those things were good for her aunt's heart.

As Mr Outhwaite seemed eager to be in charge, she decided some timely delegation was in order. 'Can you quietly spread the word that we shall commence at eight, Mr Outhwaite? And remind everyone to remain on either their own property or their lawful place of business at all costs—no matter what the provocation. Now the law is involved, and the Riot Act has been read, it is imperative the next assault remains within the bounds of it. Let us not give him the satisfaction of securing a single arrest tomorrow.'

'And tonight?' By the fearsome expression on her face and the cane clutched tight in her fist, Mrs Fitzherbert was primed and ready for more action.

Sophie glanced again at Aunt Jemima who was clearly overwhelmed and was now shivering from the cold. 'We do as the justice of the peace has ordered. We all go home and get some rest. It's been a long day and there will be no let-up tomorrow.'

'What about some soup while I read to you?' Sophie added another log to the little fire then flapped some newspaper at the smoke to encourage it to float up the chimney rather than out into her aunt's chilly little parlour. 'You have to eat something to keep your strength up.' Not a morsel had passed her lips all day. That too was most unlike her. Even during one of her feigned or exaggerated illnesses, her aunt could always eat like a horse.

'I have no appetite, dear.' Aunt Jemima burrowed into the thick blanket her niece had draped around her slight shoulders, her teeth chattering from the cold which had clearly sunk deep into her bones after a day exposed to the elements and which refused to budge in front of their pitiful, smoking fireplace in the parlour. 'I think I shall just go to bed.'

It was barely eight and they had been home a few hours. The whole time her aunt had stared mournfully at nothing. All the fight in her gone and she looked scarily vacant behind the eyes.

'I will fix this.' Sophie gripped her hands as she knelt before her. 'You will not lose your home, I promise.'

'You cannot promise me that, dear, and you know it.' The bleak resignation in the older woman's eyes broke Sophie's heart. 'As much as it pains me, we need to make plans because I sense my time here in this house is done.'

'We are not beaten yet, Aunt. I shall think of something to save us!' She had to. 'Please try and have some faith in that. Conserve your strength and allow me to worry about this house.'

'It feels like grief having to say goodbye to the place and so daunting to have to start again somewhere unfamiliar. But change is inevitable, I suppose, even at this late stage of my life.' Aunt Jemima sighed as she glanced around the room she had lived in since the day she had been born, as if it were for the very last time and she was consigning it all to memory. 'I always thought I would die here—in my own bed—especially as I haven't that long left.'

'I haven't that long left' had been a phrase uttered near weekly in all the time Sophie had lived here with her aunt. She usually ignored it, glossed over it with a dismissive flick of her wrist or roll of her eyes, but for some reason that did not feel right tonight. Not when it seemed a very real possibility.

'Please don't talk like that.' Her aunt's defeatist tone brought a lump to Sophie's throat as she helped her up the stairs to her bedchamber.

'Why? When it is the truth? I know my days are numbered and so do you.' She paused halfway up to touch her chest. 'This old heart hasn't the strength to last much longer.' Which was what worried her niece the most.

'Nonsense! You have years in you yet and good ones too. Even the overly cautious and non-committal Dr Able said as much.' To Aunt Jemima he had. To Sophie privately he had expressed his concerns about her aunt's dizzy spells and increasing bouts of breathlessness.

In case her own concerns leaked, Sophie changed the subject while she prepared the icy room for her aunt, re-iterating the success of today and reminding her of the villagers' plans for a further but more subtle protest on the morrow with more optimism for its success than she actually felt. She knew it was unlikely that a few angry placards placed in windows and front gardens would have much, if any, impact in dissuading any potential buyers, but in her current depressed and fragile state she would not tell her aunt that. Or even admit it to herself because she had no better plan to fix things.

She continued a stream of cheerful chatter as she settled Aunt Jemima into the antique four-poster bed which was so large and so old this entire bedchamber had to have been built around it. Both her aunt and her father had been born in this bed. Her grandfather and great-grandfather too. It was as old as the hills, yet the carved oak bedstead was still as solid as a rock—unlike the cracked and crumbling plaster walls surrounding it. And unlike her beloved aunt who did not look the least bit convinced by her niece's laboured buoyancy.

'We *need* to make plans, Sophie.'

Tears of hopelessness pricked her eyes which she would rather die than allow her aunt to see as she tucked her in tight. 'Tish tosh.' She flapped the truth away as if it were of no consequence. 'Even if the worst happens, we still have a bright future ahead of us. I am an educated woman who is not without skills and will easily find work.' Or at least she hoped the years of teaching the poor children of the parish their letters and assisting some of the less educated farmers with their monthly accounts and correspondence would be useful attributes in the big, wide world. 'So we shan't be homeless or penniless and we certainly won't starve. I shall find a carpenter to dismantle this ungainly monstrosity of a bed and reassemble it in our nice new home somewhere close by where we shall both have a grand new adventure...' Onwards and upwards. Always onwards and upwards. No matter what.

'We?' Aunt Jemima cupped her cheek with her frozen bony hand. 'You are a good girl, Sophie—too good, and that worries me as much, if not more, than losing this house.'

'I am the last thing you should worry about.'

'But I do, dear. Incessantly. I have worried about you and your future for years.' The older woman gripped her hand, forcing Sophie to stop fussing and listen. 'But only in the last few days have I come to the conclusion that my fate and yours shouldn't be intertwined. It isn't fair on you to feel bound to a silly old lady near the end of her days when you are so full of life and deserve so much better.' Her aunt sighed. 'That is why I am going to write to your father.'

A pointless waste of time as well as an unpalatable one. 'He has made it crystal clear that I am dead to him.' He would never forgive her, which was one enormous hurdle to any sort of reconciliation, and she would never forgive him either, which was an insurmountable one. Hell would have to freeze over before she ever spoke to that man again when she blamed him for all that had happened. 'He will always be dead to me. I would rather live under a bridge than on his shilling.' She tried to tug her hand away than discuss *him* or the reasons she despised him for a second longer, but her aunt would have none of it and patted the mattress. Insisting Sophie sit when all she really wanted to do was run out into the solitude of the woods and howl at the full moon and curse fate when it had already punished her enough. Already taken all bar one of the lives she had cared about the most.

But Aunt Jemima held her fingers tight and tried to have some of the conversation which Sophie hadn't ever been strong enough to have. 'When you first came here, you needed me so very much, Sophie.' Just that subtle reminder robbed her of all breath, so she turned away and determined not to listen. If she refused to listen, then she didn't have to remember. 'And because I liked being needed after so many years alone, as one month turned to twelve and the years rolled by, I convinced myself that you still needed me. But I knew, deep down, that I was being selfish in not encouraging you to spread your wings and find your own path the moment you were healed. It was wrong of me not to do that, and I am sorry—but now it is time. Your future and mine should not be intertwined for ever when you deserve to forge your own path.'

'I have and it is with you.' She wanted to flee. Wanted to cover her ears with her hands and sing to block out all the words. All the memories. The soul-crushing awfulness that had almost killed her too.

Because she knew that, Aunt Jemima's fingers tightened about her wrist. 'It isn't, dear, and it never should have been. You were always meant for more than this.'

She gestured to the room. 'The dull, impoverished existence we currently suffer is not the future I want for you, and I will not allow it to be so.' She stared deep into Sophie's eyes to let her know that her next words would be the most stubbornly profound. 'To that end, I have decided that I shall throw myself at the mercy of my brother, remind him that he promised our parents he would take care of me to the bitter end and insist on his charity—alone.'

'You are overwrought, Aunt.' She smiled kindly to dismiss that outrageous nonsense, even though her heart was racing nineteen to the dozen at the bombshell. Like so many things she could not bring herself to talk about, they never mentioned her father. Ever. 'And clearly not thinking straight if you could possibly imagine that I would leave you to flounder alone with him while I...'

Her aunt silenced her with a chilled finger to Sophie's lips.

'If this last week has done anything positive, dearest, it has forced me to take stock of things properly, and I realise that somewhere in the last ten years, our roles have become reversed. For nowadays you no longer need me, but I seem to rely on you for everything. I have allowed myself to become a burden to you and because you are a kind and generous soul you have allowed me to make those demands upon you—and all to your detriment.'

'I would never consider you a burden!' Sophie shook her head, mortified that this kind, sweet angel would ever think such a thing. 'After all you have done for me...all you have risked and sacrificed for me...' Saying just that aloud made all the terrifying buried emotions churn. Emotions she had kept tightly bottled for a decade in case the full force of them destroyed the husk of her spirit which had survived. From the day she had arrived here, sodden to the skin and broken inside, they had never talked about the tragedy. Not in direct terms. They skirted on the periphery occasionally—tactfully— but never mentioned anything specific because Sophie could not cope with it. What happened had happened and that was that. Stoic avoidance was easier. Avoidance was what kept her sane. Kept her putting one foot in front of the other. Onwards and upwards. Always onwards and upwards!

Never look back.

'Things I did gladly, child, as you have always been the daughter I never had—but I would never forgive myself if I allowed you to continue to sacrifice all your best years simply because you feel misguidedly beholden for something which happened so long ago.'

'I am thirty, Aunt. My best years are long behind me.' Panic swirled now. It's tentacles wrapping around her throat and choking all her organs.

'If I were thirty again I wouldn't waste them on the rigid strictures of spinsterhood or be curbed by society's expectations. I would be more like Mrs Fitzherbert. I would have adventures. Live my life exactly as I wanted. You are a clever girl, Sophie. Sharp as a tack and resourceful. The world could still be your oyster so go grab that chance with both hands. Without me holding you back, you could start afresh somewhere new. You could become a governess or become a well-to-do lady's companion. Free of me, you might even meet a nice man and have a family all of your own. There is still time for that too.'

The pain was swift and devastating but there was no skirting around the unpleasantness this time. 'Never mind that I am soiled goods and not at all the sort of woman a nice man would ever consider.' That ship had long sailed. Sailed and sunk to the bottom of the ocean with all her youthful hopes and dreams and she had made a pact with herself never to trawl those murky depths. There were monsters there. Man-eating monsters who had no mercy.

'Not all men are your father, Sophie. Some would see beyond your past. If you went somewhere new, nobody would even know what happened to you and you could reinvent yourself as you see fit. Start afresh.'

'I couldn't lie about what happened!' The flash of temper was instinctive as the past threatened to smother her. She sucked in a calming breath and fiddled with her aunt's bedcovers until the wave of grief and anger subsided, forcing it all back inside where it could do no harm. Dead and buried.

Dead.

And buried.

She sucked in a ragged breath which did little to calm her as she could not have used a more ironic and helpful metaphor to help her rebottle her past if she had tried.

Only when she was convinced her voice wouldn't falter did she continue. 'As unpalatable as it all is...' She brushed it away. Ruthlessly stuffed it all back into the bottle and jammed the cork back inside. 'I cannot erase history.' Aside from the fact she never revisited that history, she would not dishonour it with a denial. He deserved more than that.

She was also not prepared to discuss the topic in more detail than she just had.

Ever.

Not even to her beloved aunt. Some wounds never

healed over, even after a decade. 'I am not without skills. There will be other jobs I can do to keep us afloat, so please do not lower yourself to asking for my father's help. Not that he will help you any more than he helped me. He cast you adrift too when you helped me, so we are in this together and that is the end of it. You are stuck with me.' Sophie smiled and patted her aunt's hand with affection, then stood to blow out the bedside candle and snap the old-fashioned four-poster's heavy velvet curtains shut, determined to end this awful conversation but worried sick by it at the same time. 'A good night's sleep is what is needed here.'

A good night's sleep and a miracle.

She bustled to the door, trying to act with a breeziness she did not feel, wishing her heart wasn't racing and the contents of her stomach weren't on the cusp of making a reappearance or that the stoppered bottle inside where she kept it all was in grave danger of shattering at any second. 'Good night, Aunt Jemima. Sleep tight.'

Her aunt sighed behind the velvet, clearly not the least bit convinced by the forced optimism and determined to have the last word. 'All we have achieved today is delay the inevitable, dearest.'

'It isn't inevitable yet.' But even as she uttered those words she knew her aunt was right. At best, all she had achieved today was a stay of execution. At worst, she had hastened their fate by completely alienating Lord Hockley. 'Something will turn up. You have to hold faith in that.'

'Not for me it won't. But I have faith something better will turn up for you if you are brave enough to allow it.' Her aunt's face appeared from between the bed curtains, smiling wistfully at Sophie as if that too were for the last time. 'And I will rest easier knowing that I was finally brave enough to give you that chance.'

It sounded too much like a final goodbye and it split what was left of Sophie's broken heart in two. 'You are overwrought, Aunt. Tired and exhausted. That is no state to be making life-changing decisions in. I *will* fix this.'

She had to.

Even if that meant throwing herself at the mercy of Lord Hockley and begging him to somehow spare Willow Cottage from the sale if he spared nothing else. That was if he would even see her, of course, which after today would also need a miracle.

Chapter Eight

Rafe signed the final letter and placed it on the stack at his elbow then slumped back in his chair to stare at them all in disgust. Blasted woman and her blasted barricade! Thanks to her, instead of showing potential, eager buyers around his estate and having his pick of them, he now had to resort to begging them to return.

He had no clue how many would after today's debacle and in all fairness he couldn't blame them. Who on earth would want to buy a place where the inhabitants were so barking mad and belligerent that they would lay siege to the road and hold the entire estate hostage in order to get their way? He certainly wouldn't touch it with a barge pole if he had a choice in the matter. A rebellious, revolutionary and ramshackle village was the last thing any sane person would wish to spend their money on, especially when he had advertised the place as an idyllic oasis of peaceful tranquillity.

Wearisome Whittleston-on-the-Water was as far from idyllic as it was possible to be, and despite his best intentions to live that quiet life he more than deserved, he hadn't had a moment's peace since his long-lost relation had saddled him with it.

He dreaded to think what they had said to all the carriages to make them turn around. What threats or malicious slanders they had employed to scare them away before he could have the protestors forcibly removed. All he knew with any certainty was that every carriage had turned around and hightailed it back to the city without argument so whatever they had been told must have hit home and might well have put them off this godforsaken place for ever. It certainly would have done him.

Blasted woman and her blasted barricade!

And damn and blast his own cowardly shortsightedness too. If only he had had the foresight to be honest about his plans to sell from the outset, and the common sense to work with the witch rather than turn her against him. When he knew from his father's example that burying his head in the sand was never the correct solution to any problem. But Rafe had been so determined to be shot of the place he hadn't listened to all his years of military training to take a moment to pause and take proper stock of the situation before marching forth. Especially when he also knew that the quickest way to cause dissention in the ranks was to pay scant regard for the thoughts and feelings of them, so was it any wonder that he now had a full-scale mutiny on his hands? One that could have been avoided if he hadn't been so blinkered and determined to remain detached at all costs.

He was certainly paying for that now—in inconvenience and guilt.

Blasted woman and her barricade and her blasted, soulful big brown eyes! He was concerning himself with her plight in particular, and disproportionately, because something about her got to him. It had from the first moment he had set eyes on the witch, damn her.

What was it about her that mined through his well-fortified defences? What was it that made him wonder about her so when he had trained himself to never ponder women beyond the carnal? And certainly never to ponder the sort who wouldn't be interested in the fleetingly carnal. Because that sort would certainly never ponder him and his responsibilities for very long. Of that he knew first-hand. Any serious interest any woman had ever had in him had waned the second they realised that he came with Archie. That his commitment to his brother was non-negotiable. That he would not have him sent away or banished to obscurity. And that perhaps whatever had caused his brother to be the way he was, was somehow contagious. Never mind that Archie had always been more a blessing than a curse as far as he was concerned. A lovable, joyous ray of exuberant sunshine if you bothered to take the time to get to know him and did not treat him like a leper.

Which, of course, the blasted witch hadn't. She would be much easier to loathe if she had behaved like all the women had before. Much easier to dismiss from his niggling conscience.

Just as he had at least twice in the last hour, he wandered to the window. He stared into the gaping silver hole of the full moon while he pondered exactly what he was going to say to the harridan when he requested a truce tomorrow. Something he should have done earlier rather than losing his temper when all the chants of 'Shame on you!' had got to him disproportionately too. Something he should have rectified later when actual shame had set in and he had realised he had made a total hash of things so far. That was something she would doubtless make him eat a mountain of humble pie to rectify. If she would allow him to rectify it at all now that he was her sworn enemy.

What a damned, totally avoidable mess.

He huffed out a breath which steamed the glass, then rubbed it away with his palm to stare at the first hint of the sunrise on the horizon. The bright, orange glow filtered through the bare trees, sending shadows over the tangled branches that made them seem to dance in silhouette against the night. He shook his head, annoyed at himself for losing track of time and a night of sleep while he wrote all those blasted begging letters, and annoyed with the new brown-eyed bane of his life for making him have to write them in the first place, then frowned to stare back at the clock.

He had witnessed enough dawns all over the war-torn continent to know that the sun never rose at half past two in the morning, so rubbed away more condensation to study the strange anomaly better.

That was when he noticed the thick, black fronds of smoke snaking across the surprised face of the moon and panicked. Because in his extensive experience of all that war, he knew without a doubt that there was never any smoke without fire.

'Use the stream behind the house! Form a line!' Rafe shouted and pointed instructions to his servants as they raced towards the cottage, praying they had brought enough buckets to make a difference but fearing there weren't enough in the world to tackle this blaze.

Where once had been Miss Gilbert's roof was now only half thatch, half a raging inferno. Flames had blown out of a downstairs window and spewed into the night. The naked, twisted boughs of wisteria were also alight, the fire engulfing the entire left side of the building and suffocating the front door.

As he secured his horse at a safe distance, he scanned the shadows outside for any signs of life, praying she and her aunt had escaped to safety long before now. That prayer proved to be swiftly unanswered when her head poked out of a bedchamber window, and a wild Miss Gilbert appeared through the smoke screaming and clutching a cat. She held it out, leaning precariously over the sill until the animal squirmed above his outstretched arms. By more luck than judgement, when she dropped it, he caught it, the animal's splayed claws scratching his cheek in its panic to be free before it wriggled out of his arms and ran away.

'Your turn!' Rafe held out his arms again in case she jumped but she shook her head.

'My aunt is trapped!' Her pretty face was obscured by soot as she pointed behind her frantically from above. 'The door is jammed! I cannot get her out!' Then, to Rafe's horror, instead of climbing out of the window like any sane person would, she inhaled a lung full of fresh air then disappeared back into the choking smoke.

'Miss Gilbert!' He shouted upwards through cupped hands. 'Sophie!' Even his loudest bellow was smothered by the roar of the fire, so he ran towards the front door where the wisteria around it dripped flames, spitting lethal sparks like bullets until the searing heat of the burning wood pushed him back.

'Bring that here!' Rafe yelled to the first man he saw clutching a full bucket of water as he stripped off his coat, then dunked the garment in it. After wrapping it around his face and head, he lunged at the door again and managed to kick it open, only to recoil in the nick of time as the rush of air fuelled the fire beyond and sent it raging. His wet coat heated instantly, scalding his skin even as he staggered backwards away from the flames, until he ripped it off then stood impotently at the hopeless sight ahead.

The hallway was impassable. The narrow stairs had morphed into a burning pyre of crimson, hissing wood. Once that gave—and Rafe was in no doubt that it would and soon—it would likely take the upper floor, the unstable thatch and the ladies with it.

Unless the smoke got them first.

Or they burned alive before he could get to them.

Miss Gilbert emerged again at the window. Impervious to his screams to get the hell out before it was too late, she paused only long enough to suck in more fresh air and then she was gone again, leaving him simultaneously raging at her noble stupidity and terrified she would perish at any moment.

He dashed around the back of the house and kicked open the back door, only to discover that too was beyond hope because the fire had penetrated both the narrow beams which held up the ceiling and the wood behind the cracked plaster. He could not see past the blazing curtain of the door into the hallway and didn't fancy his chances under the timbers.

As he ran back around the front, a mob of villagers rushed towards the cottage from the opposite end of the lane, clutching more buckets and dragging barrels in carts. Someone must have seen the fire and raised the alarm as the pealing bells of the old Norman church added to the cacophony.

'The ladies are trapped inside!'

One of the burly farmers who had flanked her earlier, the bearded one the size of a tree, sprinted to his side as if he too realised the cottage was a lost cause and this was now a matter of life and death.

'I'm going up!' Rafe gestured to the broken window above, hoping the ominously smoking wisteria trunks beneath it would take his weight. 'That is their only way out.'

The farmer nodded and without arguing used all his brute strength to boost Rafe halfway up the trellis, and he hoisted himself the rest while the ancient, heated branches groaned around him.

'Sophie!' He tumbled into the smoky room in his haste to get to her, his lungs instantly rebelling at the acrid, hot air which filled them. 'Sophie!'

Like her, he sucked in a chest full of air from the window then ran towards the glowing landing, stopping short of the door as she stumbled back through it, coughing and fighting for breath.

He caught her as she collapsed against him, her limp hand wafting away from the advancing sea of flames snaking up the staircase. 'Back room...can't open door.'

He half walked her, half dragged her to the window, and when she tried to fight him to get back to her aunt, he shook his head.

'I'll get her!' He pushed her towards the window. Thankfully, the burly farmer had organised a circle of villagers who all stood waiting with a blanket stretched between them to catch her. 'You need to get out now!'

'No!' The whites of her eyes wide, she clutched at his shirt trying to fight him off. 'I'm not leaving without her!'

'Oh, yes, you are!' He hoisted her into his arms and wrestled her onto the windowsill, and she fought him every step of the way.

'Let go of me!'

Blasted woman was going to be the death of him! Literally.

It took all his strength to unpeel her clawed fingers from himself and then the window frame, and with one almighty push he managed to send her tumbling to safety. As the blanket collapsed around her like a co-coon, Rafe filled his coughing lungs again, then dashed back to the door.

The smoke from the staircase was thick and black here, stinging his eyes and clogging the back of his throat with soot, but he pushed onwards, using one out-stretched palm to guide his way and his other arm as a shield against the smoke, then plunged onto the landing in the direction she had pointed.

He hit the door with a thud, then scrambled to find the handle and open the thing—but only a sliver. Some-thing was blocking it from the inside.

Something big and heavy and unyielding.

Using his shoulder as a battering ram, Rafe bashed his body against it repeatedly, managing to move it barely an inch at a time until it finally gave enough for him to squeeze inside. He lunged towards the dark silhouette of what he hoped was the bed, then groped for an eter-nity around what felt like heavy curtain while he bat-tled his way in.

When his fingers touched something unmistakably human, he dragged the old lady towards him, then flung himself over her as part of the ceiling crashed down, missing them both by inches.

As Rafe coughed out the cloud of shattered plaster which seemed to have coated his lungs, the remaining beams above creaked and rumbled as they warped within the carcass of the roof, and he knew he had scant minutes—perhaps seconds—to get out.

It took everything he had left to gather the old woman's lifeless body into his arms and haul her off the mattress, then to drag the dead weight of her backwards over the splintered, smoking carnage which now littered the floor.

What was left of the staircase had transformed into a fiery pit which threatened to swallow the landing whole—but still he ploughed on. His only hope the single broken window to freedom. The only way out.

With one last heave he dragged the body in his arms towards it.

Six feet.

Five feet.

Four...

There was a noise. A terrifying, rumbling, wood-splitting sound that caused blind panic before something hard and heavy hit him across the back, knocking the last precious air out of his body as it crushed him.

His lungs were on fire.

His ribs refused to move.

Every airless breath futile as his constricted chest heaved in desperation and his head spun. He saw the face of the bearded tree man at the window as he fell to the floor. Heard shouts and then a crash as something else collapsed. Felt pain.

Searing pain.

Tasted blood.

His blood. Not good.

Not good!

Rafe tried to move. Tried to fight. Tried to think. Tried to breathe.

But nothing happened.

Then the fire and the noise, the chaos and the pain, seemed to float away around him. The world contracted to a pinprick.

Until even that went black.

Chapter Nine

Sophie hunched over the steaming cup not really tasting the contents because she was in such a daze. It was precarious, the physician had said.

Precarious.

If Aunt Jemima survived the next twenty-four hours then perhaps she would recover. If not...well, frankly that did not bear thinking about. Nothing about what had happened tonight bore thinking about. It was all so dreadful.

All so hopeless.

Her aunt's lungs had been exposed to too much smoke. Her pulse was sluggish, and she remained unconscious and unresponsive. That, as she had overheard the grave-faced doctor whisper to the vicar when he had assumed she wasn't within earshot, wasn't a good sign.

Because she did not have the capacity to comprehend it all at the moment, Sophie had decided to not to think about it. Worrying would not change the outcome, nor would blaming herself or castigating herself for not acting differently sooner. As she had done all three things incessantly for the last few hours and they had only led to the very real chance of pitying tears of remorse and despair which would help no one, she had also decided to do as she had always done when her world imploded. To exist only from moment to moment and deal with whatever each dictated.

Right now, on the good doctor's advice and while Reverend Spears was sat keeping watch by her aunt's bed, she needed to drink something to ease her scorched throat. Hence she was sitting here all alone. On the floor of the vast but cluttered landing of Hockley Hall, still in the soot-stained and ruined nightgown which was the only item of clothing she possessed that had survived the fire. As it was apparently the only thing she knew of that she still owned which hadn't been destroyed in the blaze, that too felt significant. Although in what way she did not have the capacity to contemplate nor was she inclined to when not thinking about such things was always easier.

'Are you all right, Sophie?' Archie edged towards her from the staircase, bright blue eyes so like his brother's as wide as saucers as if he had no earthly idea what to say or do to make things better.

She sympathised. She had no earthly idea either, so she nodded.

'I am as all right as I am going to be.' Because he was anxiously rocking from foot to foot, clearly lost without his brother, she patted the floor beside her. 'But I could do with some company.'

He sat and then shuffled closer so that their arms were touching, then rested his head on her shoulder. 'Cook says that Willow Cottage is all gone. Burned to the ground.'

'Half of it burned...the rest of it collapsed.' She had stood dumbstruck as her house seemed to fold in on itself in a big cloud of debris. Her home, all its contents and memories, gone in mere seconds. Wiped from the face of the earth because she had been so consumed by self-pity that she had forgotten to dampen down the piti-ful fire in the parlour in their rickety, smoking chimney before she had gone to bed. 'It turns out that wattle and daub isn't as resilient against flames as brick.'

'What's wattle and daub?'

As giving this sweet man a history lesson seemed a better use of her time than curling into a ball and weeping inconsolably, she told him in great detail, cer-tain that if she gave in to the hovering tears they would never stop.

'Cook says that you were lucky to get out alive.'

'We were.' Although that luck had been dependent on the bravery of Lord Hockley. If he hadn't got to Aunt Jemima and dragged her out of danger, then she was under no doubt her aunt would have been flattened. And if Ned Parker hadn't managed to lift the beam and haul both her aunt and her tenacious rescuer to the window in the nick of time, then two people would have died a hideous death tonight. Ned's big boots had barely hit the ground when the roof finally gave, then within seconds the walls crumbled with it.

And all because Sophie had allowed her emotions to consume her—albeit briefly—and as a consequence had forgotten to kill the pathetic, measly fire in the par-lour grate.

It did not seem quite so pathetic and measly now though. Nor did the guilt which went with it. If her aunt died because of her neglect…

For the sake of her tenuous grip on her sanity, So-phie forced herself to do an about-turn on that dark path.

Forced herself to smile at Archie. 'Your brother was the hero of the hour.' Or at least the main one to her mind.

'Will he get another medal like he did for Waterloo? Papa told me Rafe had been a hero there too, but he has always been the brave one. I get scared easily. Were you scared, Sophie?'

'Terrified.' She still was, but for very different reasons.

Archie wrapped his arms around her and smothered her in a hug. 'You are safe now, so everything is going to be all right.'

'That is good to know.' For Rafe perhaps it might all be all right. He was young and fit and in possession of a strong body that would soon repair. Her Aunt Jemima's was old and weak. Her health and her heart had been failing for some time. Not that Archie needed to be burdened with that knowledge when he had been so distraught earlier. He had been in a terrible state when they had carried his brother's unconscious, battered and blackened body into the hall.

'The doctor needs a big table from somewhere.' Ned Parker stepped out onto the landing, his face grave behind his thick beard. 'As solid as we can find.' His eyes darted to Archie, and he softened his tone to avoid causing him more distress. 'He's going to try to reset the shoulder.' But Archie's eyes widened again anyway as he swallowed hard.

'Good.' She squeezed the young man tight in reassurance before she released him. 'The sooner they mend your big brother's shoulder, the sooner he will recover. It must be very painful for him right now.' Although perhaps not quite as painful as it would be when the physician forced the dislocated joint back in its proper place.

The last thing Archie needed to hear was Rafe scream-ing in agony. 'Perhaps you can tell Walpole we need a big table up here immediately and then once that's done go and help Cook make Rafe a cup of tea. My aunt is convinced a nice cup of tea fixes everything.'

Happy to be of use, Archie hurried off, leaving her alone with Ned. 'How is he?'

'Surprisingly alive and upright for someone who had half a roof fall on top of him.' Ned shook his head as if he couldn't quite believe it. 'Apart from the right shoul-der—which looks nasty—he's managed to escape with surface wounds and a hacking cough. It's too soon to be sure, but the doctor reckons he'll make a complete recovery.'

Sophie slumped in relief, glad that at least there was some good news in this tragedy-filled night. 'Can I see him?' She needed to thank him. Needed to see for herself that he wasn't still in the dire state he had been in when Ned had manoeuvred his limp body out of the window to the waiting hands below.

Ned shrugged his big shoulders. 'I don't see why not—although I should warn you that he's not decent.'

'Do I strike you as the sort who will faint at the sight of a naked man?' If anything, Sophie was more the sort who revelled in the sight of one, as her body's scandalous reaction to Lord Hockley's bare chest at his bedcham-ber window last week was testament. She had always thoroughly enjoyed one—although Ned didn't know that. Thankfully, nobody here beyond her aunt knew that Miss Sophie Gilbert, the outwardly prim and dusty spinster on the shelf, was no stranger to the pleasures of the flesh.

'He's crotchety too.' Ned shrugged, his expression

bewildered. 'But to give him credit, a lot less crotchety than I would be in his position.' The gruff farmer huffed out a sigh. 'It's going to be difficult to hate the bastard after tonight, isn't it?'

'He saved my aunt's life.' Something for which she would be indebted to him for ever, even if Aunt Jemima did not pull through. 'He could have left her. Saved himself.'

'Yet it never occurred to him.' Ned huffed again. 'If I hadn't seen it with my own eyes, watched him throw himself over her while the roof collapsed, I'd never have believed it. Then there's his brother...' He stared towards the staircase, brows furrowed. 'Who knew he had a brother?'

Sophie had, but it hadn't felt right to share that with anyone. Not when Lord Hockley was so protective of Archie. Even as they had carried him indoors in agony, he had masked it for his sibling's sake. Reassuring the young man that all was well and that he would be as 'right as ninepence' in no time.

She followed Ned into the bedchamber, then stood awkwardly on the threshold while the doctor listened to his patient's chest. Lord Hockley was semi-reclined, propped on several plump pillows in the centre of the bed. His eyes were squeezed closed in pain and his teeth were clenched, but he made no sound as Dr Able prodded and probed around his distended, twisted shoulder. Somebody had cleansed the worst of the soot from his body, but even under the warm candlelight, Lord Hockley's complexion was pale.

As if he sensed her, his eyes opened. 'How is your aunt?'

That those were his first words said a great deal about

the sort of man he was deep down. 'Sleeping.' Sophie's gaze flicked towards the physician's briefly to gauge how much he had revealed, and the doctor subtly shook his head, his eyes pleading with her not to say anything to upset his patient before his own ordeal was done. 'We'll have a better idea of her condition in the morning.' If she survived what was left of the night. 'I cannot thank you enough for saving her.'

He seemed uncomfortable as he brushed that away. 'And Archie?'

'Is in good spirits and keen to be helpful. He just went to help your cook make you some tea.'

'Is the house still filled with strangers?' The concern for his brother was written all over his handsome face.

She shook her head. 'Walpole sent them all bar Ned away, so calmness has resumed downstairs.'

'Good.' He exhaled, then coughed, wincing as he sank back on the pillows. 'Sorry about your cottage. Ned here tells me it is gone.' She could tell he felt bad for not being able to save that too.

'They are only walls, my lord. Everything I care about came out alive.' At least for now they still were. She edged a little closer to the bed and tried to smile despite having nothing to smile about. 'I should also thank you for saving Socrates too.'

His fingers went to the long cut on his cheek. 'As you can see, your ungrateful cat already thanked me in his own special way.' The sentence came out a little slurred and he frowned. 'And clearly the laudanum that was forced upon me is finally working. On my tongue at least although my blasted shoulder still hurts like the devil.'

'With such a small dose it'll barely take the edge off.' Dr Able's gaze locked with hers and he rolled his eyes as if getting any of the drug into his stubborn patient's body had been a battle. 'As I have repeatedly said, I could give you more and you would feel practically nothing. Resetting a shoulder is a nasty business.'

'I prefer to be lucid.'

'I doubt you'll think that once we begin.'

'Can somebody ensure that my brother remains downstairs until it is done?' Two deep blue eyes stared at her directly. 'I don't want him any more distressed by tonight than he already is.'

'I have already made sure that he is occupied for the duration.'

'Thank you.' His obvious relief was palpable. 'He took our father's death badly and it is still too fresh in his memory for him not to panic that I am on the cusp of following suit.'

Walpole arrived with a footman and a very sturdy table from the kitchen. With Ned's help they manoeuvred it into the bedchamber. Sophie was about to leave to check on her aunt when the doctor caught her arm and pulled her to one side just before the door. 'He seems to trust you far more than he does me, either that or his gentlemanly politeness prevents him from refusing a woman.' Despite his whisper, his tone was frustrated. 'Perhaps before you leave you could convince him to accept more laudanum before I begin?'

Chapter Ten

'I can hear you and whether the plea comes from a woman or not, the answer is still no.'

Dr Able sighed at Lord Hockley's matter-of-fact comment. 'The procedure is going to hurt, my lord. Much more than I think you could possibly imagine. It has been some time since your injury, and your muscles have contracted too far for me to be able to push the ball back into the socket without a fight. It will be so much easier if you are relaxed.'

'I am as relaxed as I am going to be so let's just get it over with before they contract some more.' Lord Hockley tried to get himself out of bed with only his good arm, and they both hurried towards him to help. 'And we shall do it without any blasted laudanum and that is my *final* word on the matter.'

Without the shield of the blanket, he was apparently only completely naked from the waist up, so she was spared the onerous task of attempting to avert her wayward eyes from his most distracting places. They still noticed enough to see that he was as perfect a specimen of manhood as she had ever seen. However, the dislocated shoulder wasn't the only bad wound his big body had experienced. There was a starburst scar the size of her fist marring the bottom of his ribs and another jagged slash just beneath it. Both long healed over but both had clearly been earned on the battlefield and confirmed his claim to have spent too many years in the service of others.

As he stood, she wrapped her arm around his middle to avoid his bad arm, and then wished she hadn't because he was as solid as he looked. His skin was warm and smooth beneath her fingers. The muscles beneath bunched taut with the pain.

They got him to the table without incident, and then after two failed attempts, and much to his disgust, got him upon it only after Ned lifted him up. She could tell his weakness embarrassed him and dented his manly pride, but he thanked Ned regardless and allowed her and the doctor to assist in lowering him to lie flat. Prostrate, the rounded head of his humerus bone protruded above his pectoral muscle. The beginnings of a ferocious bruise bloomed over his collarbone and down his arm. He had to be in agony. Agony which was about to get worse before it subsided.

Without thinking, Sophie tenderly brushed his hair from his face. 'Take some more of the laudanum, my lord. Please.'

The slight shake of his head was his only answer, but his eyes flicked to the door and she knew his reluctance had more to do with his brother than himself.

'Are you worried about Archie?'

'He needs me here and he needs me to be invincible.' His jaw stiffened, and he turned to Dr Able. 'Do it now.' Ned stepped forward and that earned him a glare. 'I understand this is necessary and can assure you that I *do not* require restraining.'

'Actually, I have asked Ned to steady your legs, not restrain you.' Dr Able stripped off his coat and tossed it to one side, calmly taking control. 'Massaging the joint back into place will take some time and I need your spine straight.'

'Massage?' Lord Hockley seemed outraged at such a namby-pamby solution. 'Can't you just pop it back in with one good shove like all the no-nonsense, cutthroat sawbones do on the battlefield?'

'I could if I wanted to risk more, and possibly permanent, damage to your bones, muscles and ligaments; however, my method is more effective.' Dr Able rolled up his shirtsleeves. 'And for the record, Lord Hockley, I perfected this technique on the battlefields of the Peninsula where I spent five years as one of those no-nonsense, cutthroat sawbones.' He gestured to the starburst scar marring Lord Hockley's washboard-flat midriff. 'Shrapnel? Ours?'

His wary patient nodded, clearly rapidly revaluating the country doctor whom he had doubtless underestimated. 'I managed to be in the wrong place at the wrong time and momentarily on the wrong side of the lines. Damn thing exploded mid-air beside me and threw me off my horse. Cracked a blasted rib to boot.'

'And if I am not mistaken...' Dr Able traced the deeper, jagged scar below it in the air with his finger '...that beauty is from a French bayonet. Did you fall off your horse again, Captain Peel?'

'How did you know I was a captain?'

'A gut feel borne out of encounters with too many cavalry captains who think they know better about ev-

erything than the higher ranks possibly ever could to rec-
ognise one when I see one.' The physician smiled then.
'It is ironic, is it not, that if I were treating this wound
in Mont-Saint-Jean as the cutthroat sawbones-in-chief
Colonel Able, I could order you to take the laudanum,
yet here, where you now outrank me and as you apparently know better, we must do it your way.'

'You were at Waterloo.'

'I was indeed, my lord.' Dr Able laced his fingers together and cracked them ominously to warm them up
for the new battle ahead. 'Are you sure you will not take
more laudanum?'

There was a brief flash of indecision before he shook
his head again.

'Very well.' The physician spoke directly to Sophie.
'I am tasking you with distracting him, Miss Gilbert.
Try to keep our stubborn soldier as relaxed as possible
and hopefully, for all our sakes, this onerous, painful
task will not take long.'

She positioned herself on the opposite side of the
table to his injury and dithered over what to say and do,
but as the physician took his bad arm and bent it at the
elbow behind his head, she instinctively lent to his eye
level and gripped his good hand. 'Try to breathe evenly,
my lord. Think pleasant thoughts.'

The pain was etched in his face yet still he managed
a wry smile as the doctor rotated his shoulder and his
fingers gripped hers for grim death. 'Such as?'

'I have no earthly idea. It just seemed the sort of thing
people say at a time like this. I am prepared to concede
that, with hindsight, it was not the least bit distracting.'

The sounds of bone cracking on bone accompanied
his grimace and his neck arched on the table, the corded

veins and muscles knotting beneath the skin. 'Tell me something diverting instead then.' Another crack and some stoic laboured breathing. 'Something about you, Miss Gilbert, that I would find interesting.'

'Alas, I fear I am as dull as dishwater, Lord Hockley. I am not the least bit interesting.'

'As you have led an entire village in rebellion and thwarted all my best-laid plans to sell this god-awful house today, I sincerely doubt that.' The 'that' came out through gritted teeth as the doctor laid a heavy palm flat against his misshapen shoulder, then he panted out the pain. 'You are vexing, indomitable and bossy to your core, Sophie Gilbert.' Her Christian name on his lips felt odd. Nice—but unsettling. 'Another born captain who thinks she always knows best.'

'Only a captain?'

His chuckle was strained. 'What would you prefer? General Gilbert of the whinging Whittleston Rebel Alliance—one of the most formidable adversaries I have ever come up against. The good doctor and I could have done with you at Waterloo, Sophie.'

'I shall take that as a compliment, *my lord*.' It was a missish reprimand. A reminder more for her to maintain formality because he was still technically the enemy who held the future of the village in the palm of his hand—but something about him called to her anyway and it wasn't just gratitude.

He choked out a laugh, which turned into a racking cough, until he groaned as the doctor rotated his shoulder with more force than he had previously. 'Good grief, woman!' His clipped tone was likely more down to the rigid angle the physician was keeping his arm in than actual anger at her. 'Now is no time to be prudish! Not when I am in my drawers and am quite convinced you are quite naked under that prim soot-stained nightgown.' She was—but now she was worried he could see right through all the billowing layers of thick flannel to all the too bountiful, unbound curves beneath. That they all could.

'I think we're almost there.' Wordlessly, Dr Able braced her and Ned for the worst as he planted his knee on the table for purchase, and all concerns about her distinct lack of modesty evaporated in her concern for him. 'Take a deep breath in now, my lord, and hold it until I tell you.'

'I suppose it's too late to take up the offer of that laudanum now?' That he could crack a joke at a time like this was impressive.

'Just grip my hand, my lord.' She gripped his for all she was worth, hoping he would absorb some of her strength until the deed was done.

'But I might break your fingers... *Sophie*...and then you would be unable to hold your giant "Shame on you, Lord Hockley" banner at your next protest.'

He was teasing her. Distracting her, drat him, because he could see that she was worried, and he wanted her to feel better. His ingrained and thoughtful nobility was humbling.

Charming.

It made him utterly too likeable to boot.

'Fear not. I am a tough old bird... *Rafe*...and as the bossy general of the whinging Whittleston Rebel Alliance I shall simply order Ned to carry it in my stead.' She smiled and stared deep into his eyes. His held hers unwavering as he took a deep breath, then growled through his teeth as the joint finally slid home with an unimpressive pop.

As his fingers loosened, she found herself stroking his face, hers mere inches from his. 'All done now.' Then, embarrassed by the unexpected intimacy of the last few moments, she let her hands fall as she stood. 'I shall go tell Archie that his stubborn big brother is still invincible and leave you to rest.'

'Bring him up. Nobody will get rest unless he sees that for himself.' Poor Rafe no longer looked pale. He looked grey. Or perhaps green. Yet still determined to martyr through for the sake of his sibling.

'I will fetch him and allow him to see you briefly on only one condition.' His deep blue eyes could narrow all they wanted, but somebody had to save him from himself, and if he wasn't going to listen to the doctor, Sophie would make sure he listened to her. 'And that is that you take the blasted laudanum, you obstinate, noble fool, and entrust me with taking care of Archie tonight. You are no good to him—or anyone—like this.' She narrowed her eyes right back at him. 'And as the most senior officer here tonight, that is my *final* word on the matter.'

Chapter Eleven

After a peculiar and fitful night, Rafe awoke disorientated, his body aching from head to toe, and his mouth as parched as the interminable Spanish plains in the middle of a baking Mediterranean summer. He touched the strapping around his shoulder to assess the damage beneath for himself and was relieved to discover that he could probe his entire shoulder without hitting the ceiling in agony. It hurt, of course it did, but nowhere near as much as it had last night.

As he gingerly flexed his limbs and stretched his spine before he risked moving it any further, he tried to work out whether he had dreamt of Sophie in a laudanum-induced haze or if she had tended to him in the night. She had definitely been there for the bandaging. He had a vague recollection of that. But after, when he had a feeling it had been she who had mopped his brow and supported his head while she fed him water in between the peculiar nightmares the drug and the pain gave him, he wasn't entirely certain.

If it had been a dream, it had been a vivid one as he had felt the soft press of her bosom against his body as she had held him. Enjoyed the gentle brush of her fingers through his hair as she had settled him back to sleep. The feel of his hand in hers. Her whisper beside his ear assuring him he was just having a bad dream. The memory—real or conjured—of all those things brought goosebumps to his battered flesh.

'You are awake then.' The physician strode in as if he owned the place and began to examine him without asking, pressing his palm against Rafe's forehead to check his temperature. 'There are no signs of infection or fever.' He bent and lifted one of his eyelids to peer into it. 'Any blurred vision or dizziness?'

Rafe shook his head as Dr Able picked up the hand of his bound arm and began to press down on the tips of each of his fingers. 'Any numbness? Pins and needles?'

'None.'

'Make a fist.'

He did without any issues and the doctor stepped back. 'I cannot see any signs of concussion or paralysis, so despite half a roof landing on your obstinate skull you've managed to emerge relatively unscathed. How do you feel?'

'As though all of Napoleon's Grande Armée has marched over me.'

Dr Able smiled. 'The bruising will be pretty severe for the next few weeks but will abate with time, as will the pain and stiffness. It is imperative you give your shoulder time to heal or you'll end up back at square one. Your muscles have been through a trauma and must knit themselves back together to keep that joint in place and we don't want it popping out again.' He gestured to the nightstand with a flick of his head where a folded square of linen sat alongside an array of bottles. 'That means you'll need to wear a sling for at least three weeks to help keep the strain off. After that, gentle exercise and no heavy lifting for another two months while you build your strength up.'

'Can I still ride?' Archie would be unbearable if he couldn't take him out for their daily jaunt.

'Once the sling is off, I don't see why not so long as you keep to a sedate pace. Absolutely no mad gallops or jumps which might dislodge it.' He opened a pot of salve and dabbed it on Rafe's scratched cheek. 'And avoid cats as they clearly don't like you.'

'Am I consigned to bed for the three weeks too?' Because that would drive him stark, staring mad.

'You can fester here if it pleases you, being waited on hand and foot for the duration, or you can get up and move about if you feel up to it so long as you do not push yourself too hard. I often find movement is nature's own pain relief for most things muscular and you can rest in a chair downstairs just as easily as you can up here. So long as you follow doctor's orders, I see no reason to confine you to barracks, although I doubt you would listen if I did.'

It was said with good humour and that was how Rafe took it. 'How is the old lady?'

The doctor's face clouded. 'Not quite so hale and hearty, I am afraid. She hasn't yet regained consciousness and her breathing is still a cause for concern. All we can do now is sit and wait—but at least she has survived the night. After all the time she spent in the smoke, that in itself is a miracle.'

'And Miss…'

The doctor's smile was a little too knowing, as if he had been expecting him to ask about her. 'Sophie is sitting with her despite being dead on her feet and in dire need of some rest herself—but like you, she won't listen to me and seems determined to block it all out by keeping herself busy.'

'I think I would do the same.' It was the only way Rafe had survived the war. 'When the world is crashing around your ears, it is the practical and mundane that keeps you sane.'

Dr Able shot him a wordless soldier-to-soldier, officer-to-officer glance. 'Only for so long.' They had both witnessed and doubtless personally experienced the unspoken emotional breakdowns which were also necessary to keep one sane and knew, from all their battlefield experiences, that sometimes those suppressed emotions ate something alive from within. 'She has lost her home and all her possessions in one fell swoop and has apparently no other family beyond her aunt who might not make it—yet aside from the fact that she hasn't allowed herself to stop for a minute since last night, I've not witnessed any evidence that she has shed a single tear. Not even in private. She is too matter of fact. Too calm. I worry she is in shock.' Which now made Rafe worry about her too. People occasionally died of shock. 'Yet it is obvious she blames herself for what happened.'

'She shouldn't.' His heart bled for the vexing minx. Misplaced guilt was soul destroying. That he knew only too well. 'Fires happen. Especially at night when a neglected candle melts and topples.'

'Or somebody neglects their responsibilities.' An odd answer which sounded a great deal like a superior's admonishment. But then Dr Able—*Colonel Able*—had that way about him. 'Your brother is outside, pacing the landing and beyond eager to see you if you are feeling up to it.'

'Of course I am.' Even if he weren't, he owed it to Archie to pretend to be, so Rafe shuffled to sit higher on the bed so that his brother would see he was in fine fettle. 'Send him in.'

Archie entered artificially subdued, holding himself back despite his obvious relief at the sight of Rafe sat up in bed rather than on the cusp of snuffing it. 'You missed breakfast. I wanted to wake you, but Sophie said you needed your sleep, so I ate it with her instead.'

'Don't tell me...' Rafe squeezed closed his eyes and touched his temple as if he was reading his brother's mind. 'You had boiled eggs again.'

He giggled. 'Wrong! I had toast and jam. Sophie made it on the drawing room fire and we washed it down with chocolate. At least I had chocolate. She had tea and no toast, which I could not understand because it was delicious.'

The blasted woman really wasn't looking after herself at all, yet had the nerve to nag him into following doctor's orders last night. The classic do-as-I-say-but-not-as-I-do dichotomy that he had always chaffed against in the army.

'This afternoon, when her aunt wakes up, I am going to help her see if any of her belongings survived the fire and find Socrates because he ran away last night and went to hide in the trees. But Sophie says he wouldn't have gone far because he's old and creaky and set in his ways. She reckons he'll be sat on what is left of the doorstep, waiting to be fed and sulking because she never gave him his breakfast on time. Or his luncheon.'

'Luncheon?' Surely Rafe hadn't slept through the entire morning. 'What time is it?' He pointed to his charred and ruined waistcoat on the chair in the corner and Archie fetched his watch.

'It's two something.' His brother passed it over as his ability to read time only extended to the small hand—which was a vast improvement on what he had been able to do before Rafe had taken over as his guardian.

'It's ten minutes to three!' He hadn't just missed the morning but most of the day! 'I was expecting visitors.' The second flurry of potential buyers after he had lost all the first to her blasted barricade.

'Sophie told Walpole to send them all away because you needed your rest.'

'Oh, I'll just bet she did!' In every cloud there was a silver lining, and his shoulder had inadvertently given her the perfect excuse to thwart his sale of Hockley Hall yet again. 'Of course the witch sabotaged me while I slept!'

Archie's face fell. 'Sophie isn't a witch. She's kind and lovely and my friend.' The wounded expression turned to one of admonishment, which was a rare thing indeed when his brother usually looked up to him in everything. 'You are being mean, Rafe.'

The guilt was instant and perhaps not entirely misplaced this time. 'I just want to sell this damned mausoleum, Archie. The quicker it's gone, the quicker you and I can go and raise our horses somewhere miles from everyone. I didn't mean to be mean about your friend.' A friend who likely had more on her mind today than thwarting his sale.

'It's all right.' His brother's bad mood evaporated in a single smile. 'Sophie warned me that you were bound to be as tetchy when you woke up as you were in the middle of the night.'

'You were here in the middle of the night?'

'Only for a little bit until Sophie sent me to bed when you started shouting in your sleep. But she stayed up to look after you and her aunt.'

Which meant Rafe hadn't imagined her tender ministrations in his addled state and that made him feel even more guilty for his petulant outburst accusing her of sabotage. Guilty and more than a little uncomfortable that she had tended to him in his hour of need. He wasn't used to being vulnerable in front of another or relying on anyone but himself. He certainly wasn't used to being soothed back to sleep by a gentle pair of feminine hands.

Archie patted Rafe's hand as if he were a child. 'Sophie said people are always grumpy and unreasonable when they are in pain, and that you are bound to be just as unbearable for the next week because of your shoulder. Maybe longer if it hurts too much. She said I have to make allowances and remember that it is the pain talking—not you—and that if you snap at me I should count to ten and then forgive you instantly.'

Rafe would have folded his arms in belligerence if both of them had worked. Instead, he had to settle for a put-upon sniff. 'Sophie has clearly had plenty to say about me while I have been sleeping. It's a wonder I did not awaken with my ears burning. What other pearls of wisdom about me did she share with you while I was drugged up to my eyes?'

Incapable of keeping any secrets, Archie sat on the mattress and ticked off the list on his fingers. 'She said that while you are an invalid I have to be the big brother and I have to look after you because you are going to need my help. That I have to keep a close eye on you but that I must be subtle about it because you are too proud and too stubborn to ask for anyone's help—especially mine. That you are the best big brother in the world, a brave hero and too noble for your own good…'

'She called me a hero?' His brother nodded. 'And noble?'

Archie nodded again. 'And she said that because you always put me before yourself, you would feel bad about being incon-*passinated*…?' He frowned over the mis-pronunciation.

'Incapacitated?'

'That's the word!' Archie slapped his thigh. 'I knew that you would know it.'

'What else did Sophie say?' Suddenly Rafe needed to know everything. Especially as some of it sounded a great deal like praise and for some inexplicable reason he apparently craved hers.

'Only that for my sake you would try to pretend that you were all right when you weren't so I must make sure that you do not try to do too much. I must do as much as I can for you and to report any pig-headedness to her immediately so that she can tell you off.' His brother sighed like a wise old sage as he patted Rafe's hand again. 'We are both expecting her to have to do that quite a lot in the next few days. For your own good, of course.'

'Of course.'

'Sophie says that sometimes some people are too stubborn and proud for their own good and that you are one of them.' A door that swung both ways. 'It is our job to save you from yourself and pick up the slack.'

Yet who was going to do the same for her? And why

the blazes should he care when he had already gone above and beyond, and she wasn't his responsibility?

But he did. Someone had to look after the witch in her hour of need and save her from herself. And the horror of searching through that smoking ruin down the lane.

The weight of the world once again resting on his lone good shoulder, Rafe ruffled his brother's hair. 'So… now that the tables are turned and you are under strict instruction to look after me for a change, you might as well get started. I am going to need a nice hot bowl of water, some soap and a flannel before you help me get dressed, then we are both going to organise a search party to find your new best friend's damned cat.'

Chapter Twelve

An hour later, Rafe hovered outside the sickroom uncertain. As much as it felt wrong to intrude on another's grief, it felt more wrong to leave Sophie to it all alone. Especially as she apparently *was* all alone if the physician was to be believed. He hoped she had some family somewhere for both their sakes. Someone who would take her and her aunt in—or just her if the old lady never awoke. He was already agonising what would become of her if she didn't, and despite several lectures to his niggling conscience that her future really was not his problem, something about her made it seem as if she were.

Even though he hardly knew the woman.

Even though she had sabotaged his plans and turned the entire village against him.

Even though he had saved her life and her aunt's and her blasted cat's and ruined his shoulder in the process, so he had already gone above and beyond.

Even though he owed her, nor anyone for that matter beyond Archie, nothing and had faithfully promised himself he would never allow himself to be so beholden again!

Even though…

He ran his frustrated good hand through his freshly washed hair and allowed himself a quiet growl. *Damn it all to hell!* Blasted woman had been nothing but trouble since the moment he had first set covetous eyes upon her.

He blamed her sometimes soulful, sometimes skewering, sometimes sparkling and always savvy dark eyes for that. He had always had a penchant for big brown eyes. Probably because his were so blue and had always been drawn to the different. As a young officer keen to sow his wild oats, while his comrades chased after the fashionable, pretty perfection of the blonde English roses swarming the regimental balls in obvious search of flirtation, he had always gravitated to the bold and less impressed brunettes. The bolder the brunette, the better. Give him a sharp, clever, witty tongue any day over a shallow and simpering miss whose preferred method of conversing was with her artfully batting lashes.

He'd wager every penny of his new fortune that Sophie had never felt the urge to bat her lovely dark lashes at a fellow in her life. Her expressive eyebrows, however, had a language all of their own. Behind that door, he already knew that they would be sad. Scared. Exhausted. Yet when he entered she would mask all those emotions out of pride irrespective of the fact her entire world had just imploded. And for all his lofty aims to remain detached from everyone in this godforsaken village and all of their problems, he couldn't ignore that. Not from her and certainly not after her compassion towards him and his brother last night.

Strangely nervous though heaven only knew why, Rafe steeled himself before he tapped on the door, then slowly pushed it open in case she needed a few moments to compose herself. 'How is she?'

'There has been no change.' The soot-stained nightgown was gone, replaced by one of the maid's dresses, and a pale and drawn Sophie seemed surprised to see him. Then that was replaced by awkwardness at being caught looking so lost—exactly as he had predicted. Instantly she sat straighter as the ghost of a smile whispered across her mouth. Fearless, proud and stoic to the bitter end. 'You look better though, so that is a relief. How is the shoulder?'

Rafe stared down at the sling which did, to its credit, ease some of the discomfort. 'A bit tender but thankfully back where it is supposed to be. I shall apparently make a full recovery.'

'Does Dr Able know that you are up and about?'

He nodded at the subtle admonishment. Smiling as he recalled Archie's comment about pig-headedness and her threats to give Rafe a good telling-off if he did not comply. 'The sawbones has given his express permission but has put me on light duties for the next few weeks. Absolutely no galloping, lifting or wrestling mad cats.' Which he supposed brought him neatly to his flimsy excuse to visit her. 'And speaking of mad cats, Archie is desperate to hunt for yours because it's missed its breakfast— so I said I'd help him on his quest. Any ideas where we might find the snarling monster?'

'He will probably be hiding under his favourite walnut tree by the stream, but I fear your rescue mission will be futile. Socrates is a cantankerous old thing with an irrational aversion to all males. He really will not come unless myself or Aunt Jemima calls him.' Her voice caught on her aunt's name, and she covered it by fussing with the old lady's blankets. 'I shall fetch him later once she wakes up. You have gone to too much trouble for us as it is.'

'Fear not, it won't be me who goes to any trouble.' He pointed to the sling. 'I will simply bark orders at my brother and my staff while they hunt for your vicious pet.' How to say the next bit as gently as possible? 'We are also going to see if we can salvage anything from the...'

'Wreckage? The pyre? The ashes.' She shrugged as if she was matter of fact about the loss of her home. 'That is also very kind of you, but I suspect that quest will be just as futile. You were out cold, so you did not see it, but there really wasn't much left of the place after they dragged you out. Thank goodness the cottage had the good grace to wait for that before it collapsed like a house of cards else it would have taken you both with it.' She couldn't look at him and instead gently stroked the unconscious woman's hair in much the same way as she had his in the middle of the night. 'We both owe you our lives. I really cannot thank you enough...' Her voice caught again and he couldn't bear it.

'No thanks are necessary. I was merely first to the scene and only did what anyone would have done.'

She shook her head. 'You didn't give up. You risked your own life to save a stranger you barely know and then stayed with her even when the roof began to give way. Ned told me that you used yourself to shield my aunt from the falling beams.' Had he? Rafe couldn't remember. 'Few would have done that and whatever happens now...' She brushed the old lady's head again as if she were lingering over the last goodbye, a maelstrom of emotions swirling in her lovely eyes. 'I shall never be able to repay you for such selfless bravery.'

'There is nothing to repay.'

'I dare say that is just as well.' She forced a smile which did not touch her eyes. 'For we have nothing left to repay you with.' She rearranged her features before she turned to him properly in case her pain showed through her tough façade, unaware that the deep furrow which remained between her brows had the power to pierce his heart. 'However, in the spirit of gratitude, you will be pleased to hear that I have decided to resign my commission as General Gilbert of the whinging Whittleston Rebel Alliance and burn my *SHAME ON YOU, LORD HOCKLEY* banner forthwith…although I suspect that burned with all the rest of our belongings so…' She turned away again as emotion choked her and without thinking he closed the few feet between them to wrap his good arm around her shoulders and tug her to his chest.

'Oh, Sophie… I am so sorry.' Beneath his fingers her body trembled as she pressed her entire weight against him, and he realised with a start that he wanted to be there for her. Wanted her to lean on him. Wanted to carry her burdens. 'It will all be all right, Sophie.'

It was his turn to tenderly stroke her hair. To whisper words of comfort in her ear. To try and distract her from the pain.

For a few moments she burrowed against him. Her breath sawing in and out against his middle as she fought for control, and he wanted to tell her that she did not have to pretend for him. That despite the sling he had broad enough shoulders for her to lean on. That they were in this together—whatever happened. That she could count on him.

Always.

Always?

Because that realisation caught him off guard, the words he wanted to say refused to come and instead he pressed his lips to the top of her head and hugged her tight in case he actually said them.

'I promise everything is going to be all right.'

A ludicrous promise which he knew as he uttered it was an outright lie. An empty platitude which eased nothing. He couldn't magically restore her home to the way it was nor replace all the irreplaceable belongings or memories eaten by the fire, and he certainly did not have any sway over fate's plan for her aunt. The old lady's life still hung in the balance and there wasn't a damn thing he could do to change that except pray for a miracle.

She knew it as well because for the briefest moment he felt all of her hopelessness before she masked that too.

'Of course it will be all right.' Too soon she stiffened in his arms as he felt the effort it took to bottle all her feelings ruthlessly back inside. 'Of course it will.'

She stood as an excuse to sever the contact and fussed over the blankets again to avoid revealing the acute distress she was in. 'Wallowing in a pit of self-pity is never the answer, is it? Onwards and upwards is.' Then she snatched up the water jug on her aunt's bedside. 'This has been sat here for hours and must be stale by now.' She hugged it tight to her middle as she scurried to the door, intent on keeping herself busy in case standing still crushed the remnants of her spirit. 'She'll want fresh when she awakes. Or more likely tea.' The stoic smile quivered until she mustered the strength from her bottomless well within to nail it in place. 'According to Aunt Jemima, a nice cup of tea solves everything.' And with that she fled.

* * *

As she had said, there wasn't much left of Willow Cottage. Apart from two jagged remnants of the back wall which jutted from the smoking debris like broken teeth, all that remained was soot and rubble. Rubble that had already been sifted through by Ned Parker who had pipped Rafe at the post and thoroughly done all of the practical and achievable good deeds he had wanted to do personally for Sophie in her hour of need.

However, rather than be grateful that the enormous and gratingly handsome young farmer had saved him the job, he found himself irrationally jealous of the fellow instead—despite the fact Rafe owed him his life. And despite the fact he had no earthly reason to be jealous, absolutely did not want to be nor fully understood exactly why he was. It was most unlike him.

'I couldn't let Sophie do this.' The mighty oak cleaned the charred cover of a book on his trousers before he tossed it into the cart with the few other paltry belongings he had managed to rescue while Rafe had been sleeping off the laudanum. 'And knowing her, she'd have found her way here some time today to rifle through the rubble. What a dreadful business this is.'

'But thankfully, nobody died.' Yet. Though that might well change at any moment. 'I am indebted to you, sir, for saving my life.'

Two massive and perfectly working shoulders shrugged in dismissal. 'After you saved both Misses Gilbert, it seemed churlish to leave you in the flames— as much as I was sorely tempted too.' Ned folded his arms, no doubt hoping his bulging biceps would intimidate the enemy. 'How's Sophie bearing up? That woman

is as stubbornly proud as anyone I've ever encountered.
I suppose she's putting a brave face on it all?'

The tree clearly knew her well. Perhaps cared for her
deeply. Both things chaffed.

'She is. Hasn't stopped or slept a wink since last night
despite Dr Able putting several fleas in her ear about
the need to rest herself. I left her sat with her aunt.' And
with the overwhelming desire to slay dragons for her.
'Although I suppose it is understandable that she would
want to be by her side.'

Ned's face clouded. 'The good doctor doesn't hold
out much hope for Miss Gilbert.' He shook his shaggy
head as if he still couldn't quite believe what had happened despite being stood in the centre of it. 'Poor Sophie. She's devoted to her aunt. I can't imagine what she
is going through. When I finally got home, I couldn't
sleep a wink for worrying about her. Figured long before the sun came up that I might as well channel all
that worry into doing something useful by saving what
I could.' They both stared at the blackened imprint that
had once been her cottage. 'As you can see, not much is
salvageable. A few trinkets and knick-knacks, most fit
for nothing but the ash tip, but they might bring her some
comfort. Once the roof gave way, what the flames didn't
destroy, the collapse did.' He kicked the piece of char-
coal near his giant foot, the blackened carvings etched
into it marking it as once part of a piece of furniture.
'They're only things, I suppose. Nothing living to mourn
yet I dare say she'll mourn them keenly.'

'At least her cat survived.' And at least that was something he could do for her. 'My brother and I are going
to try to find it.'

So far mute and wide-eyed next to him as he tried to

comprehend the scene, Archie nodded. 'Socrates hasn't had any breakfast.'

'Oh, yes, he has.' Ned held out his arm and pulled up his sleeve to reveal it was peppered with deep scratches. 'Spiteful thing bit a chunk out of me when I finally caught him. I had to wrestle him into that basket, and it was a struggle, I don't mind admitting. What possessed Sophie to take in a feral cat is beyond me when I warned her not to.' He hoisted the hissing basket out of the cart and handed it to Archie. 'I'll leave you the pleasure of delivering the vicious beastie to his mistress, young man. Just make sure all the doors and windows are closed before you release him, as old Socrates is in a worse mood than he usually is and there's no telling how he'll react to a strange house or the strangers within it unless he's contained.'

Then Ned beckoned over one of the grooms Rafe had brought with him as he began to unhitch his cart from his horse. 'And if you don't mind, my lord, I shall entrust you with delivering these things back to her.'

'You rescued it all, therefore it should be you who takes it to her and receives all the credit.' Sometimes Rafe loathed his noble streak and ingrained sense of fair play.

Ned waved that away. 'I shall stop by later once I've been to the village. I've set the ladies the task of procuring some essentials—clothes and unmentionables and the like. As close as I am to Sophie, I have no clue what feminine necessities her and her poor aunt will need.'

As close as I am to Sophie... Was that a polite, territorial warning? 'That is very thoughtful of you, Mr Parker, and please, feel free to call whenever. She needs her friends now more than ever, not that she would admit it. Or are you and she more than friends?' *Why the blazes had he asked that?* Annoyed at himself for caring when he had long ago sworn off such nonsense regarding women, Rafe aimed for nonchalance. 'I am too new to know the local gossip.'

The tree hooked his fingers in his belt. 'There aren't many people whose company I can tolerate for long, but Sophie is one of them.'

A cryptic answer which left him completely in the dark, and apparently the only one the gruff farmer was prepared to offer as he led his horse away to tie it to a tree. Then, using just his own brute strength, Ned manoeuvred his enormous cart around to attach it to one of Hockley Hall's horses.

Rafe suppressed the urge to ask for further clarification on the particulars of their relationship and instead tried to seek some to the other burning questions he had about his vexing new houseguest. 'Dr Able said that Sophie's aunt is her only family.'

Ned nodded, anger replacing his reticence. 'The only one she speaks to, at any rate. She's estranged from her father.'

'Her father is still alive?'

'Last I heard he was—but I know better than to enquire about him from her. Mention anything to do with her past and she gets a tart look about her before she changes the subject. Woe betide any fool who presses her further as she has a temper on her.' Ned pulled a face which said that he too found the witch a bit too formidable at times. 'All I know is her old man lives in the city somewhere. Some sort of merchant, Mrs Fitzherbert told me as she knew him man and boy and long before my time. Oriental silks and spices, I believe. Used to come here once in a blue moon to visit his sister when I was younger, all puffed up with his own importance in his fancy carriage, but stopped after Sophie moved in with her. The money he sent the poor old dear stopped too—or so I reckon—around the same time, though I can't confirm it. The Misses Gilbert would rather suffer in silence than admit they were struggling, and Sophie would rather starve than accept any charity—even from me—but I know the last two years especially have been particularly tough for them.'

'Her father provides no financial support whatsoever?' Such an abdication of family responsibility it beggared belief and wasn't how Rafe had been raised. By his father at least. His mother had no sense of responsibility whatsoever but had been out of his life for so long he preferred not to spoil his mood by thinking of her.

'How that bastard sleeps at night when he's abandoned two of his womenfolk to poverty is a mystery to me—but then some people have no conscience, do they?' He jabbed a meaty finger at the smouldering debris. 'Your cursed cousin certainly didn't, and now poor Sophie is homeless as a result. It's a good job that bastard is dead as I'd have strangled him myself last night for his part in this.'

The venom in that accusation took Rafe back. 'His part?' His mystery second cousin had been dead for months, so could hardly be blamed for what happened last night.

'Sophie's been begging the bastard for years to fix the chimney. Damn thing was a death trap. An accident waiting to happen and she knew it. The pair of them had to freeze to death in winter because they couldn't risk keeping the fires burning overnight unattended. But that old miser was too tight to even repair let alone rebuild it as it needed, but still had the cheek to raise their rent every year when he knew they were struggling. Makes my blood boil.'

It was making Rafe's boil too. 'I never knew that her cottage was dangerous.'

'Never took the time to find out either, did you, in your hurry to be shot of us all.'

'I... I...' Clearly some of the blame for the fire rested on Rafe's shoulders now too and the bile rose in his throat at the realisation. 'If I had known...'

Ned stayed him with a raised palm, and an unexpected expression of sympathy. 'You didn't know, and to be fair to you, I have a feeling you would have done something about it if you had. I might not like what you're planning as my loyalty lies with the village, I'll make no bones about that, but I know a decent man when I see one and...' His eyes flicked to Archie who was peering through the wicker basket, trying to calm the obviously furious and bucking Socrates inside with some soothing words. 'We all have our own responsibilities, Lord Hockley, and must do what we think is best for the ones we love. Besides, I am indebted to you for saving one of my favourite people last night so that makes you all right in my book.' The bigger man slapped Rafe on his good shoulder with such force he felt it in his knees. 'Tell Sophie I shall stop by later. And tell the stubborn wench that if she doesn't take some time to rest in the meantime, to expect me to put a bigger flea in her ear than Dr Able.'

Chapter Thirteen

'Sophie.'

Her head snapped up from the mattress where it must have fallen forward. Her eyes blinking away the darkness in case the voice she had heard hadn't been in her dream as she groped for her aunt's hand. The fingers moved against hers. Tried to grip back but lacked the strength.

'I am here, Aunt.' Without letting go she scrambled to her feet, ignoring the protests from her spine after goodness knew how many hours sat hunched in the same chair, while she turned up the lamp on the nightstand enough to see her aunt's pale face. Her eyes were still closed but the slackness which had been around her mouth and features was gone.

'Sophie?' It was barely a whisper. A scorched, dry rasp but her heart still soared with hope.

'Shh...rest easy.' She smoothed her hand over the older woman's face, sensing her panic and disorientation and not wanting to put any more strain on Aunt Jemima's heart than it had already endured. 'You've had one of your turns, that is all.' That is what they called the little bouts of light-headedness, tiredness and confusion which had plagued her since her health had begun to fail. Minimising and glossing over the important as usual because that was easier. 'But it is over now and Dr Able has assured me that there is nothing to worry about. He wanted to see you when you awoke, no doubt to fill you with new pills and potions to add to your collection.' Aunt Jemima had always put great stock in both, seeing them as categoric proof over the years that all of her many invented ailments were real. Up until her heart condition was diagnosed, they had all been gentle herbal tisanes which he brewed and labelled specially with fanciful scientific names that sounded impressive. 'I shall just fetch him and be back in a moment.'

Unsure of the hour or of who might still be up, she dashed into the dimly lit landing and summoned the footman Rafe had put expressly on the watch in case she needed something and dispatched him to send for the physician. Perhaps ludicrously, and despite the servant informing her that it was two in the morning, she also ordered tea simply because her aunt also put such great stock in its restorative powers. By the time she returned a mere minute or two later, Aunt Jemima's eyes had opened enough to see that she wasn't in her own bed.

'You are at Hockley Hall.' Sophie smiled as she hastened towards her, thinking on her feet but clueless as to what the older woman remembered or not. 'The doctor was worried about the cold at home and…' She would hide the awful truth about the rest of their predicament for as long as she could. What her aunt did not know couldn't hurt her and the whole truth would likely kill her right now. 'We both agreed you would be better off here for the night.'

If that seemed far-fetched after the Riot Act had been

read at the barricade and she had gone to bed with Lord Hockley very much the enemy, her aunt was too weak and too ill to notice. Instead, she closed her eyes once more while she allowed her niece to feed her sips of water from a spoon.

For the next twenty minutes she lapsed in and out of consciousness, the disjointed periods of lucidness marred by obvious signs of physical discomfort and distress which Sophie did not have the skills to alleviate. As time ticked by with excruciating slowness, and the bouts of discomfort became more protracted, all her initial relief was eaten away with an overwhelming sense of impotence when all she could do was watch. There was laudanum on the nightstand, but Sophie did not dare give it to her aunt until the doctor had made his assessment in case that did more harm than good. Aunt Jemima had been unconscious for more than twenty-four hours. Too much of that potent drug might well send her back into oblivion and possibly for ever.

When she could stand it no more and was about to march out to scream for answers, she heard the sound of footsteps near the door and almost sighed aloud. Except it wasn't the doctor who entered the sickroom. It was Rafe.

'The doctor will be here presently—or so he said to my man.'

'I hope so…she's in such pain.'

He glanced at the bed where Aunt Jemima had lapsed back into unsettled, laboured unconsciousness, then back to Sophie as if he could sense all her fears. 'I am no doctor—but on the battlefield it was always the casualties who made no noise which we had to be most worried about. It might not look it at the moment, but her current distress is a good sign.' He moved closer to lay a hand on Sophie's shoulder, the reassuring weight of it making her yearn to lean against him again to absorb his strength. 'It means her body is fighting again—at last.'

'Of course it is.' As the emotion threatened to bubble to the surface, it took all she had to keep it locked inside.

She made the mistake of glancing his way and her gaze locked with his much too intuitive one. He squeezed her shoulder in sympathy and solidarity and just that nearly undid her. She wanted to look away— but couldn't. Told herself to pull away but couldn't do that either. As if he could see into her mind and her heart and her soul, his intense blue gaze softened and he stroked her cheek, and against her better judgement she leant against his palm, allowing her eyelids to flutter closed to prevent the hovering tears from forming. Yet they did anyway. With such speed and decisiveness, she was powerless to stop them.

'Soph…' Her aunt's feeble whisper, broken in half by a racking, dry cough, snapped her back a split second before she disgraced herself and fell apart.

She leapt to her feet and directed all her attention back to the older woman in case he saw how close she had come to the edge of her reserves. Yet once again Rafe was right there beside her and used his good arm to help lift Aunt Jemima enough from the mattress that the coughing could be productive. To her complete horror, as the hacking subsided, the residue left in the handkerchief was gritty and black.

As her aunt collapsed exhausted back on the pillow, he stroked Sophie's arm, his reassurance a whisper now in case it distressed the woman in the bed. 'Trust me, that is a good sign too. I had the same.'

That was when Dr Able arrived, took stock of the situation and shooed them both from the room so he could get to work.

After an eternity of pacing the landing while Rafe sat silently watching her from the footman's abandoned chair, the physician finally emerged from the bedchamber and shrugged. 'It seems the immediate crisis has passed. Her pulse is stronger. There are no signs of fever or infection. Her breathing is still laboured—although that is to be expected—and both her eyes and her throat are red raw. But those will ease with time. And his lordship is correct, your aunt has inhaled a great deal of smoke and soot which her lungs are working hard to expel now that she has emerged from the coma. Such things, in my experience, are always better out than in.'

All music to Sophie's ears. 'Will she make a full recovery?'

Dr Able shrugged again, his expression wary. 'I think it's still too soon to make long-reaching predictions—especially given her underlying heart condition—but the initial signs are encouraging. Much more than they were this time yesterday. Things could change though so we must always err on the side of caution.'

'Oh.' Deflated, Sophie sat in the chair Rafe had just vacated. 'So the crisis hasn't passed completely. The worst could still...' Rafe's comforting hand landed on her shoulder again.

'This time yesterday, you weren't certain Sophie's aunt would ever regain consciousness or even survive the night and yet here we are. Another night later and she is still going strong and fighting to be awake. Surely that is more than encouraging, Dr Able, and surely you can give Sophie a tad more encouragement than you just have?'

'Medicine is never an exact science, my lord, so I cannot in all good conscience promise a complete and miraculous recovery so early in the day. Especially in a body of such advanced years…but…' He sighed under the weight of Rafe's glare. 'I am prepared to concede that I am hopeful that things are progressing in the right direction and her current condition suggests she could make a reasonable recovery at this stage although not perhaps a complete one.'

'That is good news.' Solid, capable fingers squeezed her arm in reassurance.

But Dr Able still tempered it with caution. 'At her age, she will not bounce back as rapidly as Lord Hockley has. She was in the smoke for longer, so there will be more in her lungs and I will have no way of knowing how extensive the damage has been for several weeks yet, or whether it has all had an adverse effect on her heart. The next few days are critical and they will not be easy. Her body has taken a battering and we need to build her strength up.'

All very worrying but at least with glimmers of hope, so Sophie decided to focus on that.

Her aunt began to cough again, and Dr Able rushed back inside to tend to her, insisting on doing it alone, leaving Sophie with Rafe.

A barefoot and rather rumpled Rafe, she now noticed. One who looked as if he had stumbled into the untucked shirt and breeches he was wearing. Even his sling was askew and twisted wrong as if donned while not in full control of all his faculties. 'Did the footman wake you when I sent him to fetch the doctor?' Because the more she stared at him, the more it appeared he had just fallen out of bed. 'He shouldn't have done that when I warned all the servants that you need your rest.'

'I gave him strict instructions to wake me if anything happened and as I pay his wages I dare say that still supersedes your bossy swathe of orders.' He smiled as he came towards her. 'But talking of rest, I cannot help noticing that you are in dire need of some yourself. You look exhausted.' Gentle fingers brushed her cheek in concern, the overwhelming intimacy of the innocent gesture clearly taking them both by surprise as he quickly retracted them. 'Now that she has regained consciousness, you should go to bed.'

Sophie shook her head. 'I am not leaving her alone until the crisis has passed.'

By the stubborn glint in his bright blue eyes Rafe was about to argue but the doctor returned and ushered them back into the sickroom where Aunt Jemima was propped semi-upright on a nest of pillows. 'I have made her as comfortable as possible, and this position will help with the cough and her breathing. I have also given her a sleeping draft made from valerian rather than any laudanum as that will be gentler on her system but should still be strong enough to ease some of the pain and help her rest. Rest and fluids are the best medicine at the moment. I shall return first thing to check on her progress.'

'You are not staying?' Panic gripped Sophie. 'But what if…'

A large, reassuring hand slipped through hers. 'She's sleeping, Sophie. Right now, she seems neither in any distress nor in any pain.' He laced his fingers through hers and inexplicably that eased her distress. 'Right now there is nothing more to worry about than keeping her in that state while her body heals.'

Dr Able agreed, his gaze flicking to Rafe's in some unspoken conversation before he smiled at her. 'I am not a betting man, Sophie, but if I were, in my humble medical opinion, the odds of the worst happening in the next few hours are slim.'

Rafe's fingers tightened around hers and he tugged her to face him. 'So go to bed, woman, at least until the sleeping draft wears off.'

'Not until...' Rafe stayed her words with a finger to her lips and they seemed to blossom into life beneath his touch.

'Just for an hour. You are dead on your feet.'

'But...' The pressure on her lips intensified.

'Go to blasted bed, you obstinate, stubborn wench, and entrust me with taking care of your aunt for the next hour. You are no good to her—or anyone—like this.' The finger on her lips moved to trace her cheek, leaving a trail of tingles in its wake. 'And on behalf of the eminently qualified Dr Able and myself, be in no doubt that that is our *final* word on the matter.'

The wretch had solemnly promised to wake her after an hour and reneged. Instead, he'd left her to sleep long past breakfast. Sophie awoke naturally with a start, dashed to her aunt's bedroom in her nightgown and was met by the sight of Dr Able snapping closed his medical bag while her aunt slept soundly, and Hockley Hall's housekeeper was sat in the chair beside the bed.

He was more optimistic than he had been in the small hours, and reported that she was doing well enough that he had given her enough laudanum to knock her out cold for the next few hours so that the healing powers of sleep could work their magic. The housekeeper, he also informed her, had been fully briefed on how to take proper care of his patient until he returned this afternoon, so he was prescribing Sophie a big breakfast back in bed followed by a long, hot bath because he felt she needed them more than Aunt Jemima needed her.

An hour later, refreshed, clean and fed, that appeared very much to be the case as Aunt Jemima was not only still sleeping with the housekeeper on guard at her side, she was snoring.

Which left Sophie not quite knowing what to do with herself.

Self-conscious and well aware that she was only a guest in this strange, cluttered house on sufferance, she went downstairs in search of Rafe, to say goodness only knew what only to see no sign of him or anyone in any of the main rooms. She hesitated at the door of his study, then decided not to enter. Not so much because it felt wrong to do so or because she might interrupt him while he was working, but because she had a vague recollection he had told her that that was where he had put all the items Ned had managed to salvage from the fire and she wasn't anywhere ready to face that ordeal yet. Instead, she followed the noises coming from the kitchen where she found Archie sat chatting to the kindly faced cook.

'You look better,' said Archie, beaming, while he pointed to his face. 'The ugly shadows have gone from beneath your eyes.'

The cook shushed him. 'Don't be so tactless, young man. You never refer to a woman as ugly, especially to her face.' She rolled her eyes at Sophie who couldn't help smiling at the ill-considered compliment.

'I wasn't calling Sophie ugly. Just the dark, puffy shadows.' Archie seemed quite baffled that anyone could take offence at his words. 'They made her look old and haggard.'

'And you certainly never call a lady old to her face either.' The cook admonished him with a lacklustre wag of one finger then pushed the mixing bowl towards him so he could lick the remnants of the cake mixture from the sides with his finger. 'You have to remember your manners, Archie. Old and haggard indeed! Apologise immediately.'

'There's nothing to apologise for.' Sophie smiled at them both. 'I saw myself in the mirror last night and almost screamed at my reflection I looked so dreadful. Archie is only being honest.'

'See,' said Archie with a fingerful of cake batter. 'Sophie knows I am her friend and would never say anything intentionally mean to hurt her. I was only being honest.'

'Would you like some more tea, Miss Gilbert?'

'No...' She had drunk so much she was swimming in the stuff. 'I was actually looking for the master of the house. Is he around?'

Cook looked to Archie who ran his finger around the rim of the bowl before he answered. 'Rafe's gone out with your cat. He tied him to a rope.'

'I beg your pardon?' Surely she had heard that incorrectly...unless Socrates had attacked him again and Rafe had decided enough was enough. 'Why has he tied him up?' She might owe him her life, but she would not stand by and allow cruelty to a defenceless animal, no matter what her vicious cat had done to deserve it.

Archie laughed. 'He hasn't tied him *up* with the rope, he's tied him *to* the rope. It was very funny to watch. It took him and Walpole half an hour to catch him and get it around his neck.'

All manner of dreadful scenarios skittered through her mind. 'Is your brother going to hang my cat! For I swear if he does that or drowns him in the river there will be hell to pay!'

Archie blinked at her outburst then barked with laughter again. 'Of course he isn't! Rafe would never do such a thing. He's taken Socrates for a walk so he can get his bearings and…' His voice dropped to a conspiratorial whisper. 'So he can do his business outside rather than in the middle of Rafe's study like he did this morning.'

'Oh.' The image of Rafe striding the grounds with her curmudgeonly cat on a string made the corners of her mouth twitch too. 'I take it he left him his calling card.'

'He did!' Archie thumped the table this time as he giggled. 'And Rafe stepped in it when he went to deliver Socrates his breakfast!'

Poor Rafe—but she couldn't help laughing too.

'I am amazed you slept through that commotion,' added the cook, also grinning. 'Thanks to your cat it's been an eventful morning, although it is probably just as well as the air was filled with all manner of expletives which are wholly unsuitable for a lady's ears.'

'Oh, dear. I do apologise. If you point me in the direction of a bucket and scrubbing brush, I shall clear up the mess.' And face the remains in the study. It had been pathetic to avoid them in the first place when what awaited her in that room wasn't going to be anywhere near as terrible as what awaited her down the lane. But then avoidance was what she always did.

A realisation which pulled her up short because there was no skirting around the inescapable fact that she and Aunt Jemima were now homeless, no matter how much she might wish to ignore that frightening truth. Her aunt might well be taken in by her father on sufferance but Sophie…

No! That skirted too close to all manner of things for comfort and churned the murky seabed filled with monsters. So she pushed it back down to smile at the cook. 'I should probably also clean poor Rafe's boots.'

'Oh, the mess is all long gone, my dear, so do not trouble yourself. Why don't you put your feet up and read a book in the drawing room?'

Archie tugged at her sleeve. 'I am going to the stable to help Mr Ruddock exercise the horses in a minute if you want to help, Sophie? They need a good run because they didn't get one yesterday.'

'Thank you but no. I think I'll take a walk instead.' She needed to blow the cobwebs out of her mind which seemed so filled with fog she could barely think straight. A brisk walk would restore her equilibrium and lift her mood. She hated feeling so despondent and lost.

'All right—but don't go down the lane.' Archie pulled a face of horror. 'Rafe has given strict instruction that you are not allowed to go there and see the dreadful state of Willow Cottage all alone.'

Chapter Fourteen

By the time he had realised where she had gone it was too late, and she had been gone a good fifteen minutes before he returned. Despite Archie's warning for her not to visit the remains of her cottage alone, of course the witch had done so because she was so determined to put on a brave face she would refuse all help because that was the way she was made. He recognised a kindred spirit when he saw one and Sophie was so proud and noble she put him to shame. Rafe had no idea what a dreadful blow it had been when she had first witnessed the devastation, but as he hurried around the bend and saw her stood before it, her posture was entirely defeated and her lovely face bleached of all colour. She looked desolate. Heart-wrenchingly desolate and lost. Her brave face and expressive eyebrows so downcast it physically hurt to witness it.

She sensed his approach and briskly made herself busy by bending to rifle through the rubble.

'You are supposed to be resting.' She avoided his gaze as she spoke. 'And I know for a fact you have had a very eventful morning thanks to Socrates.'

'You are supposed to be resting too, madam.'

'I was ordered to have a good night's sleep and I have.'

Rafe stopped on the periphery of what had once been the cottage, ridiculous and innate good manners dictating that he should not enter her home until invited. 'I did not want you to see this alone.'

'I saw it the night it collapsed in a ball of flames, so this is hardly a shock.' She bent to move a big chunk of plaster from the ground so she could investigate beneath rather than glance at him.

'I am so sorry for what happened. If you had told me about your chimney, I would have had it fixed. You have to know that, Sophie. I would never have…' She stayed him with a raised palm but still refused to meet his eyes.

'The state of the chimney was hardly your fault. Your predecessor though…well, that is another story. But I dare say he is already burning in hell for his shocking neglect of his tenants and the extortionate rent he charged them.'

'A small consolation and an eternity of roasting in brimstone hardly seems punishment enough for this.' He stared out at the remains and wished he knew how to fix it for her. How to make amends. Even if he rebuilt it, it would never be the same. The soul of the cottage was gone along with all its memories and sentimental contents. Things that not even the Almighty could replace. 'His neglect was criminal.'

'It was.' She stood to dust off her hands, then rested them on her hips while she surveyed the scene in her customary matter-of-fact manner. 'Once I am done here, I might wander past the churchyard and spit on his grave.'

'I shall join you.' His long-distant second cousin had a lot to answer for. 'We can spit like camels together.'

She tried to smile but didn't quite manage it. 'I shall be sure to come fetch you once I am done. In fact, I might even invite all the villagers and we can all dance on his grave once we've all run out of spit.' The tense, flat line of her eyebrows proved the bravado was taking its toll on her. In case he noticed, she bent to heave another large chunk of rubble out of the way and he just wanted to grab her and haul her into his arms and reassure her that he certainly wouldn't judge her if her real emotions broke through. In case he did, he caught her elbow instead.

'Ned has already been through this with a fine-tooth comb.'

'I know...' She gestured to the angry sky above. 'But it looks like we are due a storm, so I wanted to sift through it all myself in case Ned missed something of significance before it gets washed away into the stream.' To prove her point she picked up the scorched, carved panel Ned had kicked and discarded yesterday. 'This, for example, is part of Aunt Jemima's bed. It was a family piece, well over a hundred and fifty years old, and both she and her father and grandfather were born in it. The bed might be no more, but this small memento of it might bring her some comfort.' She brushed it down and put it to one side, still avoiding his eyes, then carried on with her search. 'It is a task which only I can do.'

As polite a *go away* as he had ever heard.

'Many hands make light work, and I might only have one usable one at the moment, but I should like to press it into your service.'

She hesitated before answering, clearly wanting to be

left but also aware that he wouldn't leave her. As if she sensed he was as stubborn as her when he put his mind to it, she went for admonishment instead of argument. 'Dr Able said no lifting, so you cannot.'

'Anything heavy and only with my bad arm. You have my solemn pledge I shall only use this one.' He raised his good palm up as if swearing an oath. 'If it doesn't fit in this...' He waggled his hand for good measure. 'I shall leave it to your burly beau to shift.'

Her dark brows furrowed. 'I have a burly beau?'

'Ned isn't your paramour?'

The eyebrows shot upwards. 'Of course he isn't? Wherever did you get that idea?'

More importantly, why the blazes did he vocalise it? 'The pair of you seem close, that is all. I am not privy to any local gossip.' Rafe stepped over what had once been the threshold and crouched to examine the floor with as much nonchalance as he could muster. 'But you are single and so is he, so it is a natural assumption to make.'

'We're friends, nothing more.' She forced a smile as if the mere thought amused her. 'Never mind that I am much too old for him.'

'Are you?' He made a great show of scrutinising her, trying to distract her from the onerous task at hand by making inane, charming conversation while they worked side by side. 'Then you have aged well for an old hag.'

'Less of the old hag, thank you very much, for I am only thirty and hags are at least double that. I believe the correct terminology for a woman of my years and circumstances is *past her prime*. A phrase which is usually always followed by *the poor thing* and trust me that is bad enough. Besides, I have already been called old by a Peel this morning. Old *and* haggard, I believe were his exact words.'

Rafe winced. 'Archie tends to say whatever pops in his head with little consideration as to whether it is appropriate. I doubt he meant it how it sounded. If it's any consolation, he thinks I am old and wizened too and I have only three paltry years on you.' He found the twisted remains of a buckle and held it up in case it meant something to one of them, then tossed it when she shook her head.

'Archie is what? Eighteen? Nineteen?'

'Close.' Rafe found a stick and began to use it to move the dusty layer of compacted soot next to his feet. 'The rascal turns one and twenty at the end of the month. Wants a puppy in honour of the milestone. Plans to name the mutt Mary irrespective of the sex of the thing and will make my life a misery if I do not find one in time.'

'One of Ned's sheepdogs has just had pups. He might be tempted to part with one of them.'

'Any bitches?' Not that Rafe cared as he'd pay a king's ransom for the dratted thing to make his brother's wish come true. 'Only it seems cruel to saddle a boy dog with the name Mary.'

She smiled then it melted as she uncovered the remains of a book that was barely recognisable as such. 'Beyond hope.'

'I fear you are correct. A favourite volume?'

She traced her finger along the fire-frayed edge. 'My mother gave me this the year before she died. I always meant to read it and now...' Realising that her matter-of-fact façade had briefly slipped, she shrugged to knock it back in place. 'It was a book of poems and I have never really been one for poems. As you might have gathered,

I prefer direct speech to flowery language. I have always been the same.' She stared at the book, lost again for a second before she forced that away.

'It's hard to lose a parent. I know because I have lost both—although to be fair only one to death. I had mislaid the other, or rather she mislaid us the year Archie was born.' He wasn't usually one to share confidences, and especially not that one which still cut deep, but hoped that if he shared one of his, she might feel more inclined to unburden herself. He suspected she needed to. That everything was boiling up inside like steam in a kettle and that was never healthy.

'Your mother left?'

He nodded while he concentrated on the stick which he prodded in the ashes. 'My father, God rest him, was a constant source of disappointment to her and his youngest child was the last straw. She ran away with a shipping merchant and none of us has heard hide nor hair of her since even though she moved to Bristol not ten miles away.'

'I'm sorry.' And he could tell by the crinkle between her eyebrows that she was.

'It is what it is. To be honest, I rarely think of it. It's always easier, isn't it, burying things rather than airing them? Hurts less.' Myriad complicated emotions skittered across her features before she masked them, giving him a window into how hard she worked to bury everything at all cost. 'Perhaps not always the most sensible course of action, though.' He paused his search to study her, to see if his words were getting through, but she had turned her back to him. 'Sometimes they fester, and that is never good.'

'I suppose not.' She had retrieved another damaged book, or at least that was what he assumed it was, then discarded it as if it was of no consequence. 'But it's sad for Archie to have grown up without the love of a mother.' She was deflecting. Such a subtle diversion from the topic, she had become a master of it. Rafe decided to play along until the convoluted path provided the perfect opportunity for him to circle back.

'He knows no different and has always had me and my father so he has grown up smothered in love. My father and he adored one another.'

'Just as you and he adore one another.' She smiled as she briefly gazed his way. 'I doubt many older brothers would give up a successful career in the army to care for a younger sibling.'

'Soldiering was always a means to an end.' The little square of soot he had been mining was now exhausted, so Rafe stood to stretch his limbs then moved to a different patch. 'My father excelled in being a devoted father, but not much else, so somebody had to put food on the table and a roof over Archie's head.' In that respect, Rafe had had to grow up fast. He had also had to be the one to push his brother to reach his full potential, because his well-meaning and self-sacrificing father had no clue where to start, but it felt disloyal to his memory to criticise the way he brought Archie up. 'And we certainly couldn't afford to send me to university to train for any other career, so I ended up in a uniform. It was no great sacrifice to discard it.'

He jabbed his stick in a fresh layer of debris and set about excavating it. 'Fortunately, there was still some money left in the house to keep us going after my father passed and I paid his creditors, so once we sold up we moved from Somerset to the capital. A fresh start in Cheapside. Miles away from the indelible stain of my poor father's crushing debts. Gutter Lane to be exact, just off it, but Cheapside sounds so much better and, in truth, Gutter Lane is a misnomer because it is actually a rather pleasant road.'

'I know. I grew up in Cheapside.' The second she let that slip she stiffened, her dark eyes shuttering. 'It was always an excellent place for shopping.' That was said with such breeziness they might have been at a summer garden party rather than in the charred ruins of her home. Clearly the estrangement from her father and her childhood home still hurt too. More emotions she had buried and likely festering away unchecked while the stubborn witch denied it.

Instead of prodding the ground, perhaps he should prod her a bit to get her to open up. Dr Able was right. All this stoic but deft avoidance was unhealthy. 'Ned said your father still lives there.' She stiffened some more. 'Would you like me to send word to him about what has happened?'

He assumed he would see some glimmer of regret or longing for family in her expression. The need to reconnect to her kin back home now that she had lost everything here. What he did not expect was anger. A fury so visceral and all-encompassing it shimmered off her in waves. Almost as if she were a firework and he had inadvertently lit her fuse. 'If that is your unsubtle hint that your hospitality is finite and you want rid of us, kindly say so!'

'Whoa!' Rafe instinctively held up both palms until his torn shoulder protested and he was forced to settle for just the one. 'Where on earth did that come from?'

Her fists were clenched. 'I am not being shipped

back to my father! I would rather sleep in the street than darken his door again!'

'I wasn't for a moment suggesting you would be shipped anywhere, and my hospitality extends for as long as you and your aunt need it.' A rapid retreat seemed the most prudent in case she used those fists on him. 'I merely asked if you would like me to write to contact him. I thought it might bring you and your aunt some comfort. Heal some rifts.' He spread his palms placatingly. 'Mend some of the broken bridges because I had heard the pair of you were estranged. In my unique and clumsy way I was trying to help but I can see now that it was a bad idea.' He huffed out a sigh, feeling dreadful that he had kicked that particular hornet's nest and more dreadful that she carried so much pain. 'I am sorry, Sophie. I did not mean to upset you or add to your distress.'

Her cheeks coloured as she swallowed back her anger, as if she too was surprised by the strength of her outburst. 'And I am sorry as well. I should not have overreacted.' That mortification at her overreaction was written all over her lovely face, and by her expression and her posture she looked ready to run. Although why and where he had no clue—but it bothered him. Everything about her reaction to this tragedy bothered him. *She* bothered him. Far too much than he was prepared to contemplate. 'I am already heartily ashamed of myself for it. But...' While she struggled for the right words to explain it he gestured to the carnage in sympathy.

'At this precise moment, if anyone is entitled to overreact, it is you. That you are so calm and reasonable about everything is a miracle, all things considered.' And a huge worry. He'd watched men lose their minds on the battlefield for less, and once lost they could never find it again. 'If I were you, I'd be rocking in a corner somewhere with my head in my hands or ranting to the heavens at the unfairness of it all.'

'That wouldn't help my aunt.'

'It wouldn't—but it might make you feel better. I quite enjoy a good rant and rave. Its cathartic. When life gets on top of me, I gallop to a field somewhere and then bellow at the sky. I like to slam the odd door too. And stomp. I always feel unburdened after a good stomp. Between you and me, I'm not afraid to admit I've succumbed to the waterworks a time or two too. Because that helps as well.' Rafe was prepared to wager his entire inheritance that the buttoned-up, matter-of-fact warrior before him hadn't allowed herself to shed a single tear in years. 'I wouldn't judge you for it if you did, Sophie... because if I might be so bold as to suggest it, you look like you need to.'

She ignored him to heave a big beam to one side to free another book from the rubble. It was filthy but otherwise complete. 'Aunt Jemima's Bible.' She used her skirt to remove some of the dirt from the cover. 'She will be glad this survived although it might need recovering.' She was changing the subject and he had no choice but to let her. 'There's a bookbinder in Hornchurch not far from here who always does a good job. He recovered Mrs Fitzherbert's prized collection of Marlow's plays. They were family heirlooms passed down from her father, but they were falling apart after too many years of being loved. They looked as good as new when they came back. I shall take this there too.' Without stomping, she walked to the edge of the destruction to place the book with the carved fragment from the bedframe, then took herself to the furthest point of the rubble from him to continue her search. No doubt putting as much distance as she could between herself and the uncomfortable conversation Rafe was failing to have with her.

In case he tried to restart it, she turned her back to him and carried on wittering about the skills of the bookbinder in Hornchurch in great detail. Thwarted, he sighed and resigned himself to listening.

People dealt with grief in their own way, he supposed, and in their own time too. There was no point in trying to hasten the process if she wasn't ready to deal with it. It had taken his father two years of futile hope before he accepted that his wife wasn't coming back. Even then he had still held on to some. Probably still held it until the day he died too as Rafe had found her enamel likeness in his bedside table when he had packed up his father's things.

Maybe it was easier to hold that hope than to face the stark acceptance?

And what did Rafe know about such things anyway? He was no better. Love, in all its forms, was a tricky, complicated and destructive emotion. His one serious foray into romantic love had ended in heartache and he had used that horrid experience to erect tall battlements to prevent him ever succumbing to it again. The love for family was even more complicated. He both hated his mother for what she had done and yet part of him yearned for her still. And in his youth he had both loved Archie more on the back of it while resenting him at the same time. That resentment had grown, he was ashamed to admit, as Rafe had strode from boyhood to manhood, and in the army he had cultivated a persona that had a brother, but one he never talked about in detail. When that course of action bit him royally on the arse and he had had his heart stamped on, he had resented Archie more. Yet the overwhelming love he had for the scamp had never waned, and once their father had died, it was as inconceivable to Rafe that he would not drop everything to protect and care for him as it was that he would drop Archie for a woman.

It was all so complicated, he preferred not to think about it much nowadays. But unlike Sophie, at least he had thought about it. Thought about it and come to terms with it. It was what it was, and if he had his time over, there wasn't much he would change. No matter what he had felt inside, no matter what unfair resentment he had had towards his brother, or his mother, or his father and his crushing debts, Rafe knew, without a shadow of a doubt, he would still be exactly where he was now. By Archie's side. No matter what the sacrifice.

His stick found something hard and, while he philosophised, he chiselled it out, then cleaned it with his thumb. The small hexagonal leather trinket box looked like the sort people kept jewellery in, so perhaps this was indeed something one of the ladies thought precious. 'Sophie, I think I've found something.' She turned as he opened it and held it out to her, pleased with himself. But instead of joy that the gold wedding band had survived the fire, she recoiled in horror then froze.

Almost as if she had seen a ghost.

Chapter Fifteen

Sophie hadn't thought of the ring in a decade.

Hadn't thought about it.

Hadn't looked at it.

Hadn't been able to do either.

Hadn't dared.

Yet now, seeing it again, as shiny and new as it had been when Michael had also held it out in his palm smiling, it seemed to hold the power to transport her back to that fateful Tuesday a decade before.

The day before her life was supposed to start. And the exact day it ended.

She could see his face. Taste his kiss. Feel the warmth of the rising summer sun on her face as she waved him goodbye from her bedchamber window. Just as it had that fateful morning as the dawn broke, her tummy fizzed with excitement and anticipation for the adventure to come. So eager for a mad joyous dash to Gretna that he had only just suggested as he had given her the ring he had saved for months to buy her. The solution to all their problems and a glorious act of rebellion which thumbed their noses at her unreasonable father and all his cruel machinations.

Freedom and for ever were only twelve hours away. Just as soon as Michael finished his last shift at the docks and collected his final wage.

Only twelve more hours.

She remembered thinking that as she floated back to her bed and snuggled under the covers on the exact patch that he had warmed. Her hand fluttered to her belly. To the new life which quickened within. Half her, half Michael. A happy accident, yet a welcome one because it was a testament to their enduring love against all the odds stacked against them. Certainly not even one her father could deny, although they had agreed not to tell him yet. They would save that wonderful news for after the wedding when their 'unthinkable' union was a fait accompli, and he could no longer stand in their way. She planned to write him a letter from wherever they set up their new home on the day she turned twenty-one. To let him know that he hadn't beaten her or broken them. That they would live happily ever after just to spite him. One final act of rebellion before she cut all ties with her controlling and ambitious sire for ever.

She felt another hand touch her arm that wasn't Michael's, dragging her back to the present and yet another tragedy she was trying not to think about. All so overwhelming and hideous she had bottled it with her past the moment the walls of the only sanctuary she had left crumbled to dust.

As if seeing it all for the first time, the scale of the devastation around her suddenly pulled the ground from beneath her feet as her entire world imploded properly for the second time.

'Whose is it?'

'Mine.'

'You were married?'

She shook her head, the pain of that day suffocating her alongside the pain of this. 'He died.' Against all her better judgement and the voice of sanity screaming in her head to run away as fast as her legs would carry her, Sophie reached out to touch the thin gold band. Then her hands fluttered to her stomach again when the usual denial failed to numb the agony. 'So did our child.'

And just like that, like a volcano erupting inside of her, unstoppable and unrelenting, everything spewed out in a tumbled rush because the ring had rendered her powerless to stop it.

Sophie told him everything.

From the forbidden three-year love affair with her father's clerk, to her father's vindictive reaction when Michael had begged for her hand in marriage. How he had dismissed him on the spot and had him thrown out of his lodgings. How he had blackened her beloved's name in Cheapside ensuring that no decent business would employ him so he had been forced to take manual, back-breaking work at the docks. How he had done everything in his power to stop her from seeing him. How they had thwarted his plans to separate them by meeting in secret whenever they could, how they had plotted to run away together. How Sophie had pawned all the jewellery she had been left by her mother while Michael had worked all the hours God sent to save enough for them to escape. How her tenacious lover had still managed to sneak into her room that night while the house slept to present her with the ring and to plan their elopement.

Then, as her legs gave way and she crumpled in Rafe's stunned arms, she recounted every second of that dreadful week in graphic detail. Waiting for Michael in the churchyard of St Paul's for hours and hours clutching a small bag of belongings and with his ring in her pocket. The mad dash to his shabby lodgings in Whitechapel when he failed to materialise. Learning the news of the accident when, in desperation, she had ventured to the docks. Of the crane snapping and sending its heavy load to crush him as he unloaded more cargo on the dockside below. Staggering back home in a daze and crying on her maid's shoulder. Collapsing on the mattress only to be dragged from the bed by her hair and beaten because the maid had told her father she was with child. Being tossed on the street. The two-day walk to her aunt's, her heart shattered into a million pieces, sleeping in fields when she could not walk another step. Existing only for the life still growing within her while wishing she were dead too. Willing the unbearable pain to end because it hurt so much.

'What happened to your child?' Rafe's voice was soft against her ear as he held her close, and Sophie realised they were somehow sitting under the shelter of a tree near the stream. Rain splattered heavy on the leaves overhead because the threatened storm must have started but she had been too distraught, too bombarded with all the hideous memories, to notice.

'I miscarried the night I arrived here.'

That had been the final blow. One too cruel for her bludgeoned spirit to bear. She had lost herself then. Lost all sense of reason. All sense of purpose for goodness knew how long until she had decided to ignore what had happened. To lock it away where it couldn't hurt her and ruthlessly never think of any of it again. Self-preservation rather than self-destruction. Not so much a new chapter but a rewrite of the whole book. One that started when the suffocating darkness had lifted and never looked behind.

His strong arm tightened around her, and he sighed. A long, shocked, hopeless sigh which somehow said more than any words ever could. When he finally spoke, it wasn't with empty platitudes or any philosophical non-sense about time healing all wounds, yet once again it was somehow more appropriate.

'Hell, Sophie. Bloody, bloody hell.'

Thunder rumbled overhead to punctuate that point and the rain fell harder, punching though the flimsy leaves above to drench them, yet still neither of them moved. Bizarrely, the silence and contact felt a fitting and symbolic end to the sorry tale she had just told in more graphic and honest detail than she had shared with her aunt on her first night here—or even with herself since.

They were both soaked to the skin before Rafe spoke again. 'And I thought fate had dealt me a shocking hand.' He exhaled into her hair, his warm breath heating her sodden locks momentarily until they reminded her she was freezing. 'If he were kicking up daisies, I'd visit your father's grave today too and spit on that. Or bet-ter still, I might just gallop to Cheapside and spit in his face. Right before I slam my fist into it!'

'I cannot allow you to do that. You're not allowed to ride, remember.'

She wasn't sure where the humour came from when she felt as if the truth was eating her and she was dying inside, but it popped out regardless and caught them both unawares. Rafe's response was part huff, part sur-prise and part laugh, but whatever it was, it triggered the same in her. Within seconds and still clinging to one another, they were laughing hysterically but at heaven only knew what.

But it felt good.

Necessary.

As cleansing as the rain which pummelled their faces and seeped through every fibre of their clothes.

To her complete surprise when her emotions were all over the place and her head and heart were filled with all the memories and grief she had banished for ten years, Sophie still slept away the entire afternoon. Aunt Jemima was wide awake when she finally checked in on her and remained so for most of the evening. While still in some pain and as weak as a kitten, her aunt was well enough to complain incessantly about all her new ailments and well enough that she was able to eat a whole bowl of hearty soup before the sleeping draft Dr Able stopped by to give her took effect. He was delighted with the progress, which for a cautious man spoke volumes, and that at least soothed one of Sophie's churning emotions which had decided it would be suppressed no longer.

Feeling fragile, battered, vulnerable and more than a little embarrassed by the way she had broken down in front of Rafe earlier, she was quite content to remain ensconced next to her snoring aunt all night. But, and no doubt at Rafe's insistence, Sophie was once again relieved of her post at the sickbed by the housekeeper who ushered her out and ordered her to go down to dinner which was being expressly held for her.

'The ladies of the village delivered some gowns this afternoon while you were sleeping, so I have taken the liberty to have a couple pressed and laid out in your room, Miss Gilbert, for you to choose from as it is hardly appropriate for you to be wearing that old scullery maid's frock in perpetuity. Mrs Fitzherbert has also asked for your measurements so that the sewing circle can make some proper outfits for you that fit.'

That simple kindness brought fresh tears to her eyes when she was certain that she had cried so many today there couldn't possibly be any left. 'It has been so long since I had any clothes made I hardly know.'

'Then I shall measure you myself later before you retire for the night. Would you like a maid to help you dress and do something pretty with your hair now?' The woman's eyes glanced at the sorry state of her coiffure which likely resembled a bird's nest after it had been rained then slept on.

'Good gracious, no. You have all already gone to far too much trouble for me as it is and I wouldn't want to delay your master's dinner any longer than it has been. I am used to dressing myself.'

'If you change your mind...'

'I won't.' And in case the housekeeper pressed the offer further, she hurried back to her bedchamber and then groaned at the two choices she had been given.

The first was an austere, high-necked and matronly brown crepe which she just knew had to have come from Mrs Outhwaite who was always buttoned up in such expensive but dowdy garments. The second screamed Isobel Cartwright because while it might have been a subtle shade of green velvet with very sensible long sleeves, the neckline on the bodice was as daring as its flirty owner. The first gown risked Archie telling her she looked old and haggard again. The second would likely make her look a scandal. She glanced down at her chest and winced at the prospect because while Isobel's bosom was undeniably generous, she was nowhere near as well-endowed as Sophie.

Caught between the devil and the deep blue sea, she plumped for Mrs Outhwaite's monstrosity, but it was so tight around her generous bust she could not do it up without the risk of the seams popping the second she sat down. Which left her with Isobel's inappropriate cast-off or the tatty scullery maid's frock which was still damp from the storm, covered in dirt and soot and hopelessly crumpled from her exhausted afternoon nap.

Isobel's it was then.

Ten minutes and much futile hitching up of the bodice later and she found Rafe and Archie in the drawing room. Archie unexpectedly in a pair of spectacles while he read to his older brother from a book.

'There was a dog so wild and…and…' Archie screwed up his face. 'I can't read this.' He pushed the book towards his elder brother in defeat.

'Sound the word out.' Not wanting to interrupt what was obviously a lesson, she hovered in the doorframe while Rafe smiled at his sibling.

'It's too big!' The youngest Peel glared at him in disgust then counted the letters out. 'There's ten letters! Ten!' He had the same stubborn glint in his eyes that Rafe got when he wouldn't budge. 'You need to read it because I cannot!'

'A word with ten letters is just as easy to read as one with four. Sound it out, Archie, or you'll never know what happened to the dog.' Rafe tapped the book with all the patience of a saint and closed his eyes, the ghost of a smile on his lips while his brother grumbled. 'Which would be a great shame when you love Aesop's stories about dogs more than all his other fables combined.'

'*Miss… Miss…chev…*' Archie traced the word with his finger. 'Mis—chev—ous.'

'Good. Now say it all together a bit faster.'

'Mis—chievous. *Mischievous!* Like me!'

'Excellent! Exactly right.' Rafe grinned and Archie beamed in triumph, as pleased as Punch with the praise. 'And yes, you are mischievous. When you are not being insufferable, manipulative and demanding, of course.' The half-hearted insult was accompanied by an affectionate ruffle of his brother's hair.

'I hope my puppy Mary will be mischievous too, then we can be twins.'

As Rafe rolled his eyes at the unsubtle nag, a chuckle escaped her lips and he sat up a little straighter before he turned towards her. 'Good evening, Sophie.'

'Sophie!' Archie forgot his book in his haste to bound over to her. His hug was so exuberant he knocked off his spectacles. 'You look pretty and not the least bit old tonight! Doesn't she look pretty tonight, Rafe?'

His gaze flicked the length of her as he politely unfolded himself from the chair. No mean feat when it was too low for his tall frame, and he only had one arm for leverage. 'She does indeed.' She could tell by the way his eyes lingered that he appreciated Isobel's cast-off significantly more than she did, and somehow that gave her a little more confidence in it. 'Green suits you.' Then he winked and that did odd things to her insides. 'It has obliterated all signs of any previous haggardness completely.'

He didn't look too bad himself. The dark blue coat did wonderful things to his shoulders, even with one of them supported by a pristine white sling, and the buff breeches he had paired with them hugged his cavalry officer's muscular thighs like a second skin.

'Thank you.' She bobbed an exaggerated and insincere curtsy, then aware she was displaying a lot more flesh than she had in years, fought the urge not to wrestle with the daring neckline again. 'You both look handsome too. Especially you, Archie. Did you tie that splendid cravat yourself?' The plain but neat knot was a mirror of his brother's.

'I did. And I tied Rafe's because he couldn't do it with only one hand.' Archie preened like a peacock at his own brilliance. 'Although he helped a little.' He held up his thumb and index finger an inch apart, earning him an insincere glare from his dashing sibling.

'By that he means he ruined at least six before he decided to listen to my instructions.'

'Rafe normally ties both our cravats.' Archie touched his knot and frowned. 'He likes his to look boring like this one—but I prefer a mathematical. I couldn't do that on my own even with Rafe's instructions.'

'My stubborn little brother ruined a further six trying before I decreed enough was enough.'

'Couldn't your valet help with the mathematical?' Hockley Hall was teaming with servants. 'I presume you have one?'

'We inherited one alongside all these dusty antiques.' Rafe's good arm swept the clutter filling the room while he pulled a face. 'He is as old as the hills and as dour as these dowdy draperies. I doubt he has the first clue how to tie a cravat in a modern style.'

'Oh, dear.' He was using his charm to put her at her

ease. His way of telling her not to feel self-conscious for earlier.

'Oh, dear, indeed, madam.' He made a great show of adjusting the cuff that poked out of his sling as if he were an outrageous dandy. 'While I am happy to delegate the day-to-day maintenance of my wardrobe to the fellow, I suspect his sartorial expertise leans more towards dressing curmudgeonly old earls rather than one in his absolute prime.' All evidence of the affectation disappeared with his shrug. 'Besides, I am used to dressing myself.' She sympathised and rather approved of that.

'But I dressed him tonight,' said Archie. 'And I dressed me too. Do you like my new waistcoat?' He tugged it to sit smooth. 'Purple is my new favourite colour. It used to be crimson, but I changed it last week when this arrived back from the tailor. What's your favourite colour?'

Her eyes locked with Rafe's, amused, then were dazzled by the depth of them. 'Blue.' She hadn't meant to say that as she had always had a penchant for purple herself, but the word was out and she could not claw it back.

'The same colour as my brother's waistcoat!' Was it? She had been so absorbed in admiring his eyes and the way he filled his coat and breeches, she had missed the flash of bold sapphire silk adorning his chest. 'That is a coincidence as Rafe's favourite colour is brunette.' As soon as Archie said it with a loaded wiggle of his golden eyebrows, the eldest Peel winced.

'And on that note, I think it's time for dinner.' He raised his good elbow. 'Shall we, Miss Gilbert? Before my horrid brother says something else to mortify one of us.'

Just as it had been earlier, his arm was comforting and solid, but this evening it was also disconcerting. Sophie was honest enough with herself to realise not all of that was due to the dark secrets she had spilled out of nowhere. The rest was down to the odd effect he had on her. The increasingly odd effect which wasn't merely a result of the undeniable physical attraction she had for him. There was something else beyond that, and the more she got to know him, the more she liked him. Really liked him. Enough to be drawn to him in a way she had not allowed herself to be drawn by a man since Michael.

Which was a worry—but not one she had the capacity to overindulge now when there was so much else fighting for attention in her overwhelmed brain.

Chapter Sixteen

Rafe did his best to keep the dinner conversation light and buoyant as he suspected she needed it—at least in such a public setting. Archie was a great help with that because he chatted incessantly and was so delighted they had company he could barely contain himself. Unsurprisingly, there was the odd moment where her smile was false and her eyes troubled, but she quickly recovered. Or seemed to. After all she had told him, it was a wonder she managed it. Especially as she had confessed, as her tears had finally subsided and they walked back to the house, that she hadn't allowed herself to think upon any of it since her awful tragedy had happened. Hadn't been able to, she had said, in case the grief broke her.

He could tell by the slight redness in her eyes that she must have cried several times since her breakdown in the rubble, and as much as he hated thinking of her in such silent pain alone, he also knew that it would all be cathartic in the long run. People had to grieve. It was unnatural not to and grieving went through many stages before it began to wane, as he knew from personal experience.

He had mourned the loss of his mother even though she hadn't died, and almost eighteen months on from the death of his father, he was only just at the stage where he could think of him fondly without feeling the bitter sting of loss. With Archie's visceral and heart-wrenching reaction to also deal with, alongside all the legal, career, financial and personal ramifications of their father's sudden and unexpected passing, Rafe's own grief had been pushed to the back of the queue. He had been angry for months as a result. Angry and lost and not sure what to do. But once he had found his feet and accepted that this was his new reality, that it was what it was and hardly either his father's or Archie's fault that Rafe now found himself a sole parent, bizarrely it had all got easier. That was when he had started to contemplate the future again rather than coping moment by moment. He made new plans and actually looked forward to carrying them out. Now—unwanted and troublesome new inheritance aside—he was rather content with the way his new life was going. Aspects of it were still bittersweet and always would be, and he would be a liar if he did not admit that sometimes he pondered how his life could have been different, but it wasn't, so that too was something he accepted.

While Archie waxed lyrical about how wonderful his life was going to be as soon as his promised puppy arrived, Rafe watched her stare sightlessly into her post-dinner nightcap and wished he knew how to expedite the hideous grieving process for her. Or at least ease some of her burdens.

There was every chance she had already purged the shock and anger in those devastating initial days, but all the hurt which inevitably came after had not been allowed an outlet so it was likely as fresh today now that it was out as it had been a decade ago when she had buried it. But the past was just one aspect of what she was coping with. There was also the fresh and separate grief of losing her home. And if that weren't enough to cope with all in one go, it was still shadowed by the dark cloud of her aunt who, while infinitely better than she had been, wasn't out of the woods yet.

He had no control over any of that but at least there was something he could do. And he would prefer to do it when they were alone. He swirled the last dregs of his brandy in the glass and glared at his brother. 'No ifs or buts, it is bedtime.' Archie was a nightmare if he stayed up past midnight. Largely because he awoke like a cockerel at dawn no matter what.

'I'm not tired.' The younger Peel said this while stifling a yawn. 'Why don't we play cards or charades or something?'

'Because when you are as old, decrepit and haggard as Sophie and I are, we need our sleep and we are both clearly exhausted. As are you.' Rafe pointed to the door with his glass while he hoped his eyes conveyed to Sophie that he wanted her to stay put. 'Bedtime, young man, and that is in order.'

'I shall go to bed when you and Sophie go to bed.' Like a pugilist in the ring, his gaze locked and held with Rafe's.

'We shall follow you up presently—but first I need to talk to her and what I need to say is private.' He thought he'd add that in case she offered to walk his brother up the stairs.

'What private things do you need to talk about?'

'If I told you, then it wouldn't be private, now would

it?' He shot his brother a pointed look and maintained it until he capitulated.

'I hate answers like that!' Archie huffed as he stood, severely put out. 'But I suppose I shall still see Sophie at breakfast, luncheon and dinner every day anyway seeing as she lives here now, doesn't she?'

Neither of them expected that question. While Sophie blinked, awkward, Rafe floundered, his gaze flicking to hers uncomfortable. 'Sophie and her aunt…'

'Are merely guests until my aunt is well enough for us to leave.' She smiled at him as she came to the rescue. 'We certainly cannot live with you.'

'Why ever not?'

She brushed Archie's cheek tenderly before she answered. 'Well, for a start, you will be moving to your little horse farm in another part of the country and Aunt Jemima and I need a new home here in Whittleston.'

'But Rafe is so rich now he could buy a huge horse farm with plenty of space for you and your aunt to join us.'

Her dark eyebrows quivered while she tried to think of a suitable answer to that objection, but settled once she smiled again. 'As generous and tempting an offer as that is, I am afraid it wouldn't be at all proper. It would be scandalous if a pair of old spinsters moved into the same house as a pair of fancy-free bachelors like you and Rafe. It just isn't done, Archie.'

To cover his relief at that diplomatic and unarguable statement, Rafe sipped his drink, then promptly spat it out when his brother responded with the unthinkable.

'If you marry Rafe you could move to the farm with us and not be scandalous at all.' As this was apparently the most sensible solution to all their problems, Archie turned to his choking brother, grinning as if he had just invented the wheel. 'Sophie is lovely, Rafe. Kind and pretty and not haggard at all now that she's slept. And Papa always said you needed a nice wife.' He spread his palms, beseeching. 'Especially as neither of us liked your fiancée when we met her.' He pulled a face of disgust at Sophie who was, for want of a better word, dumbstruck at the suggestion. 'Annabel is horrible. Papa said she was mean and vain and full of her own importance.'

Her expressive eyebrows shot skyward. 'You have a fiancée?'

Rafe opened his mouth to answer but Archie did in his stead. 'Not any more he hasn't because Horrible Annabel called it off! Broke Rafe's heart she did too, so I doubly hate her now.' Oblivious to Rafe's wince of pure mortification, the wretch continued undaunted.

'She had brown hair too—but yours is much prettier, Sophie, and I think your face is prettier too now that you've had some sleep because your eyes are nicer than hers were. And they are brown.' Archie nudged Rafe with as much subtlety as a rock shattering a window and smiled with glee as if the reading of the banns was already a fait accompli and he had his brother to thank for it. 'You love big brown eyes too, don't you, Rafe? You told me that last week when I pointed Sophie's out to you, and now that she's proved she's as lovely inside as she is on the outside and not at all the nagging old harridan that you thought she was, she's the perfect choice. I am already quite decided that I want her for my new sister.'

Rafe blinked at this logic, his cheeks heating before he shook his head, baffled at the unexpected and cringeworthy turn this evening had taken. 'Bed!' He pointed to the door. 'Bed right this second or I swear I'll *never* get you a puppy as long as I live!'

Those were the magic words, those and the daggers shooting out of Rafe's eyes at his annoying sibling, because Archie hightailed it out of the room and up the sweeping wooden staircase in a thunder of boots.

Alone, and only after a door slammed above them, Rafe offered her an embarrassed smile. 'I'm sorry about all that.'

She waved it away with a chuckle. 'Archie will be Archie.'

'I just wish he would forget to be so resolutely Archie all of the time.'

'So…' She couldn't resist teasing him a little. 'Aside from your penchant for brunettes with brown eyes, did Horrible Annabel really break your heart?'

Rafe sighed as he settled back in his chair, even though his toes were still curling inside his boots. 'I was young and foolish and proposed before I really knew her. Any decision taken in the heat of the moment should never be trusted because it is always wrong. Especially concerning matters of the heart.'

'I shall take that as a yes then.' She sat back herself to stare at him, those beautiful, big brown eyes quizzical. 'Why did she call it off?'

He sighed again while he weighed up whether to lie or not, then he jerked his head upwards rather than answer.

'Because of Archie?' That came out more outrage than a question and he shrugged at her response, not wanting to trust it even though a part of him did. 'Whatever for?'

'All manner of reasons.' He tried to act nonchalant, hoping it sounded as convincing as he intended. 'Because we barely knew one another. Because we were too young to march down the aisle. Because she wasn't sure of her feelings.' Oh, good grief, this was painful. But after this afternoon, it felt wrong not to be as brutally honest with her as she had been with him. 'Because she did not see herself as a nursemaid. Because she felt I had been disingenuous about him before she accepted my proposal. Because she had assumed his condition was caused by a difficult birth or an accident or some such, and because she desperately wanted children of her own and she wasn't prepared to risk having them with me.' The minutest drop of bitterness leaked into his tone before he banished it with a decisive thump of his empty glass on the side table. 'Suffice it to say, there seemed to be no talking her out of so many objections, so we bade each other a polite adieu.'

'Oh, Rafe…' The pity clouded her eyes and brought a lump to his throat as she leaned forward to squeeze his hand. 'I am so sorry.'

'It is what it is.' He swallowed past the lump to force a wry smile. 'With the benefit of hindsight it was for the best because Archie is right: she was—is—mean and vain and full of her own importance.' He unfolded himself from his chair to retrieve the decanter in case her intuitive dark eyes saw how much that crushing rejection still hurt, or how much it churned up the previous crushing rejection from his own mother.

'She was—is—also as shallow as a puddle.' Incensed on his behalf, Sophie snatched the decanter from his hand and topped up both their glasses with more brandy. 'Good riddance to her, I say, for if she cannot see past her own upturned nose then she doesn't deserve you *or* Archie.' She thrust out his filled glass huffing. 'Aren't some people just dreadful excuses of humans? Horrible Annabel, my callous father, your selfish mother. Your dreadful, money-grabbing, conscienceless predecessor.' She waved her glass to encompass the cluttered drawing room Rafe had inherited. 'They don't possess a decent bone amongst them. I want to knock all their heads together. Or better still—knock their worthless teeth out!' As the same fire she had displayed at the barricade or when she had first hoisted her *SHAME ON YOU, LORD HOCKLEY* banner returned with a vengeance, he couldn't help but laugh.

'There she is!' He toasted her with his glass. 'That's the indomitable Sophie Gilbert I know. I knew she wouldn't disappear for long.'

'Yes...' She averted her eyes, her teeth worrying her plump bottom lip and drawing his to it like a moth to a flame. 'I lost her for a little while earlier... I am so sorry about that.'

'I'm not.' Was it the right time for him to offer his theories? He supposed it couldn't hurt. The woman was always too hard on herself and in just a few days they were more friends now than enemies. An irony which was not lost on him when he avoided anything more than transient, superficial relationships with women nowadays. Yet it was undeniable. They were friends—or at least they shared the bond of kinship which was almost the same. 'Bottling such things is never wise. I've seen it time and time again on the battlefield after comrades have fallen. The men that keep all that pain inside risk letting it fester and turn to poison. Releasing it is much healthier. A bit like lancing a boil. It hurts like the devil while it's happening but it is only once it is all out that the healing starts.'

'I sincerely doubt I shall ever get over it.' She was talking about Michael, he realised, Michael and their unborn child—not the loss of her house. By comparison, clearly that tragedy did not come close to the first she had suffered.

'You loved him a great deal, didn't you?'

'I did.' It felt churlish to be envious of that, but he did. Annabel had never loved him with such unbreakable and resolute fervour. He had known that at the time, deep down, but like a fool he had ignored it. Rushed in even when his own head had warned him to proceed with caution.

Without thinking, she touched her chest. 'His death broke my heart.'

'Hearts mend.' He shrugged, not quite believing that rot himself. 'Or so they say.'

'Did yours?' A question which deserved an honest answer.

'Again, with the benefit of hindsight, I don't think it was ever broken in the first place and certainly not in the way it should have been had I truly been in love. It was more bruised...' At the disbelieving quirk of her eyebrow, he laughed without humour. 'All right, I'll concede to bludgeoned but it emerged intact. Intact but jaded. Jaded enough to avoid all romantic entanglements since.'

'You shouldn't give that awful woman that much power. You should find someone else to skip off into the sunset with purely to spite her.'

And there was the rub. The undeniable reality of his situation. 'But it wasn't one woman, Sophie. It has been all of them. Annabel might have been my only serious romantic skirmish, but I've dealt with that sort of prejudice and rejection all my life. Enough to put me off any sort of attachment for good.'

'So you have given up women completely? I do not believe that.' The look she shot him was loaded with innuendo. 'A man who can charm the birds from the trees as effortlessly as you do would have no trouble charming women, and no matter how noble you are, you do not strike me as a saint.'

'All right…perhaps I haven't abstained completely since Annabel…' He paused and bit his lip. It felt odd discussing such things with a woman, and an unmarried one to boot, until Rafe reminded himself that Miss Sophie Gilbert was, by her own admission, no blushing virgin. 'But those relationships are always superficial and transient. I know better than to seek anything beyond that, for however strong and sincere the initial attraction seems, it always withers on the vine once they learn of my particular responsibilities. Although to be fair to the fairer sex, it isn't just the women who recoil from it. It has a similar effect on everyone who comes near us—as if Archie's condition is catching.'

'Ignorant people always fear what they do not understand.'

Because the genuine sadness swirling in her lovely eyes brought the lump back to his throat, he diverted the same question back to her. 'But I am quite content nowadays with my status as a social pariah, hence I am eschewing all contact with the human race voluntarily for a life filled with non-judgemental and less fickle horses in the middle of nowhere. All much safer for everyone and most especially me. Why have you not ventured forth again yourself?' His hand flapped to encompass her appealing figure and face. 'You are as far removed from an old hag as it is possible to be.' Which was about as much of a compliment as he was brave enough to offer when she appealed to him too much.

She swallowed as she closed her eyes briefly, then sighed as she allowed him to see her pain and the sheen of fresh unshed tears in her eyes. 'I cannot do that again. Cannot risk it as I fear the stitched-together remnants of my heart would not survive another loss. It's safer up on my shelf, gathering dust.'

'Lonely though.' Which struck him as such a huge shame when she clearly had such an enormous heart.

'So is raising horses in the middle of nowhere, so people in glass houses shouldn't throw stones.'

'Talking of houses.' Rafe sat forward. 'I want to re-build yours. It is the least I can do after my dreadful, money-grabbing, conscienceless predecessor neglected its upkeep for so long that his neglect left you homeless and almost killed your poor aunt.'

She shot up from her seat like a firework and shook her head, lost for words. Before her pride got in the way and she refused him, his logic and a stark reminder of her circumstances tumbled out in a rush as he closed the distance between them.

'You have nowhere to go, Sophie.'

'Yes, we do. Mrs Fitzherbert has offered to take us both in until we can find our feet again somewhere. We shall be moving there just as soon as my aunt is well enough.'

That was news to Rafe—but it did not change the facts. 'And how exactly will you find your feet again with no money. No family. Nothing that will give you the start you and your aunt will need to begin afresh. If it was just you, I have no doubt you would triumph over

this adversity and flourish. You are formidable and resourceful and as stubbornly vexatious as anyone I have
ever met. But you aren't alone, Sophie. Like me you
have the responsibility of another to consider, one who
is too fragile for the long road which would undoubtedly
lie ahead if you trod it alone. I know how that feels and
it isn't pleasant. The guilt along the way would crush
you long before you both reached your destination. I've
robbed Peter to pay Paul for years to keep Archie safe.
Sold my soul to the army, then sold all that was left of
the family silver to put a roof over our head this past
year while worrying endlessly of what would become
of him if something happened to me and fate left him
all alone. It's been suffocating and I wouldn't wish it on
my worst enemy.'

He smoothed his hand down her arm, beseeching
her not to put pride before a fall. 'This isn't charity, Sophie—it is compensation. A debt owed to your aunt by
the house of Hockley because she has been a good tenant
for over sixty years, and she has not been treated fairly.'

She might not take it for herself, but she would take
it for her aunt. If he had to go to her aunt behind her
back and twist the sick old lady's arm into accepting the
offer he would do that too. Whatever it took to see this
stubborn minx here right. 'By some miracle I now have
more money than I could possibly spend in one lifetime.
The rebuilding of your cottage won't even make a dent
in it and my cousin's debt to you must be repaid. I would
never sleep soundly again if I didn't.'

Indecision furrowed her expressive eyebrows. Pride
and need warred in her lovely eyes. But she was waver-
ing, thank God, as common sense prevailed. Or he hoped

it was prevailing. In case she still had reservations, he sugared the offer some more.

'Your aunt would have the freehold obviously, so it wouldn't be sold along with the rest of the estate when Archie and I leave. It would always be yours, no matter what happens.' That was the last argument he could think of to counter any objections. Or perhaps there was one more. 'I am not going to take no for an answer, Sophie. Whether you want me to or not, I am going to rebuild Willow Cottage and the deeds will say Gilbert.' He smiled, his tone gentle and pleading. 'And that is my final word on the matter.'

She smiled too, a little bewildered and a lot overwhelmed. 'I—I don't know what to say.' More tears gathered and one spilled over her lashes. Before he thought better of it, Rafe reached out to brush it away with his thumb, then tugged his hand away when it had the overwhelming urge to trace the shape of her face. 'That will mean the world to my aunt.' He wasn't doing it for her aunt, but he wouldn't admit that aloud. 'How can I ever hope to repay you for all that you have done for us?'

She reached for his hand and just that touch conjured a hundred images in his mind, all of them inappropriate. In case his imagination decided to run riot with one or two of them, he tugged his hand away and used it to lead her towards the door. 'You have already resigned your commission as General Gilbert of the whinging Whittleston Rebel Alliance. Trust me, that is payment enough. But enough gushing, we are both on doctor's orders to get plenty of rest. It's long past both our bedtimes.' Like an idiot, he succumbed to the ingrained good manners which dictated he offer his hand again to assist her up the stairs and was sorely tempted to haul her into his arms instead when the contact sent ripples of awareness throughout his body.

Unsettled, and improperly aroused and feeling like the biggest cad for being so, Rafe made small talk all the way upstairs then bade her a hasty goodnight at her door to go and have a long, hard talk with himself. Alone in his room, he decided to pace rather than sit, rationalising that it was better to give his body something to do to distract it from what it had made plain it wanted to do while he pondered his odd and uncharacteristic reaction.

What was it about her that called to him so?

The attraction was more than physical. There was no denying that. There was something about Sophie which tempted him to want more, in a way he hadn't allowed himself to want in a long, long time. Yet it was a pointless and futile yearning. Because even if she was the one woman in the world able to adore and accept Archie as no eligible woman ever had, she was still hopelessly in love with another man and only just grieving the loss of him. That was an obstacle no amount of his inappropriate yearning was ever going to surpass.

Of course it wasn't.

Only an idiot would attempt to compete with a ghost, and Rafe prided himself on not being an idiot any more when it came to women. Sophie's heart belonged to another and likely always would. And just because he had some inappropriate feelings stirring for her which strayed away from the carnal did not mean she felt any for him.

Of course she didn't.

Only a blithering idiot would confuse the first shoots of a blossoming friendship with anything else, and his heart was just too jaded to risk anything beyond that anyway.

Of course it was!

And that was that.

He was probably still tired. Very definitely a little over-wrought after the day—correction—*days* that he had just endured. He wasn't thinking straight.

Wasn't thinking straight.

Besides, the pair of them had been thrown together in a crisis and that had made everything seem more charged. Made his understandable physical attraction to the witch, who was frankly too damn attractive for her own good, seem like more. When it wasn't.

It wasn't.

All was calm. He was still in control.

He sighed in relief as he shrugged off his sling and then his coat. There was nothing to worry about. Nothing in the slightest, because even the physical attraction was a consequence of their enforced proximity and perhaps the charged response to all their shared confidences today. He had held the minx in his arms for goodness' sake and she was a glorious armful. There was no denying that either. Physically, she was exactly the sort of woman his eyes and urges were drawn to. He might well be immune to romance and all the unpleasantness that went with it, but he was still a hot-blooded male and there hadn't been much of an outlet for all that hot blood in the last year and a half. A simple enough predicament to fix once his damn shoulder was mended. All he had to do was visit a tavern and use his charm on a lusty tavern wench, and he would be as right as ninepence again. All was well and all would be much better if he had a good night's sleep.

As his bed beckoned like a lifeline, Rafe used his feet to slide off his boots while he tugged his shirt from his waistband. He tried to undo the knot in his cravat with one hand and, when it wouldn't budge, tried to assist with his bad arm and his torn shoulder screamed in pain. Frustrated he tugged on the stupid thing while cursing Archie's too-tight knot, only to tighten it worse as he wrestled with it.

In desperation, he staked to the washstand to grab his razor, and was about to cut the dratted thing off when he remembered that his good hand wasn't his good hand at all. It was his left hand, and Rafe was right-handed. If he were incapable of untying a paltry knot with his left hand, he'd likely cut his own throat if he attempted to slice it off in a temper.

Annoyed, at both his predicament and his lingering arousal despite the long lecture with himself, he marched out of his bedchamber intent on waking Archie to help him, but as the door slammed behind him, it was Sophie who emerged onto the landing.

'Is everything all right, Rafe?'

As his necktie now resembled a noose and he was clutching a cutthroat, it clearly wasn't, so there was no point in lying. Worse, if indeed things could get worse, the vixen had unpinned her hair and it fell in soft, tactile, silken waves to her waist to taunt him some more. 'I can't undo Archie's blasted tie!'

She laughed at his anger. A soft, feminine, come-hither sort of sound which played havoc with the unruly, awakened beast in his breeches.

'Let me help.' Her seductive hips undulated as she came towards him, yet she was clearly oblivious of their deadly effect because she invaded his personal space to study the source of the problem, sending an alluring waft of soap and Sophie up his nostrils as she tackled the knot. 'It's just a cravat, Rafe. Nothing that requires this much dudgeon.'

When her fingertips brushed the exposed skin above his collar, he almost groaned aloud, so he channelled the sage words of his favourite colonel instead to help him withstand the torture.

Stay calm...

Remain in control at all costs.

It didn't help, so he gritted his teeth, trying to pretend they were the fingers of the hag Mrs Outhwaite or the ancient Mrs Fitzherbert instead. That didn't work either so he gritted his teeth as hard as he could until the blasted knot finally came free.

'There...all done now.' Like a wife, she smoothed his lapels, and he made the fatal mistake of gazing into her gorgeous big brown eyes. That was when something odd happened in his chest. Something odd and unsettling and wholly unexpected.

Because he wished, just for a split second, she actually was his wife—and that scared the living daylights out of him.

Chapter Seventeen

Walpole entered the study and bowed despite repeated assurances that such ridiculous formality was unnecessary. 'You have a caller, my lord.'

'Oh, good grief, not another one. I thought I told you to tell the villagers that the Misses Gilbert are still not receiving visitors yet.' Now that her aunt was lucid, Sophie was spending almost every waking hour with her and quite a few more when her body screamed she should be asleep. She was dead on her feet and her aunt had barely risen from the dead. 'What part of *convalescing* do those nosy idiots fail to understand?'

'This gentleman isn't from the village, nor is he here to see the Misses Gilbert. Mr Stephen Bassett is here expressly to see you, my lord.' Walpole bowed again as if kowtowing was something he had always done in this house as a matter of course. It was clearly going to be a hard habit to break him of. Rafe blamed his long-lost and dead as a doornail cousin, who probably favoured the rule by fear approach of leadership. In the absence of any real respect, he supposed that was the only way the odious scoundrel ever got any.

'I do not know a Mr Bassett.' Although something about the name Stephen Bassett rang a bell for some reason. He scrunched up his face while he searched his memory then offered the butler a one-shouldered shrug when he drew a blank. 'What the blazes does he want?'

'It is regarding the sale of the estate, my lord, and he is insistent it is urgent.'

Rafe groaned. 'Of course it is.' With everything else going on this past week, he had forgotten about the sale—or depressing lack thereof—because the alluring witch upstairs and her devoted familiars had thwarted it at every turn. The stack of letters he had written to all the potential buyers the whinging Whittleston Rebel Alliance had scared away was still piled on his desk seven days on, because he had neglected to post them. Why he hadn't was a mystery when they annoyed him every single time he glanced at them, never mind that his odd reaction to the comely distraction upstairs made it imperative he sell fast too. That was an attachment and a complication he did not need when his long-planned quiet life was also within reach, hence he had been keeping his distance since the odd incident with the cravat. When good manners dictated he couldn't keep that distance, Rafe made sure they were chaperoned by Archie. His boisterous brother made the perfect boundary between his irrational urges and the vixen who stirred them because there was not a cat's chance in hell of acting on them with Archie glued to Sophie instead like a limpet.

'Does Mr Bassett want to complain about my plans for the estate like everyone else in this godforsaken hole? Because if he does, can you inform him that I only see whingers on days without a Y in them.'

'Actually, I might be in the market to buy it, old chap.'

Much to Walpole's horror, a dark-haired gentleman of about Rafe's age sauntered through the door. 'For the right price, of course.' The stranger held out his hand as he strode towards the desk. 'Stephen Bassett.'

Quietly impressed at the bare-faced cheek of the fellow, Rafe took it and shook it.

'This is a large estate close to London. The only one, I believe, currently on the market.' Rafe allowed his eyes to wander to the stack of correspondence on the desk so that Bassett's followed, then shrugged. He really did need to post all those blasted letters now, he supposed. More for Sophie's sake than his own. He'd promised her the final choice out of two and a promise was a promise. Especially when she would have to live cheek by jowl with the decision. 'Assuming you also make me an offer—' He tapped his stack of unposted correspondence with all the confidence of a man teeming with offers. 'I should first like to know what you intend to do with my estate, Mr Bassett.' He didn't want to care. Shouldn't care when he owed this place nothing and could not wait to be shot of it, but to his complete surprise, he did.

Her again.

Blasted woman was getting under his skin!

'What do I intend to do with it?' Bassett looked baffled that Rafe had even asked the question. 'Why live in it, of course.'

'I do not care, Sophie!' Her aunt was agitated and belligerent, exactly as she had been for the last three days. After nearly ten days of being so frail she could barely stay awake for more than a few minutes, she was finally well on the road to recovery. Her appetite had returned, she was building up her strength and the hacking cough which had made the doctor so worried had completely subsided. While such robustness was good to see, and a huge weight off Sophie's mind, it was also wearing. There were only so many ways to placate her without telling her the truth and she had always been a bad and demanding patient. 'I want to be in my own bed in my own house!'

And there it was. The demand she had made near hourly since yesterday too. It was exhausting fobbing that off. Exhausting and stomach churning. The guilt at lying and the reality of what Sophie had to eventually say had given her acid.

Aunt Jemima threw back the covers. 'I am not staying in that horrid man's house for one more night!'

There was clearly no more eventually because the time had come. 'That man saved your life, Aunt.' Sophie locked eyes with Dr Able across the bedchamber. He was busying himself mixing medicines, but he was here tonight in case her aunt took a turn on hearing the bad news they all agreed couldn't be put off any longer. Not when her friends knocked on the door insistently every single day without fail, and she and Rafe had run out of excuses not to allow Aunt Jemima visitors. Especially Archie who seemed determined to sneak in via any means possible whenever their backs were turned, convinced he could cheer her up and back to her old self in no time if only they would let him. They hadn't because the youngest Peel was incapable of keeping a secret and they both knew that all the forewarnings in the world would not prevent him from accidentally blurting it all out within seconds. 'If it hadn't been for his bravery, you would have died.'

'What?' Her aunt paused in her attempt at getting out of bed to stare at her.

Sophie took her hand, wishing there were an easier way to soften the blow she was about to deliver. 'You have been so poorly, so very poorly, and distressed that I did not wish to burden you with more. But I lied to you, Aunt, when I said you had had one of your turns while we were out walking.' Unseen over her aunt's shoulder, the doctor had abandoned all pretence of working to watch the proceedings carefully, and he nodded when Sophie hesitated, reassuring her that the time had come. Aunt Jemima had made exceptional progress fast, he had said. He couldn't be certain that this blow wouldn't send her recovery backwards, but he thought it unlikely that she would die on the spot from the shock of it. He also had a potent sleeping draft standing by—just in case.

'What are you talking about?' The panic in her eyes added to Sophie's guilt. 'If I didn't take a turn on the lane then what happened?'

'There was a fire...at the cottage on the day of the barricade. You were trapped inside, and I could not get to you. Rafe... Lord Hockley...risked his own life to get you out.'

'But...' Aunt Jemima stared down at her arms as if noticing the healing cuts, bruises and blisters for the first time. 'A fire?'

Sophie nodded.

'Was it bad?'

She nodded again and squeezed her aunt's instantly limp hand. 'We were both lucky to get out alive.'

The elongated pause was gut-wrenching while her aunt digested this.

'And my house?'

'Is gone, Aunt. Rafe's staff and the villagers tried their hardest to save it, but the flames spread too fast through the old beams and there was nothing to be done.' She would spare her all the gory details of that for another time. For now, as Dr Able had suggested, she would stick to the bare minimum as little more would go in because it was all so much. This was her aunt's worst nightmare come true. She was homeless—yet not in the way she had originally feared. Somehow, being evicted seemed like the kinder option now that the worst had happened. At least then she would still have her things.

'But we are safe and that is the main thing.' Sophie would focus on the positives—because there were positives if you dug deep enough and she would cling to those like driftwood in a storm. 'Even Socrates survived unscathed. And the good news is Lord Hockley has promised to rebuild your cottage—the plans have already been drawn and the foundations will soon be laid.' Just as soon as Ned and Rafe's staff finished clearing the site of debris. 'And he has made sure that it will be all yours this time. The deeds will be in your name. No court in the land would ever be able to make you leave it so all your worries about the future are over.'

'But I do not want a new house… I want my old house. The house I grew up in.'

'I know…' She wrapped her arms around her aunt and rocked her like a baby. 'But there was nothing to be saved so we must rebuild. We are safe and still together and we must make the best of things. We have a great deal to be thankful for…'

Chapter Eighteen

'How did she take it?' Rafe stopped pacing the darkened landing to stare at her. That he had been pacing at all an hour after Dr Able left said a great deal about him when it was late, and he had already gone above and beyond. So above and beyond it was humbling. Yet here he was at midnight, waiting, to check on her and that warmed her.

'Well…she knows.' Sophie sighed as she consoled herself with that. 'And I was able to be the one to tell her, but I am not sure it has sunk in yet.'

'It is a lot to take in.'

'I expected hysterics at the very least because she has always erred on the dramatic and we have lost everything so some hysteria would have been understandable—but even without it, it was still dreadful. Worse, in fact. I think I would have coped better with an outpouring than I did with her stunned silence.' Sophie was so battered by it all, she would have gladly let him envelop her in one of his fortifying, one-armed hugs if he offered. He didn't, nor had he touched her so much as by accident in the week and a half since he had comforted her in the remains of her ruined home. Yet part of her was still sorely tempted to request one. Rafe seemed to possess the unique ability to make everything feel better. 'The silence was awful.'

He started towards her, then stopped himself as if he too was wary of the physical. Wary of the mutual attraction which she was often convinced was reflected in his eyes. Or at least she had convinced herself was reflected in his eyes when theirs met and locked with more frequency than Sophie was comfortable admitting—even to herself.

To confirm that suspicion, he tucked the arm which wasn't in a sling behind his back. 'If I know your aunt, as I believe I am coming to know your aunt, that silence won't last long.' His smile told her that he had overheard all her most recent insults and the twinkle in his disarming eyes informed her that he was completely unoffended by them. 'She does like to complain.'

'There is that.' Oh, how she wanted to just lay her head on his broad shoulders and listen to his irreverent take on things for the next few minutes rather than return to the oppressive and relentless ordeal of the sickroom, where she was forced to be an over-attentive nursemaid or left alone too long with her tangled thoughts.

Thoughts of Michael. Of the child they had lost before it could even be called a child. Of the cottage—both the old and the promised new. The village. Her guilt at no longer having to worry about her own future when everyone else's was still up in the air.

Sophie was desperate to move onwards and upwards, needed to do that for the sake of her own sanity now that she had purged herself of the pent-up and festering emotions which had been holding her back. But current circumstances entrenched her resolutely in the now. All so overwhelming, a one-armed hug from this complex, vexing and dangerous but solid man would help no end as he felt like a calm port in a storm. He had certainly been her rock and her anchor since the fire.

She was also prepared to concede that succumbing to the urge to fall into his big, strong arms wasn't prudent. Not when it had felt so good to be in them and she couldn't seem to stop thinking about being there. And certainly not when some of those thoughts weren't the least bit chaste and a few, in the last few days especially, had been downright scandalous. All part of the healing process, she supposed. She wanted to live again rather than exist, and more of her old self was emerging from the dark cavern it had hibernated in for a decade, eager to see the light. Before Michael's death, she had always been a sensual, passionate individual, and while parts of that had always leaked through the cocoon of numbness which kept her safe, she had suppressed it. Yet allowing her body to feel grief again had reawakened all the other things it was capable of. Food tasted better. The air smelled fresher. She felt deeper. Cared more. Even the outside world looked sharper and more inviting. She craved. Yearned. Hungered. Wanted it all in a hurry—exactly as she always had before fate had crushed her spirit and stolen her dreams. But since the fire, that dreadful, life-changing but somehow cleansing fire, that spirit had emerged from the ashes like a phoenix from the flames. Where once was nothing there was now a big, bright light at the end of the tunnel, beckoning her towards its warm, inviting glow.

Which meant in between the bouts of sadness and hopelessness, Sophie felt more alive, ripe and reckless than she had in a decade. There was no denying the ripeness had a lot to do with Rafe.

Aside from his undeniable physical attributes there was the heady allure of him to contend with—Rafe the man. The much too likeable, logical, reliable, generous and beguiling man. A combination which was, frankly, much too dangerous for her bludgeoned heart to bear. One that, in another life without all her tragedy, would be exactly the sort she would have been tempted to risk for ever with. Just like Michael yet completely different in every single way—from his looks to his background to his character. Which was a ridiculous contradiction but yet still undeniable. Because just like Michael, Rafe called to her soul and made her damaged heart smile. He also made her body want again. It wanted to be touched, filled…satisfied again. And, heaven help her, it wanted him.

'It is done now, so from here on in your aunt will rally and it will get easier.'

'Will it?' She dragged her wayward mind back from the carnal and reminded it that there were more important things to consider in the now than her needy body and his much too appealing one. 'Despite reiterating that precious little survived, she kept asking about her most treasured things like her mother's pearls or her grandmother's quilt, and each time I had to tell her that the fire had taken that too, she seemed to shrink in the bed some more. It was awful.'

'Being the bearer of bad tidings always is.'

She returned his sympathetic smile as much as she was able, which meant it likely resembled more a grimace than appreciation for his unswerving moral support. 'I am still not convinced she is strong enough to cope with it all. Allowing another few days might have been more prudent, no matter what Dr Able said.'

'And risk someone slipping up in the interim?' He shook his head as he reached out to brush her arm. It was a gesture of empathy and support, lasting mere seconds, but Sophie felt it everywhere. 'What if she overheard a maid talking, or, God help us, Archie barrelled in and put his great big foot in it.' He pulled a face. 'Short of nailing his troublesome feet to the floor, there is no way of keeping him away from her in perpetuity, and certainly not when his bedchamber is but a few feet away.'

As he gestured to his brother's door it opened. No doubt because Archie had had one of his inquisitive ears pressed against it. 'Now that she knows about the cottage, can I visit Aunt Jemima now?' He held up Aesop's fables. 'I could read her a bedtime story to help her settle.'

'No! And no! And why are you listening at keyholes again when we have talked about this? Listeners never hear any good of themselves.' Rafe's exasperated expression as Archie stared longingly at Aunt Jemima's closed door stated he knew his admonishments were falling on deaf ears, but he was still going to issue them regardless. 'And how many times do I have to tell you that it isn't proper to allow Sophie to see you in your tatty old nightshirt?' He flapped his good hand up and down his brother, who seemed oblivious that the capacious but flimsy garment he refused to sleep without was hanging off one shoulder and barely covered his knees. 'And whilst I am on the subject of things I have to repeat ad nauseam because you have decided not to listen to a single word that I say, the lady in that bed is *Miss Gilbert* to you. Miss. Gilbert. Because you haven't been formerly introduced, and even if you had and were now bosom buddies, she is categorically *not* your aunt, she is Sophie's. The only blood relation you have is me.'

'For now.' Archie smiled first at his brother and then at her as if he knew something they did not, the implication as clear as crystal. 'But we could all be family soon, couldn't we?' He was as fixated on the idea that the pair of them should get married as he was with his old nightshirt and his boiled eggs for breakfast. 'You and Sophie, Aunt Jemima and me, and Mary the dog could all live together.'

Rafe pointed through the open doorway. 'Bed! Now! Before I strangle you with my bare hands.'

'Hand,' said the younger Peel, unthreatened. 'For you only have one that works, Rafe, and I am pretty sure you'll need both of them to strangle me because I shall wriggle.'

'Want to bet on that?' As Rafe started forward, his good hand raised and poised ready to throttle the rapscallion, Archie giggled and slammed the door.

'Goodnight!' There was a thunder of feet and then a thud as he launched himself at the mattress, followed by the sounds of squeaking as he burrowed beneath the covers. Finally, there was silence.

Just to have the final word, Rafe hollered through the ancient oak. 'And go to blasted sleep or we shan't be collecting that puppy on the morrow! Do you hear this?' He stamped his boot hard on the floorboards. 'That is me putting my foot down, Archibald Leo Peel!'

As he rolled his eyes her way, she laughed. 'If your intention was to be terrifying, Rafe, I have to tell you that fell well shy of the mark. We all know you will be fetching him a puppy on the morrow no matter what he does in the interim, so why bother with the hollow threats when Archie has you wound around his little finger? It is a mystery to me that you were able to command soldiers because you are as soft as down.' He would make an excellent father. A random thought which made her smile before she chastised herself for even thinking it.

Onwards and upwards meant treading a new path not veering back to the old one. Her broken heart was healing but it would never be the same, never be as strong, and it certainly would not have the capacity to cope with all that again. While she now believed it was better to have loved and lost than never to have loved at all, she also knew she could not bear to love again in case she lost it all again. No matter how great the initial temptation. 'It is even more of a mystery that you were able to lead them to victory.' Unsettled, her teasing tone felt forced. 'I declare that had Archie not shown me your Waterloo medal, I would not have believed that either. Yet apparently, once upon a time, you were considered not only a good leader of men—but a great one.'

Rafe shrugged, uncomfortable with the compliment, but did not deny it. 'Soldiers understand rules and boundaries.' In unspoken agreement, they began to stroll slowly towards their own bedchamber doors. 'And they respected my superior rank. Brothers don't.'

'How long do you think it will be before Archie sneaks in to introduce himself and read Aunt Jemima *The Hare and the Tortoise*?'

He made a show of pulling out his pocket watch, even though it was clear his frustration at his sibling had already switched to amusement at his foibles. 'As Archie's a devout early riser, my money is on six…maybe seven if he visits the chickens first to hunt for eggs, so we should

that the only skin which had touched the stays she was currently laced into was her own.

Rafe and Archie both needed and deserved more people in their lives who cared about them too. Just because they had been made pariahs in the wilds of Somerset, where perhaps the rural population were less enlightened, did not mean that would automatically happen here. Whittleston-on-the-Water was a stone's throw from the capital and, as such, much more modern in its outlook, and many of the residents, herself included, had not been born here but had still been welcomed with open arms. Welcomed and smothered and rapidly absorbed into the eclectic whole as one of them.

That Rafe hadn't was more down to his own stubborn reluctance to engage with the community than it was the villagers' fault. In trying to protect Archie, he had made himself the enemy, when she could see he wasn't enemy material at all now that she was coming to know him better and he would fit in here just fine if he stopped being so standoffish with them all. Which in turn, she supposed, made him his own worst enemy...

She needed to tread carefully broaching that or she'd become the enemy again too.

'Not so long ago there was another village within spitting distance of here. It was called Hinkwell-on-the-Hill.' He instantly stiffened at the mention so she rolled her eyes. 'That wasn't a dig either so stop being so touchy. I merely mention it for some context because there used to be a splendid haberdasher's in Hinkwell which was run by a Mr and Mrs Gresham. They had two strapping sons and one daughter.' She glanced back towards Archie's bedchamber. 'The daughter—May—was like your brother.'

'She was annoying and stubborn and obsessed with boiled eggs?'

'No, Rafe.' She caught his arm. Tried not to enjoy the solid feel of it or remember what he had looked like naked from the waist up. 'She was just like Archie.' She pointed to her face. 'So like him the pair of them could be twins.'

His head tilted as he digested this, his gaze wary but interested. 'And...?'

'And May was as accepted here by all and sundry as any other member of the community. She worked in the shop, attended the local assemblies, and nobody ever blinked an eyelid. Archie would be safe here.'

Curiosity at that warred momentarily with disbelief until his bicep hardened as disbelief won. That was when she realised she had pushed it too far too soon. That a man like Rafe—one who had real live experiences of prejudice and intolerances—would require categoric proof of such a bold claim with deeds rather than words. Real and tangible reassurance rather than just anecdotal. 'I thought you had resigned your commission as General Gilbert of the whinging Whittleston Rebel Alliance.'

'I have—but I shall always be an ambassador for them. I firmly believe you and your brother could be happy here.'

The shutters went down. 'Goodnight, Sophie.' He paused at his own door, his stormy blue eyes as cold as ice. 'Sleep tight.'

'Goodnight, Rafe.' She went to turn, annoyed with herself for poking at his exposed nerve, then changed her mind. She had to keep prodding at that exposed nerve. For both the good people of Whittleston and for him. Because he deserved so much more than the hand life had so far dealt him. 'I shall always be an ambassador for you too, because if my lofty opinion is worth anything, I believe with every fibre of my being that Whittleston could not only be the sanctuary you crave, but it would also be a much better place with you in it. As much as it pains me to admit it, you, my reluctant Lord Hockley, are one of the finest men I have ever encountered.' Then to her surprise as much as it clearly was his, she rose up on tiptoes and kissed him on the lips.

Chapter Nineteen

Stunned and shaken, Rafe blinked at Sophie while he tried to work out exactly what was going on.

His head told him that it had been a chaste kiss. A friendly kiss. A depressingly platonic and much too brief kiss. Yet while there was no denying it had been brief, there had been nothing chaste about it. At least not from where he was standing.

Chaste kisses were like the punctuation at the end of a sentence. Short, sharp and abrupt. That's why they were called a peck. Furthermore, a peck was usually administered to the cheek or the forehead, not the lips. It was affectionate and pleasant but transient. Gone and forgotten in the blink of an eye as the world moved ever on.

Pecks did not bring the world to a shuddering halt. Did not charge the air or awaken nerve endings or linger in anticipation. And to the best of his knowledge, they did not make the lips tingle and the breath erratic. Nor should they, in the usual course of things, leave the receiver of the peck befuddled and rampant, or make the bestower frown. Sophie's single quirked eyebrow over her rapidly blinking eyes suggested she was as be-wildered by the actual definition of her kiss as he was.

'What was that about?' A part of him hoped the ques-tion would break the spell. Another part—the bigger part—was perfectly content with remaining bewitched.

She answered with a baffled shrug then stared at him with such intensity and indecision it was disconcerting. 'Perhaps it is best not to over-analyse it.' Without think-ing, he used the pad of his index finger to rearrange the line of her brows, his thumb gently massaging the fur-row between them. 'Perhaps it is best to gloss over it and pretend it did not happen.'

'Perhaps…' But as indecision creased her forehead her palms smoothed down his lapels, then with a sigh of resignation used them to tug his mouth down to hers.

There was no misunderstanding the timbre of the sec-ond kiss. It started hot then burst into flames—and all initiated by her. She pushed him back against the door, plunged her hands in his hair and explored his mouth with her tongue. When that wasn't enough, her hands joined in, raking over his shoulders and his chest as if she needed to know every inch of him.

She moaned when he wrestled his arm out of the sling and filled his greedy palms with her bottom, sighing as she ground her pelvis against his already straining erec-tion before she reached behind him to open the door.

They staggered entwined into his bedchamber. Feast-ing on each other's mouths while hurried fingers fought with hairpins, buttons and laces. Sophie removed both his coat and his waistcoat in one hurried movement, then tugged the shirt from his breeches and over his head. When his uncooperative bad arm struggled to untie her gown, she turned around, holding up her hair in invitation so he could see what he was doing.

His heart racing and his body burning, as soon as the stubborn bow at the top released, Rafe slowed the pace. Not to give them a chance to think about what they were apparently about to do, but to revel in it. Luxuriate in it. He took his time with the rest of the laces and, once loosened, eased the bodice gently to expose only her shoulders so he could lay a trail of open-mouthed kisses over that sensitive flesh. She arched her neck to give him greater access, her hands covering his where they rested on her hips, then lazily dragging his up to cup her breasts.

Even through several layers of fabric her nipples were hard and puckered with need and that heated his blood further. He traced the outside of them until she moaned and pressed the full mounds into his palms, anchoring them in place with her own palms in case he stopped.

When she could stand it no more, it was Sophie who tugged the bodice down until it puddled around her feet. Sophie who turned around so he could look at her stood in only her chemise and stays. Sophie who pushed him to sit on the mattress, forcing him to be a spectator while her fingers traced the clear demarcation line between the proud jut of her cleavage and the lace edge of her undergarments like a seductive siren luring him to the rocks. Like Eve tempting Adam she began to undo the ribbon between her cleavage which held it all together, inviting him to watch as she unbound her breasts then tossed her stays to the floor.

She smiled at his sharp intake of breath as she wiggled out of her chemise, teasing him by revealing herself inch by glorious inch, turning her back to him as the fabric caught on her nipples so that he had to see the delicate curve of her spine and ripe peach of a bottom as the final barrier to his eyes and her nakedness pooled on top of her discarded dress.

Then she tugged the last few trapped pins from her hair with impatience. Tousled dark waves fell in a silken curtain over her shoulders and down her back as she bent to roll off each stocking with the practised guile of a courtesan, still denying him the opportunity to see her in all her full-frontal splendour on purpose.

'You're killing me.' And she was. Rafe had never wanted a woman more.

Her earthy, feminine chuckle was all seductive confidence, as if she knew she was torturing him, and knew he would thank her for it. The firelight behind turned her skin golden while intriguing shadows skimmed her curves.

She paused for a moment before she turned, her bold, expressive eyebrows and heated gaze confirming that she wanted this—wanted him—while giving him the opportunity to take it all in before she undulated towards the bed.

Naked, she took his breath away.

Full, heavy breasts capped with saucy dark nipples. A narrow waist which flared into seductive, womanly hips. The dark triangle of soft hair between her lovely, long legs.

Temptation incarnate with the promise of sin swirling in her beautiful dark eyes.

He caught her hand and tugged her to stand between his knees and watched her watch him as his fingertips reverently explored her body. Her eyes only fluttering closed when his lips teased her nipple. She sighed as he sucked it into his mouth, arching again to give him full access, her fingers tracing his face while they anchored it in place.

She seemed to feed on the pleasure, torturing them both by eking out every bit of it before she pushed him backwards. Her kiss was thorough and intense as she made short work of the buttons of his falls, but she tore her mouth away to watch as she tugged the tight fabric down his hips to reveal his hungry body. She made it plain she liked what she saw and his ego bathed and rejoiced in her lack of artifice.

Again, there was a confidence about her as she caressed him which inflamed Rafe further. She traced the shape of him with needy reverence, massaged the length of him in torturous, assured strokes and until his hips bucked on the mattress.

He growled as he reversed their position, and instantly she was submissive. Murmuring her encouragement as he touched her intimately, opening her body so he could pleasure it unhindered. Her hot, sensitive flesh slick and responsive to every gentle caress. Her hooded eyes locked with his as her fingers clenched the sheet.

As her passion built, she took control again, hauling him on top of her. His hardness strained towards her entrance and she tilted her hips to greet it. He hesitated, needing confirmation, and she reached between them to guide him, her body shuddering as he began to edge inside. As he adjusted position, he leaned on his bad arm and she saw him wince slightly. Quick as a flash, she rolled him on his back and took control again. Slowly lowering herself onto him until he filled her to the hilt. Then she smiled as she began to move, her eyelids fluttering closed as she focused all her concentration on taking them both to heaven.

It was then that Rafe lost all track of time and all his wits. All track of everything except the enchantress who held him enslaved as she unapologetically took her pleasure and in return gave it back to him in spades. Twice she brought them both to the edge of reason, and twice she denied them both release, the walls of her body caressing him relentlessly from root to tip until he was begging her to finish it. Finish him.

She moaned as he touched the bud of nerves where they joined, flinging her head backwards as he pushed her further and further towards oblivion. Watching her get there was the single most erotic thing Rafe had ever seen, and he ruthlessly held himself back so he could witness every second. And when she came and her body pulsed around his, she swallowed his cries of ecstasy in a kiss so carnal and so decadent he almost—*almost*—did not notice when he toppled with her into oblivion, that his body spilled into nothing.

Chapter Twenty

'There's four bitches and one male.' Ned Parker leaned his enormous frame on the gate of the stall while Archie cooed in ecstasy beside him at the boisterous puppies wrestling one another around an obviously tired black and white collie. 'Ophelia, the mother, is my best sheep-dog and has the sweetest temperament. The father is one of my hunting dogs.' He jerked his head out towards his stable yard where an enormous brute of a dog glared at them from behind a fence as if he fancied them for dinner. 'But Falstaff is his own dog. Loyal to a fault if you are one of the few humans he can tolerate, but woe be-tide anyone who annoys him.'

'He's a big animal.' Much bigger than Rafe had an-ticipated living with. 'What breed is he?'

Ned studied the beast for a moment then shrugged. 'Hard to say but I wouldn't be surprised if there's some wolf in his lineage.' *Good grief!* 'Along with a good smidge of gun dog. Take it from me, nothing beats his nose. He can sniff out a duck or a pheasant at five hun-dred yards—perhaps further.' Falstaff eyed them all like prey as they gathered around his young family. 'He's the undisputed leader of the pack on this farm, that's for certain, and he terrifies any would-be poachers.' By the looks of the huge fangs framing his massive jaw, Falstaff could rip them apart and without too much trouble.

'He's a gentle giant though,' offered Sophie beside him. 'Much like his master.' She smiled at Ned in affection and Rafe almost gnashed his teeth in irrational jealousy when Ned smiled back in the same soppy vein.

He blamed the kiss and the aftermath of it because both had knocked him sideways then left him up in the air. Hours and hours later and he was still none the wiser about what any of it had meant. There hadn't been the need to say any words during their fervent lovemaking—not that Rafe could have spoken he was so consumed and overawed by it. After they had both collapsed exhausted side by side on the pillow, he had fallen into instant, blissful sleep and she hadn't been beside him when he had woken up. He had no idea if she had slept beside him and crept out at dawn, or if she had done so the second he had drifted off. Either way he felt irrationally abandoned by it all.

Then she had avoided either breakfast—or simply him—and the window of opportunity to talk about it all had firmly closed because his brother was bouncing off the walls in excitement to fetch his promised puppy from Ned. Sophie then materialised out of hiding to join them in the carriage, as pretty as a picture and as cool as a cucumber, behaving as if nothing at all had happened between them. Which, true to form, did not bode well for his foolish heart. Not that he was even sure that he wanted it to bode well, because his irrational infatuation with the witch and the speed at which it had all escalated had caught him off guard and unprepared. Woefully unprepared and totally unarmed. Especially as he had a sneaking suspicion that, unlike Annabel, Sophie actually possessed the power to break his heart and that, frankly, scared the living daylights out of him.

'Which one is mine?' Archie was champing at the bit to get to the puppies.

'Whichever one chooses you, young man, as that is the way of things with dogs. The best, most loyal hounds always pick their own master. Therefore, once I let you in, you must stand as still as a statue and wait to see which of the pups fancies you.'

By the law of averages that meant that there was more chance of Archie leaving today with a female than not— but knowing Rafe's luck and fate's warped sense of humour, those averages meant nothing. 'Can you at least remove the boy before he goes in.' He whispered this out of the corner of his mouth so that his brother would not hear. 'Otherwise the poor thing will be saddled with the name Mary.' Which, judging by the size and fearsome shape of its father, would be a travesty of epic proportions.

'Easier said than done.' Ned huffed at the inconvenience, regarding Rafe as if he were an idiot. 'At this age it's not apparent unless you lift the blighters up to check their credentials.'

'Which is a job of less than a minute, you old curmudgeon.' Sophie nudged Ned in a way that looked a bit too flirty for Rafe's liking. 'So go check and stop being belligerent.'

With another put upon groan, and only because *she* asked him, the human tree undid the bolt to do just that, but as he opened the gate with much too deliberate slowness, he allowed Rafe's over-excited little brother to dart beneath his armpit.

'Who fancies me then?' Archie spoke to the puppies, all of whom were more interested in clambering all over one another than in him. 'Which of you fancies me as your new master?'

'Stand still, Archie.' Sophie caught his coat before he threw himself at the dogs and rolled amongst them, begging them to like him. 'You have to wait for one to come to you.'

'And Ned has to check them all first.' The moment Rafe uttered those words, one of the puppies untangled itself from the fray and studied Archie with interest. Then, as if drawn by some powerful cosmic force beyond its control, it scampered towards him and pawed at his leg.

'Looks like the dog has spoken.' Ned backed out of the stall palms raised and a smug expression on his face. 'Not much point checking those credentials now that the die is cast.'

'Hello, Mary.' Delighted, his brother bent to pick the animal up and giggled as it licked his face. 'You are coming home with me today.'

'And Mary has been christened.' Ned grinned at Rafe, enjoying himself far too much. 'Wouldn't it be marvellous if it is the only boy in the litter?' By the evil twinkle in his eye, it was obvious his burly nemesis was wishing it upon him. He reached one meaty hand over the gate and unpeeled the little dog from his brother's face. 'I need to borrow Mary for a moment, young man, then she—or *he*—is all yours.'

'And is it?' Before Ned even had time to check, Rafe knew that was a stupid question, because of course Mary would be the only boy. That was exactly the sort of prank fate would enjoy playing on him and yet another reason why he had to live miles from another living soul in the middle of nowhere.

Ned winced, though his eyes were filled with mirth as he turned the squirming pup towards them and the tiny wisp that would one day be the main feature of his canine wedding vegetables revealed itself in all its taunting glory. 'I'm afraid so.' Then he threw back his head and laughed as he handed it back to Archie. 'Good job he's going to be a huge dog else he'd never carry it off.' As his brother cradled the dog in instant adoration, Ned couldn't resist putting the boot in further. 'Mary will likely howl all night for his mother once you get him home, but that is normal. If you love Mary and play with Mary and feed Mary the best roast chicken and salmon then he'll bond with you and forget his mother in no time. You will become Mary's everything.' Rafe was in no doubt the wretch was repeating the name to cement it fast in his brother's mind.

'The name Mary isn't set in stone yet, is it, Archie? Especially now that we know your dog is a boy.' At his brother's horrified expression, he tried to sound conciliatory, knowing full well Archie would dig his heels in if Rafe tried to change his mind. 'And especially as there are some fine similar-sounding masculine names with only four letters too. Like Mark for example, which only changes one letter and suits that handsome puppy so well.' He turned to Sophie rather than Ned, hoping she would at least support him in his hour of need. 'What do you think of the name Mark?'

'I like it. It's strong. It's noble and it is majestic.' She beamed at Archie, nodding. 'Mark would be a very fitting name for your puppy. I also like Fred as that has a nice ring to it and suits him far better than Mary ever could.'

Archie hugged the precious bundle in his arms tighter, his expression utterly betrayed. 'But it has always been my dream to have a dog called Mary. Why would you crush my dreams, Rafe?'

'The dog was the dream and that has come true. You thought up the name Mary less than a month ago.' As Rafe's impatience leaked out, Sophie touched his shoulder to stay him and, without realising it, set his body alight once more.

'I say we take this little fellow home to give him a chance to settle in—don't you think so?—and wait until he reveals his true character. As I am sure Ned will agree...' She shot the malicious tree a look which warned him to keep his big, meddling mouth shut. 'In much the same way as a dog *has* to pick its own owner, the dog *also* has to pick his own name else he'll never come when called. Isn't that right, Ned?'

Ned wavered then nodded with as much reluctance as it was physically possible to put into the gesture. 'Aye— that's right.'

'So I cannot call him Mary?' Archie was crestfallen.

'Of course you can.' Sophie stroked his cheek and then the puppy's head. 'But in the same way as you have several names, Archibald Leo Peel, you might have to settle for Mary as the middle name if the dog doesn't like it.'

Slightly placated, Archie followed her to the stable yard still cradling the pup. 'But how will we know if he likes the name or not?'

'We write a whole heap of names on pieces of paper

and we spread them out over the floor, then we see which one your puppy wanders to first. After all, Archie, you want him to be happy most of all, don't you? So it is only fair he gets the final say?'

'Can I at least pick some of the names on the papers?'

'As you are the owner, Archie, you get to pick all of the names. Isn't that right, Rafe?' Her eyes lifted to his and he lost himself in them again until his poor heart ached with wanting.

'Absolutely.' *Good grief, he was in some serious trouble.*

Sophie stood in the circle of names with Archie while they surveyed their evening's work. There were twenty-two pieces of paper in total, all with a single name written in big, bold letters. Each name hand-picked by him and most consisting of only four letters. Only Aesop and Attila the Hun had more. The former in honour of Archie's current favourite author and the latter the only suggestion from Rafe who felt it fitting seeing as they had likely welcomed a mad, man-eating and marauding dog into the fold thanks to the fearsome Falstaff being the father. Sixteen of the names were unique, which meant, at Archie's insistence, there were six separate Marys dotted around the carpet.

'I think it's time to release the puppy.' She smiled at Archie who immediately clicked his fingers at Rafe, making the eldest Peel roll his delicious blue eyes.

'I suppose I should jump to it then.' For the sake of impartiality because she and Archie had laid down the names, they had decided he had the honour of carrying the bundle of fluff in and placing him dead in the centre of the circle. A spot which had been meticulously measured and which was also marked with its own piece of paper.

As Rafe stomped out of the drawing room to fetch the animal from the makeshift pen they had made him in the hallway to protect him from Socrates who had already attacked the poor thing twice, she and Archie removed themselves to opposite corners to watch the proceedings from afar. Although it did not go unnoticed that the youngest Peel took himself to the corner where he had arranged three of the Marys altogether and where he no doubt fully intended to defraud the election process despite solemnly swearing that he wouldn't.

'One bloodthirsty wolf in puppy's clothing.' Rafe returned with the squirming pup held aloft in his arm like a sacrifice to the gods and with a very solemn Walpole who had been drafted in as the referee traipsing behind him. 'Let the Grand Choosing of the Name Ceremony commence!'

The second he placed the animal on the X in the centre of the Persian, Archie began to pat his knees. 'This way, Mary! Come to Papa!'

As Rafe glared at the butler, the servant shook an admonishing finger at the flagrant cheat. 'Silence, Lord Archie. If you speak again I shall declare the result invalid, and we shall have to start again.' As Archie frowned at being thwarted, his brother came to stand beside her, sending a waft of the heady scent of Rafe straight up her nostrils to remind her of last night.

Not that Sophie needed any reminders of last night or of the fact that the pair of them had not talked about it. That had hung in the air like an ominous dark cloud all day, casting a veil of awkwardness over them both which she had diligently tried to ignore with the same stubborn determination as she had avoided being alone with him all day too. As he had made it impossible to avoid him, which would have been her preferred option in perpetuity, she had worked hard to keep them all busy as well as chaperoned by either Archie or Aunt Jemima or both all the way through to dinner. Even this—the Grand Choosing of the Name Ceremony—was happening now with great pomp and circumstance because she had engineered it that way. Simply because it guaranteed they were occupied with something other than the enormous fly she had personally shoved in the ointment right up until bedtime.

Like a coward, she had avoided the conversation and the explanation for her scandalous and wanton behaviour. She had to avoid it because she still had no earthly idea how to fully explain the complicated and tangled emotions which that mad, unguarded moment of unbridled passion had created.

How exactly did you face a man who you'd determinedly and purposely seduced so you could have your wicked way with him? Because that was precisely what she had done in hindsight. She had used him to scratch her overwhelming carnal itch and thoroughly enjoyed every single second of it.

And she had been quite shameless about it too. Driven entirely by too-long-suppressed lust and blinded by re-awakened need and a renewed thirst for life, she had behaved as little like a proper and prim spinster as it was possible to be. Rafe had seen every visible inch of her. Intimately touched, explored and penetrated a few more invisible inches. Heard her fevered cries and whimpers as she vocalised her appreciation in the most unladylike manner. Witnessed her writhing atop him in the full throes of passion as she rode him like horse until she reached the release she craved.

Or perhaps she had ridden him like a stallion.

A beautiful, wild and untamed stallion.

Given his impressive, talented and truly satisfying credentials, Rafe most definitely fell more into the stallion category rather than the nag, and she absolutely fell into the wild. She had been so wild and brazen in her quest to gallop towards fulfilment, her wayward body still throbbed scandalously at the memory of it. And, heaven help her, it was still craving more despite all the guilt which ate her from the inside.

Guilt about Michael.

Guilt about her feelings.

Guilt about her needs and about using Rafe to satisfy them.

She couldn't imagine what he must be thinking. Especially as she had revelled in every inch of his body. Greedily explored and took advantage of every single inch.

Every.

Splendid.

Inch.

She surreptitiously flicked her gaze sideways and almost cringed as she met his.

As if he could read her sinful mind he tilted his golden head towards her, his intuitive stare relentless. 'I cannot help but notice that there are six Marys and one Attila—this is hardly an unbiased election.' His deep whisper drizzled down her back and trickled through every nerve ending, including every improper one, in the most disconcerting fashion.

'Of course it is an unbiased election. I designed it specifically as such.'

'You want that poor thing to be saddled with the name Mary.'

'He won't be.' She couldn't resist a smile as the puppy tripped over his large paws while he sniffed the air. 'I am the former General Gilbert of the whinging Whittleston Rebel Alliance, remember—one of the most formidable adversaries you have ever come up against. Your words, *Captain* Peel, not mine. Do you think I entered into this without a cunning plan and decisive battle strategy?'

'To be perfectly frank with you, Sophie, I never know quite what you are going to do next.' His bemused gaze heated as he too clearly remembered all she had instigated then frogmarched to completion. 'You are a vexing enigma who is doing her level best to avoid talking to me about last night.'

Her stomach fluttered as she floundered, so she bit her lip hoping the right words would miraculously appear despite eluding her all day. 'About that…'

'No!' Archie's disgust tore through the charged air as his puppy lurched away from the cluster of Marys next to his feet. 'Here, boy!'

'Stop cheating, Lord Archie.' Walpole wagged his finger. 'You cannot make up the rules and not apply them to yourself. Miss Gilbert and your brother are sticking to them to the letter. You, young man, are not.' Because both the butler and Archie were now staring at them she used the situation as an excuse to avoid Rafe a bit longer by wandering to the youngest Peel and wrapping her arm around him.

'He has to choose his own name, Archie, and you have to be patient while he does it. Just remember, whichever one he chooses, you also chose too and at least he is avoiding the dreadful Attila so I am inclined to trust your dog's sensible judgement.' As the young man lay his impatient head against her shoulder, she could feel his brother's intense stare all the way to her soul.

The puppy gingerly sniffed several names but did not put his paw on any of them. Finally, after hovering over three of them, he rubbed his tiny black nose on one then scampered off with the paper clutched in his teeth until he tripped over it.

'What did he choose?' Like a tiger stalking his prey, Rafe sauntered over and took up the space beside her which Archie had vacated in his mad dash towards his dog, who was now in the process of tearing the sheet of paper to shreds with his little razor teeth. While his brother was distracted trying to piece it all together, he folded his arms all nonchalance and leaned towards her ear, so close the vibrations from his warm breath were like a silken caress. 'And precisely when *tonight* shall we talk about *last* night, minx? For be in no doubt we *are* going to talk about it before this day is done.'

'It's Fred!' As if that had been the name he had been rooting for the entire time, Archie beamed from ear to ear. 'Isn't that the perfect name? I thought he looked exactly like a Fred the first moment I laid eyes on him and it has four letters too. F. R. E. D.' He punctuated each letter with a kiss on the puppy's nose and then rolled around on the floor giggling as the little thing responded by licking his face to death.

'Wasn't Fred your choice?' That soft murmur sent ripples of awareness to all the intimate parts of her that he was now so intimately aware of.

'It suits him.'

'So you've said. This morning if I am not mistaken. At Ned's.'

'Can I take Fred up to bed to sleep with me, Rafe?' Soulful blue eyes, the exact shade of his distracting big brother's, widened into manipulative saucers. 'You did promise.'

'Yes, I did, and a promise is a promise.' He slanted her a pointed glance in case she tried to use his brother's retiring as another excuse to evade him. 'Goodnight, Archie. Goodnight, Fred.' He caught her fingers and hid them behind his back so the other two could not see, and the urge to lace hers within his was overpowering. 'And goodnight to you too, Walpole. Miss Gilbert and I will turn out the lights.'

Trapped and her heart racing in a combination of panic and desire, Sophie remained rooted to the spot while Rafe ushered the others out of the room. As the door closed with a decisive click he leaned his back against it. 'Well?'

Chapter Twenty-One

'I don't suppose we could just forget it ever happened?' The coward's way out and one she wasn't proud of suggesting, especially as denying her grief for so long hadn't been the most prudent course of action.

Yet that grief was all part of her jumbled confusion. Experiencing all that, opening herself to all that a second time, was out of the question, therefore she could not afford to let Rafe into her heart. Nor did it feel appropriate or respectful to Michael. Yet on the other hand, there was something undeniable about Rafe that tempted her beyond the obvious lure of the physical. A sense of wellbeing and rightness in his presence which was like a balm to her soul. Attraction and kinship. A dangerous, potent combination that she could not risk.

Exactly like Michael but not and so very hard to comprehend.

'I am pretty certain what happened last night is something I shall remember till my dying day.' He raked his good hand through his hair, unaware that, rumpled, he was even more attractive than he was neat. 'Was it just me who found it particularly...' He shrugged with an awkwardness which he rarely displayed but which her damaged heart found much too appealing. 'I am no blushing virgin myself, Sophie, and last night was…' He sighed and shook his head as if baffled by it all. 'Let us just say that last night…you…well, it was not at all what I am used to.'

Was that a compliment? A chastisement? Sheer unadulterated shock that a supposedly proper and unmarried woman could behave with such flagrant, hedonistic and enthusiastic abandon? Before her death, her mother had stuttered over an awkward conversation regarding 'stoically enduring the marital chore' which had left the sixteen-year-old Sophie dreading it. But then at seventeen, even with her and Michael's first inexperienced fumblings, Sophie hadn't found it a chore at all. Far from it, in fact. Over the three years they courted in secret, and whenever they could find an opportunity, she had never once refused Michael's advances. If anything, she had welcomed them and created as many opportunities as she could for them to indulge themselves more. Together they had experimented and learned until she fully understood her sensuality and her body as well as his. In no time, that aspect of their lives had worked like clockwork, and he had adored her passion. Encouraged it and her to be ever bolder. But Michael was from common stock and Rafe wasn't, so perhaps to his sensibilities her behaviour last night was shocking in the extreme.

'I sincerely apologise if I shocked…' He stayed her with a finger to her lips. One that lingered and traced the shape of them as he smiled.

'For pity's sake, don't apologise.' His laughter was part amusement, part wonder. 'Though I cannot deny I was both shocked and stunned, still am truth be told, but last night was wonderful. You were wonderful. So wonderful I have to keep pinching myself that it wasn't all a dream. It just knocked me sideways, that is all. Probably as much because it came out of the blue as it was…spectacular.'

Spectacular was an apt word. Her body still thrummed from the splendour of it and she smiled shyly back at him, which was ridiculous when there had been nothing coy about her in his bedchamber. There she hadn't experienced an ounce of doubt or reticence. She had been in too much of a hurry to indulge in it all.

'Are you blushing?' He brushed her cheek and she nodded.

'It's absurd, isn't it, when I am well aware that it is I who led the charge last night.'

'Well, you are a general and I am but a mere captain…' The finger tracing her cheek twirled in a stray tendril of her hair. 'You really are a vexing conundrum, Sophie Gilbert.' As if he realised he was touching her like a lover again, he withdrew his hand and fisted it behind his back. 'But I still do not understand what it all meant.' His stormy blue eyes were unsure. Wary.

Hopeful?

Surely not.

'It meant…' She wanted to say nothing but that would have been a lie—because it had meant something. A great deal, truth be told, although she did not want to pick apart why in case her heart was already involved, and that prospect terrified her more than her lack of restraint had. 'Does it have to mean anything?' Thankfully, no evidence of her sudden panic was visible in her tone. 'We are both adults after all and neither are strangers to the sport.' She hoped there was a broom big enough to sweep all this under the carpet where she did not have to ponder it. 'Being in for a penny does not mean we have to go in for the whole pound.'

He frowned at her tortured analogy. 'Pennies and pounds aside, I think we both need to understand where we stand now, don't you? What with us being stuck under the same roof at least until your cottage is rebuilt or your aunt is well enough to move elsewhere in the interim. It's going to be dashed awkward otherwise.' He dropped his voice to a disarming whisper. 'We have been intimate, madam. Gloriously intimate and we cannot undo that inescapable fact no matter how much you might wish to pretend otherwise.' There was a hint of bitterness in those words. 'If you regret what happened and have already deemed it a mistake, at least have the good grace to admit it.'

She could tell by the stubborn set of his jaw he wasn't going to allow her to fob him off with more cowardly avoidance. 'I do not regret it, Rafe.' His broad shoulders relaxed at that truth. 'Last night was…lovely.' A wholly unsuitable word for it but an inane one which suited her confused emotions better than all the alternatives her brain conjured. All of them worrying and not at all as detached as she wanted to be. 'And I have decided not to feel guilty about it.' Another truth she did not realise until it tumbled from her lips.

'I am thirty and long past the age of coquettishness, and I see nothing wrong in two consenting, over-burdened, jaded and lonely adults finding some occasional and discreet comfort in one another's arms.' Good heavens, that was an outrageous statement because it stated outright that she was open to a repeat of last night so long as they maintained strict parameters, yet it was exactly how she felt. 'It is not as if either of us want any more than that.' Best to lay out those parameters now. She was willing and content to share her body but had to protect what was left of her heart at all costs. Had to manage the guilt of betraying Michael's memory. Had to march onwards and upwards on a different path now that she had stopped numbly marking time. One which embraced both life and her womanhood but that she trod resolutely alone. 'I certainly don't. As much as I like you as a friend, Rafe, I have no desire to pursue a romantic relationship with anyone ever again. I have done that. That ship has long since sailed, and I likely would not survive another shipwreck.'

Unexpected tears pricked her eyes. Tears for the love that she had lost and tears for the love she had to deny herself. She blinked them away and strapped on some bravado, hoping the deep, unexpected and empty feeling of regret would ebb as quickly as it surged. 'Besides, I sincerely doubt a guarded cynic like you harbours any thoughts of for ever, do you?'

'Of course not!' But for a moment she thought she saw a flash of hurt skitter across his beguiling bright blue eyes before he shuddered in mock disgust. 'Perish the thought. I am still wedded to a life in the middle of nowhere, as far away from the disappointing human race as it is physically possible to be. I'd probably buy an island if one were for sale.' He smiled but it did not touch his eyes. 'And rest assured I am still determined to offload this blasted mausoleum and whinging Whittleston-on-the-Water as soon as is humanly possible. I've always preferred horses to people.'

She chuckled as she was supposed to even though it sounded hollow to her ears. 'I am glad we cleared the air, Rafe.' Except it did not feel cleared at all. It now felt thick and dense like the worst winter fog on the banks of the Thames.

'Me too. I can sleep soundly now, safe in the knowledge that you do not expect a ring on your finger and I have been spared the snapping teeth of the parson's trap.'

Her errant pulse quickened at the thought. 'My honour was not impugned, Captain Peel, so please absolve yourself of all misplaced obligation for it is neither necessary nor desired.'

'Splendid.' He smiled as he rocked on his heels. 'Good to know.'

'Indeed.' Now what? She loathed the new awkwardness which lingered between them. Loathed it and wished she knew how to fix it. Fortunately, like the noble knight in shining armour that he was, Rafe rushed in to save her.

'So...' He raised his good arm and gestured to the door. 'Exactly how did you get that puppy to choose the name Fred?' As she slid her hand through his elbow, he began to lead her to the stairs, pausing to snuff out the lamp on the mantel. 'Spill your secrets, witch.'

'It wasn't witchcraft, if that is what you are implying, more a little strategic common sense based on sound recognisance.' If he could behave as if nothing cataclysmic had happened, so could she. 'Surely as a decorated soldier you must understand that it is entirely possible to win a battle before it has even begun—so long as you've planned it correctly. Which I, as the superior strategist here, did with meticulous precision.' She let go of his arm at the foot of the stairs to waft a regal hand in the air. 'But then some of us were born to lead and others rise only as far as their own incompetence will allow,

Captain Peel.' She offered him her sauciest shrug as she skipped up the steps.

She had barely gone two feet when he caught her hand and spun her back, then gripped it tight in case she tried to escape. 'Don't make me torture the answer out of you. After a decade fighting fiercer foes than you, I know many ways to make the enemy talk.' He leaned closer. Close enough that she could smell the spicy scent of his shaving soap. Close enough that she could feel the heat of his big body and not just where their hands touched. 'Many, *many* ways.' His deep blue eyes swirled with amused challenge. 'And do not think for one minute I shall let you get one wink of sleep before I have received proper satisfaction.' Which all sounded scandalously wonderful to Sophie because her wayward mind instantly pictured him in the throes of passion on the cusp of receiving just that. She pictured herself on the cusp again too. Something else her wayward mind had been conjuring up since last night and her overwhelming impulse to kiss him.

She almost sighed aloud as she stared up into them. Those sinful blue eyes were deadly weapons and once again she was unarmed. 'Do your worst, Captain Peel, for I shall never talk.'

Good heavens above, now she was flirting. Flirting and courting danger when she knew she should avoid it. Yet here she was, sashaying up the stairs so that her hips wiggled in stark invitation, willing him to follow. 'Nothing you can say or do will ever make me tell you how I slipped out of dinner for a few moments to retrieve the piece of the expensive smoked salmon I hid during luncheon. Nor will I ever let slip how I ruthlessly rubbed the back of the piece of paper emblazoned with the name

Fred with that same piece of salmon before I shuffled it back in the pack. Or make any mention of how I then fed little Fred his first morsel of that sublime salmon to give him the taste of it because I knew he would have his father's keen nose.'

'You sabotaged the election.'

'On the contrary, Captain Peel. Everything I did was to ensure you not end up with a giant male dog called Mary.'

'So you cheated for me?'

'I prefer to think of it as an act of selfless charity because you needed my help and clearly needed my assistance.'

'I see. You are more Good Samaritan than a sneaky saboteur.'

'Of course. I am more saint than sinner, as you well know.' She stopped directly outside his bedchamber door and leaned against it like the most brazen, unsubtle hussy. 'If you ask me nicely, Captain Peel, I would be only to happy to assist you again…because I cannot help noticing that the knot your sleeping brother tied in that cravat looks awfully, *awfully* tight.'

Chapter Twenty-Two

'He has already had one offer on the land but has promised me he will not accept it until there are several suitable offers for us to choose from.' Sophie sipped her tea and smiled at the rest of the ladies of the Whittleston-on-the-Water Friday Sewing Circle in reassurance. As much as she did not want to have to contemplate Rafe leaving Whittleston, her head told her it was for the best.

In the last ten days she had got rather attached to him. Their discreet arrangement was only ever meant to be temporary, and no matter how many times she reminded herself of the importance of keeping her heart quite separate from their secret nocturnal activities, he was a charming, lovable scoundrel who appealed to it regardless. Too many more days of easiness followed by nights filled with sublime passion, and she feared she would never be able to give him up. As it was, it got harder and harder to leave him sleeping to return to her own bedchamber each night, but she knew waking up next to him would be too intimate to bear. Too revealing. Too romantic. Too much like they meant something to one another and that was a familiar, slippery slope which she wasn't prepared to risk. Nor did it seem to bother Rafe who was quite content with their arrangement as it was. By day, he was the perfect gentleman who never gave any hint or made any mention of what they did in private. Not even her wily Aunt Jemima suspected anything, which now that she was able to spend the day downstairs in a chair in the drawing room was a miracle when she usually saw everything. But by night he was...

She had to sip her tea again to hide her smile. Because at night he was the perfect lover. Attentive, generous, adventurous and vigorous. She would miss that when he was gone. 'He has invited several interested parties to visit us a week Saturday and has asked me to help him show them around the estate so I can get a feel for their characters and ask them questions.'

'Why should we trust your opinions, Sophie Gilbert, when you have nothing to lose any more?' Mrs Outhwaite glared at her across the large communal sewing table. 'Your aunt told me she is being given the deeds to the new cottage this week and the ground had barely been prepared.' Her eyes narrowed with suspicion. 'A cynic would say that your new, conciliatory attitude to the new lord of the manor has come because you've already feathered your own nest.' That stung. Probably because it wasn't that far from the truth and she experienced enormous guilt over it. 'Although goodness knows how you managed to crack through his standoffish exterior when he still avoids the rest of us like the plague.'

The insinuation was clear and, again, too close to the mark, so Sophie's cheeks heated, but before she could counter, Mrs Fitzherbert rallied to her defence.

'Are you suggesting she seduced those deeds out of him, Agatha, for if you are apologise this very minute for your filthy mind!' Mrs Fitzherbert bashed her cane on the floorboards and glared. 'Might I remind you that Sophie and Jemima nearly died thanks to his predecessor's neglect! And they lost everything in that fire! The very least he could do was rebuild them a cottage and not one of the rest of us sat around this table begrudge them that!'

Mrs Outhwaite practically withered under the disapproving stares of the rest of the group, but even as her eyes dipped to her hands contrite, she couldn't quite bring herself to apologise for the slur. 'I just don't see why Sophie should be the only one to vet the candidates when it no longer directly affects her, and we all have to live with the final decision.'

Put like that, Sophie could understand why Mrs Outhwaite felt aggrieved. 'I am sure Lord Hockley will not mind some others tagging along.' She would speak to him and suggest as much the second she got home.

Home? Where had that come from?

She brushed that errant thought away as a mental slip. 'Rafe is actually a rather agreeable sort when you get to know him.'

'Oh, it's Rafe now, is it?' Isobel Cartwright shot her a knowing glance. 'Perhaps it isn't Lord Hockley who has been seduced after all. Perhaps it is Sophie here who has had her fickle head turned.' Then she nudged her, grinning. 'Although I cannot say that I blame you if you have, for he is very easy on the eyes and fills his coats *so* well.' He filled his breeches better but Sophie bit her tongue. 'Is he coming to the assembly tomorrow?'

'I haven't asked him.' Although with hindsight, she probably should have. It might do him good to see the villagers in a social setting rather than thinking of them all as the enemy. 'But I will. I know Archie will enjoy it.'

She glanced over to the other end of St Hildelith's village hall where Rafe's brother was sat with Reverend Spears, trying and failing to teach Fred some tricks.

'I fail to understand why we are now rolling over and accepting his plans to sell the village from under us.' Mrs Outhwaite was like a dog with a bone. 'What happened to our protest? To defending Whittleston at all costs via fair means or foul?' She skewered Sophie with a look that would sour milk. 'Your words, Sophie Gilbert, in case you have forgotten. Or did all your rallying calls to fight go up in flames the same night as your cottage?' While several ladies gasped in shock at the vitriol, Mrs Outhwaite continued defiant.

'We can still thwart this sale, and I say we stop using fair means to do it and resort to foul! If that man listens to you, Sophie, then *make* him stay and *force* him to stand up to his responsibilities! Need I remind you that, against my good advice, you were elected our leader because others...' She glared at Mrs Fitzherbert. 'Believed you were the best choice to save the village.' She shook her customary quaking finger to the heavens, her voice rising an octave with every syllable. 'Thus, your duty and loyalties should still be for this village first and foremost and none of us want this land sold! Not under any circumstances!'

'She does have a point, Sophie.' Mrs Fitzherbert pulled a face as she reluctantly agreed with the other woman. 'Lord Hockley—for all his standoffishness—is obviously a decent sort beneath all the bluster with a good heart.' Her wily old eyes swivelled to Archie pointedly before locking with hers. 'I think I speak for all of us when I say we would much prefer the devil we know than some stranger with a fat purse and delusions of grandeur who will likely say anything to get his hands on such a prime piece of land.' Several ladies around the table nodded. 'If we put it to the vote, Sophie dear, I am convinced it will be unanimous that none of us want him to sell and you do seem best placed to talk him around to our way of thinking. He likes you.'

'Ned says that he looks at Sophie with *covetous eyes*.' Isobel Cartwright nudged her hard in the ribs again as she sighed with theatrical aplomb. 'And we all know that a man besotted is putty in the right woman's capable hands. If Ned is right, then you are the right woman.' She batted her eyelashes for good measure in case Sophie did not get the gist.

'You could seduce him to our way of thinking.' That came from Mrs Fitzherbert who grinned at Sophie's appalled expression at her turncoat effrontery.

'So much for filthy minds!'

'Oh, pish.' The incorrigible nonagenarian rolled her eyes. 'It would hardly be a chore. As Isobel quite rightly said, he is very easy on the eyes.' She winked at Isobel. 'I'd do it myself if I were ten years younger. I would sacrifice my virtue to the handsome brute and gladly.' She cackled at the irony as they all knew Mrs Fitzherbert had been married three times. 'And I would try to enjoy it for the sake of the village.' Several of the married ladies—including Mrs Spears the reverend's wife—tittered knowingly.

'I do not believe what I am hearing!' Sophie's cup clattered to her saucer. 'Are you seriously asking *me* to seduce Lord Hockley to get what *you* want?' Because that felt wrong on every conceivable level. 'Never mind what you are suggesting is both immoral and improper...' What a hypocrite she was to bring up propriety after last night's vigorous session which had occurred because she had indeed seduced him again and without any additional incentive or motive whatsoever. 'Might I remind you all that I owe that man my life! That he risked his own to save my aunt *and* my grumpy cat and nearly got himself killed in the process!' She was hissing now, hunched like her grumpy cat in case Archie heard and came running to assist and then tattled all of this shocking nonsense to his brother. 'He took us in! Is rebuilding our home!' She jabbed an incensed finger at both Mrs Fitzherbert and Mrs Outhwaite. 'I owe a huge debt of loyalty to him too!' The thought of her betraying him in that way was inconceivable.

'You do not *actually* have to seduce him in the physical sense.' Mrs Fitzherbert patted her hand, unaware that that stable door was already wide open and that horse had long bolted. 'All we are asking is that you use your unique influence to encourage him to see reason. Point him in the right direction. Ease him down the correct path. Wear him down with sound, logical, charming arguments that bring him around to our way of thinking.' She patted her hand again as if what she was asking were already a foregone conclusion. 'You are our Trojan horse, Sophie Gilbert. Not to mention our only hope.' Then she addressed the rest of the table in her own persuasive, Machiavellian way. 'Diplomacy is its own form of seduction, after all, and perhaps it is something we can all play a part in? If Sophie provides us with the opportunities, of course.'

As the other ladies all nodded as if the vote had already been unanimous, Mrs Fitzherbert bashed her cane on the floor again and prodded Sophie with her finger. 'Bring him to the assembly tomorrow and we can all charm him, then collectively but with subtle haste we can all seduce him into staying at Hockley Hall for ever before he accepts any offers.'

Rafe couldn't find Archie anywhere.

Nobody had seen him since mid-morning after he had helped brush down the horses. As that had only been two hours ago, and because there was no sign of Sophie or Fred the puppy either, he tried not to panic. The pair are them were probably walking the grounds together. Something the three of them had taken to doing daily at around this time. As his brother was a creature of habit, he'd likely dragged Sophie out anyway in his impatience for Rafe to finish working in his study.

To be fair to him, the meeting with the solicitor had dragged on over an hour longer than Rafe had expected. But then, they had been discussing both the deeds to Willow Cottage and Stephen Bassett's generous offer, so there had been much to talk about. Bassett had countered his original offer of the asking price to one well above it so long as no other offers were considered, and the papers were signed within the fortnight. As Rafe had promised Sophie she would have at least two buyers to choose from and because he had already arranged for ten potential buyers to survey the estate in eight days' time, they had needed to draft a letter to Bassett explaining that as politely as possible without losing him completely. If it meant losing eight thousand pounds on top of the asking price of fifty thousand, so be it, but he had to appease his conscience and he had to do right by her.

Her!

Rafe groaned aloud into the empty, cluttered hallway. Blasted woman had not only got under his skin, she was already burrowing her way into his foolish heart. Even though he knew she wasn't the least bit interested in anything beyond the physical and was still in love with a ghost. And even though she had made it plain their liaison, for want of a better word, was temporary, he knew without a doubt he was in grave danger of falling for her anyway and falling hard. In truth, he likely already had no matter how many times he tried to convince himself otherwise.

She had bewitched him and thoroughly consumed him. He already dreaded her moving in with Mrs Fitzherbert, let alone their final goodbye, but couldn't afford to draw it out for his sanity's sake or his pride's. But it was what it was and to quote the vexing minx, all he could do was forge onwards and upwards. Far better to have loved and lost the minx than never to have loved her at all.

Loved! Good grief, he was already doomed!

Blasted witch. Blasted circumstances. Blasted, blasted, bloody fate and her cruel sense of humour—because Rafe was in no doubt fate was a blasted woman too.

Annoyed at his own pathetic weakness and lack of self-control, he wandered out of the back door in search of both Archie and the conundrum of a woman who was quite content with the situation as it was, his gaze scanning the horizon for any sign. But all he saw were the gathering storm clouds above the river. Dark and ominous and filled with trouble and, for some reason, they felt symbolic which made him worry more about everything.

Some sixth sense made him wander towards the gates and out onto the lane. When there was still no sign of them at the recently cleared site of her cottage, he picked up his pace and practically slammed right into them as he turned the corner.

Sophie was carrying the sleepy Fred in her arms like a baby while his brother was tucking into what looked like a big bag of sweets.

'Where have you been?'

'To the village.' Archie grinned as if he had just had the most marvellous adventure. 'I visited the church and the market square, and we had a delicious cake from the bakery. And I met so many nice new friends.'

'Did you indeed.' True to form, Archie either ignored or was oblivious to Rafe's clipped tone.

'I did! Reverend Spears is going to teach me how to train Fred. We are starting with sit first because that is most important and will show him who is in charge. And Mrs Fitzherbert has lent me an old book filled with the most detailed illustrations of wild animals—but it was too big to carry so she's going to ask Ned to deliver it here later. And Mr Roberts from the shop gave me this liquorice which I am not supposed to eat all at once in case they give me a belly ache.' He offered the bag of goodies towards Rafe as pleased as Punch, oblivious to the fact that he had already eaten so many they had tinged his mouth and teeth with a hint of black. 'Best of all, we've been invited to the local assembly tomorrow night where Sophie and Miss Isobel are going to teach me to dance. I am so excited I feel fit to burst.'

'That is probably all the liquorice,' said Sophie, tugging the bag of sweets out of his hand and replacing it with the puppy. 'You can have the rest tomorrow.'

'I do not recall giving you permission to visit the village.' He glared at Sophie, trying not to feel betrayed, then at his brother. 'In fact, I am certain I expressly forbade you to ever set foot there.'

'Alone,' said Archie unperturbed. 'Which I wasn't because I stayed with Sophie the whole time. Didn't I, Sophie? I didn't wander off at all.'

'You didn't.' She beamed at Archie then it dissolved to a guilty smile when she turned to him. 'I wanted to thank the ladies from the sewing circle for all my new clothes. I've been meaning to do it all week and now that Aunt Jemima's recovery is coming along in leaps and bounds, and you were busy, it seemed like the perfect time. Especially after the last batch arrived yesterday.' She gestured to the pretty pelisse she was wearing, drawing his gaze to her lush figure and instantly reminding him what was beneath the garment. 'Archie was bored waiting for you and asked if he could come with me.'

'And it did not occur to you to ask me?'

'I did poke my head around the door but you were ensconced in a deep conversation with Mr Spiggot, so I didn't like to disturb. Besides, he was with me so I saw no harm in it, and as you can see, Archie has had a lovely morning.'

'You still should have asked, Sophie.' Especially as he had entrusted her with all his truth and she knew how protective he was of his brother. Especially as she knew how both he and Archie had been treated by the small-minded before.

'To hear you say no?' She was annoyed for some reason, as if he was somehow in the wrong rather than the other way around. As if she were angry at him. 'Sometimes it is better to seek forgiveness than ask permission.' She marched on ahead to avoid a scene, dragging his brother with her with a stream of inane chatter, forcing Rafe to trail behind as if the topic was closed and that was that.

For the sake of Archie, he bottled his temper until they were back in the house, but as soon as his brother left the drawing room to feed Fred his dinner, it was ready to explode.

But he wouldn't. Instead, he would channel all his training.

Stay calm. Appear reasonable. Stay measured. Remain in control at all costs.

'You should not have gone behind my back like that.'

The expressive dark brows rose as she had the temerity to roll her eyes as she dismissed that. 'We spent an hour in the village, Rafe. I hardly committed high treason.' Yet it felt like high treason to him.

'You know how I feel about Archie meeting strangers. You wilfully put him in danger. What if something had happened?'

She had the gall to scoff at his reasonable question. 'Firstly, he was never in any danger, and secondly, while the villagers may be strangers to you because you have never taken the time to know them, they are not strangers to me. If you think for one moment that I would ever put Archie in harm's way then you do not know me at all, Rafe. And if you think for one second that forcing Archie into being a recluse like you is best for him then you have misjudged everyone—including your brother.' She jabbed her finger in the direction of the kitchen where his brother had gone. 'Archie adores people, and it isn't fair to deny him the opportunity to know more of them. By confining him to this house, you are denying him the right to thrive!' She was royally furious now, and spun on her heel to turn away, so he caught her arm to spin her back.

Stay calm. Appear reasonable. Stay measured. Remain in control at all costs.

As if that was likely! Not when his blood was boiling.

'Do not presume to lecture me on what is best for my brother! A brother who has thrived exponentially under my guardianship! He couldn't read a word until I taught him. Could not count beyond five. Could not tell the time eighteen months ago...'

'And he is capable of so much more, don't you see?' She spread her palms, pleading although her gaze made it very plain she still thought him an idiot. 'People learn from other people. A wide variety of people. Your brother is not a child and I know he has the capacity for so much more if only you would let him learn.'

'Because learning how to dance in a room full of prejudice will surely be the boost he needs!'

'How do you know it will be a room full of prejudice when you have never taken a moment to know the character of a single soul in that room? But heaven forbid you should take into account their offers to help during and after the fire. The friendly daily calls to check on us since. If you could have seen Archie with them you would know they are not the enemy.'

'They barricaded the road and laid siege to my house with placards!' At her behest and under her leadership. But still!

'Because you tried to sell the ground from under them! If you had engaged with them, been upfront and honest as any decent sort would, rather than cagey and underhand, then all of that could have been avoided and they would have worked with you to reach a solution rather than against you. But you never gave them the chance to understand.'

He would go back and change that if he could as it wasn't his finest hour. However, he still would have shielded Archie. 'People are people wherever you go, Sophie, and I have met enough of them to know how they will react.'

'The irony of such prejudice coming from the lips of a man who claims to abhor it beggars belief.' He went to speak then clamped his jaws shut because he could not grope for a suitable enough answer. Sophie saw that chink in his armour and sighed. 'Bring Archie to the assembly tomorrow night. Meet them. Watch them. Give them the chance to prove to you that you might have misjudged them. And if you haven't...' Her hand gripped his as she sighed. 'What do you have to lose, Rafe, when you are leaving here anyway? At least give them a chance.'

'No. Hell would have to freeze over before I toss him to the wolves.'

'Wolves! Wolves! Have you gone quite mad?' She shook off his hand and instantly turned into Harpy Sophie again. 'You are holding him back, Rafe, because you—*you!*—' she prodded his chest with an accusatory finger '—are scared of the world not Archie. From where I stand it is not the other way around. That is also why you prefer to complain about the clutter in this dusty mausoleum than clear it away to find the beauty of this house too! You are a coward, *Captain* Peel, and I cannot bear to look at you!' She tossed back her hair and flounced towards the door, and all attempt at keeping a lid on his emotions flounced away with her.

'To be accused of fearing the world from the master of avoiding it is so rich it is laughable. At least I use my past to shape my future. You use yours to prevent having one, *Miss* Gilbert! For heaven forbid you should ever get past the sainted Michael when all the alluring promise of spinsterhood lies before you!' Her head whipped around, her fists clenched, her dark eyes incandescent and her expressive brows so knitted they merged together as one. 'And do not direct your eyebrows at me in that tone of voice, madam, when it is I who have been wronged here tonight!'

'How dare you bring Michael into this!'

'Oh, I dare, madam! I dare! For you hide your heart behind his memory like a coward and keep the rest of mankind at arm's length because you are scared that there is one of us here in the land of the living who might just have the gall to measure up!'

Her eyebrows exploded up her forehead like a firework, then the door slammed behind her with a decisive thud.

A split second later, Socrates revealed himself from his hiding place behind the sofa to hiss at Rafe and block him from following.

Not that he wanted to when he was in danger of laying his whole heart bare.

As he stalked out of the opposite door, cursing himself for already saying too much, he could not decide which vicious, belligerent cat he wanted to strangle first.

Chapter Twenty-Three

Sophie did not appreciate being partially in the wrong. Nor did she appreciate being caught between the devil and the deep blue sea. Yet there was no denying she was languishing in the doldrums dead centre of both with no clear way out of either. The villagers had put her in an impossible position with Rafe which was complicated by their difficult to define relationship. And Rafe's over-reaction to her visit to the village with Archie had made her mad at him as well as the villagers. They were all a bunch of idiots who needed their heads knocking to-gether and she included herself in that number, because she had been an idiot too.

With the benefit of a great many hours of hindsight, she was prepared to concede that she shouldn't have taken Archie on his first visit to the village without Rafe's permission. That did not mean she wasn't still furious at him for bringing up Michael or agreed with his assessment of the danger she had put Archie in. She had meant every word of her defence of the good people of Whittleston-on-the-Water even though she was furi-ous at them too for their unreasonable expectations. It wasn't fair to ask her to use all her powers of persuasion to bend him to their will. For one thing, he did not deserve to be manipulated in that way when he had been nothing but noble and decent to Sophie and her aunt. For another, it left a bad taste in the mouth with regards to both their growing friendship and their discreet physical relationship.

There was a name for women who seduced a man for their own profit, and even though that profit wasn't monetary, the name wasn't pretty and the transaction would feel the same. Mrs Fitzherbert could call it diplomacy till she was blue in the face, she still would not do it no matter how angry she was at Rafe!

All in all, with the battle lines redrawn between them, everything was now a huge mess and she supposed it was all no less than she deserved because things never ended well when one played with fire.

She tugged on her hand-me-down evening gloves and frowned at her reflection in the mirror before she came to the conclusion that not being able to stand the sight of herself had nothing whatsoever to do with her outfit.

She had to apologise. At least in part for their argument yesterday as her deft avoidance only seemed to make her feel worse. And she should probably do that before she stomped off down the lane to the local assembly as otherwise her attendance would look like another pointed dig when it was nothing of the sort. Or perhaps it was. She was so incensed by both situations she was prepared to concede her current mood was clouding everything and she wasn't being entirely rational.

But then again, neither was he...

The tap on the door put a blessed end to her endless pontificating. 'I am sorry to intrude, Miss Gilbert, but his lordship has asked me to inform you that the carriage is awaiting you outside.'

'The carriage to where?' It would be the icing on the cake if he was so aggrieved by the sour turn in their relationship, he had decided to evict her to Mrs Fitzherbert's tonight.

'To the assembly, miss. Seeing as it is raining cats and dogs.'

'Is it?' In her miserable quandary, she hadn't noticed. Yet now that she looked, rain pelted her window and wind rattled the glass in the frame. 'Tell his lordship I would not like to inconvenience him or take advantage of his hospitality any further than I already have, so am happy to walk.' It was a churlish, childish response, and one she wasn't proud of.

'Didn't I tell you she would say that, Walpole? There is nothing quite like the acrid scent of a burning martyr.' Rafe marched in and folded his arms. Both of his arms because he was minus his sling. 'But if you want to go to your blasted assembly looking like a drowned rat, who am I to argue.' Sophie's jaw hung slack in outrage.

'How dare...' She found herself staring at his raised palm.

'Ask your brows to stand down, madam. Just this once, as I dare say they have worked hard enough today already on my behalf and we need to make haste. Archie is in the carriage awaiting you in a state of fevered anticipation and is convinced you promised him the first dance, so step lively.'

Confused by his abrupt and complete about-turn, Sophie scurried after him onto the landing. 'You are allowing Archie to go to the assembly?'

'Your fault.' He did not turn around as he took the

stairs two at a time. 'So if it all goes wrong—which it inevitably will—I can blame you entirely for it.'

'I don't understand.'

He stopped dead at the bottom, and she almost crashed into the back of him. 'What is there to understand? As far as Archie is concerned he has been invited and will not hear that he is not. There have been more manipulative tantrums and tears, and so many egregious accusations, that I have been declared the heartless enemy who is ruining his life.' That final part was aimed at her because hurt swirled in his eyes. 'So for the sake of the quiet life I have been denied since I got here, and because you have turned my brother against me with your interference, I relented. So on his head— and yours—be it. I shall enjoy telling you both that I told you so when I have to charge in and pick up the pieces.' He folded his arms again; contrition, fear and murder warred in his eyes, highlighting the enormous battle he was engaged in with himself to relinquish his control.

Hers dipped to avoid witnessing his turmoil and blinked at the fancy cobalt silk embroidered waistcoat she had never seen before beneath his well-cut evening coat. 'You are coming with us.' She could not hide her surprise. 'Even though you prefer horses to people.'

'I might be spitting feathers at my stubborn brother's rebellion, but I am not leaving Archie to that ordeal alone. And…' He stared down at his boots. 'In the unlikely event that you are right and I am wrong…' He huffed as he raked a hand through his hair. 'This is an experiment, nothing more. A lesson to my brother that intolerance and ignorance thrive everywhere, and make no distinction no matter whether they hail from Somerset or from whinging Whittleston on the blasted Water.'

'They might surprise you.'

He rolled his eyes. 'They won't. But I shall make you right about just one tiny thing.' He held his thumb and index finger a fraction apart. 'I have nothing to lose when we are leaving here soon anyway.'

His loyalty and protectiveness disarmed her. His ability to go against the grain and heed her advice, even though it terrified him, humbled her. 'You are a good man, Rafe Peel.' She wanted to touch him. Kiss him. Cuddle him close and reassure him that everything was going to be all right. Fix his ruffled hair, neaten his lapels and then take his arm, but that all felt too wifely rather than friendly. Instead, she shrugged and smiled. 'What happened to your sling?'

'The sanctimonious sawbones has declared it redundant.' He was struggling to look at her without snarling. If she was a burning martyr, then he was definitely a wounded lion with a splinter in his paw.

'I am sorry I went behind your back yesterday. It was wrong of me to step on your toes, Rafe.'

He acknowledged her apology with a curt nod. 'I dare say Archie will avenge me by stepping on yours on my behalf during your dance. He has two left feet and is so excited he is particularly bouncy tonight—but as that is your fault too I have declared it your problem to deal with.' And with that, he stalked all the way to the carriage.

Several hours later and Archie, the ungrateful wretch, was having a whale of a time. He was butchering a country dance with the same enthusiasm as he had shown to the first and every subsequent dance since. His brother had eaten, drunk and been nothing but merry, lapping up every ounce of the copious amounts of attention which had been lavished on him by the locals who were bending over backwards to make them feel welcome.

Rafe wasn't feeling quite so merry. Thanks to his own reluctance to join in with the same wholeheartedness as his brother, he had been cornered for the last half an hour by Mr and Mrs Outhwaite.

'Dear Sophie said that you have already received an offer for the estate, my lord. From a London gentleman, although she was forgetful of the specifics. Could you enlighten us further? Or at the very least provide a name.' Mrs Outhwaite had him practically pinned to the wall. 'Only my dear husband here, being a respected and esteemed newspaper proprietor around these parts, also has many connections with Fleet Street and I am sure the entire village will sleep easier if we can do some digging into the gentleman's character.'

Rafe wouldn't mind doing some digging himself because a tunnel out of this claustrophobic village hall would be just the thing right this second. He had never been asked so many impertinent and personal questions in his life. It was all wrapped up in politeness, of course, but in typical quaint English village fashion, they all wanted to know everything about him from his army record to his inside leg measurement. For some reason, they all seemed to think he had a dead wife and no matter how many times he had denied any sort of wife at all, none of them seemed to believe it.

'The gentleman's name is Mr Stephen Bassett. He owns Bassett's Club in Piccadilly.' If the mostly mute newspaper propriety was as well connected in Fleet Street as his forceful wife claimed, Rafe should have seen some glimmer of recognition in his face, but he smiled back the bland smile of the oblivious. 'All I know of him is he is a former veteran of the Peninsula and has done rather well for himself since.'

His own discreet enquiries into Bassett's background had, if not set alarm bells ringing, ever so slightly raised his own soldier's hackles as the man had quite a ruthless reputation, albeit in business. But then, not being a businessman himself, or in any way, shape or form business-minded, Rafe also supposed it was a walk of life where a little ruthlessness would come in handy. The fellow had indulged in some impressive philanthropy too, so the former Lieutenant Bassett couldn't be all bad, even though a cursory glance through his well-documented donations did suggest he was selective about where he directed his charity. Favouring projects sponsored by the great and good rather than those struggling without an influential patron. That, of course, could be because all Mr Spiggot had found was the information in the public domain and there was every chance he was just as generous in private.

'Will he be coming next Saturday to view the estate with the others?' Mrs Outhwaite watched his reaction like a hawk. 'As Sophie mentioned, you had asked her to accompany you on that endeavour and is hopeful you will invite some of the other influential and upstanding residents of the village to come along.' She smiled as if butter would not melt in her mouth. 'Is that the case, my lord?'

'I would be only too happy to introduce the potential buyers to some of the people of the village, Mrs Outhwaite.' Although not this harridan who would likely scare them all off. 'I shall confer with Sophie as to what she has planned, but alas, Mr Bassett will not be attending as he has already shown himself around the estate.'

The barricade nor the protestors had intimidated the intrepid Mr Bassett and Rafe still wasn't certain if he admired that about him or if such a lack of regard for the obvious distress of others bothered him. He supposed, no matter how much he tried to ignore it, something about the owner of London's most fashionable club did not sit right with him, hence he hadn't invited him next Saturday and was eager to receive another offer in case his niggling gut feeling was correct.

'Oh, that is a shame.' If Mrs Outhwaite moved any closer, they would be intimate. 'What can you tell us about the gentlemen we will meet next Saturday?'

'There you are, Lord Hockley.' The pretty blonde flirt he had been introduced to earlier—Arabella? Isadora? Or was it neither of those?—grabbed his arm and pulled him out of Mrs Outhwaite's clutches. She hung onto his elbow proprietorially, her impressive bosom pressed against his bicep as she dragged him away. 'You promised me the final dance.'

He hadn't, because he hadn't asked a single woman to dance, not even the bewitching vixen he had arrived with and desperately wanted to. The flirty blonde waited until they were out of earshot before she giggled. 'Or at least you should have promised me this dance simply to escape that dour old battle-axe Mrs Outhwaite.' Then she giggled some more. 'No need to thank me for saving you. You can thank me by returning the favour at the next assembly when I am stuck with a dreary dullard. Or most particularly if I am stuck with Ned Parker which is always a fate worse than death.'

'Thank you, Miss…' While he searched his memory for the correct name she feigned annoyance.

'You don't remember, do you, Lord Hockley? I have made such a grand impression on you since you arrived in Whittleston that you do not know me from Adam.' She rolled her eyes and snuggled his arm a bit more. 'It is Isobel, my lord. Miss Isobel Cartwright. Not that you care one jot when your attention has been resolutely elsewhere all evening.' Her eyes swivelled to the dance floor where Sophie was curtsying to Archie and his brother was bowing back. 'If you had actually promised me this dance, I would be rightly peeved about that, but as you didn't, I will let it slide.' Bold as brass she led him to the floor as all the other dancers regrouped for the next number, then twirled before she dipped into an exaggerated curtsy.

'And what dance did I *not* promise you, Miss Isobel?'

'Why the waltz, of course, my dear Lord Hockley, as that is the one most likely to cause a splash. The Reverend Spears fears for the morality of his congregation and only allows one waltz per assembly and it is always the last dance. I make a point of always dancing it with someone dashing because it vexes Ned in the extreme and he never dances it because his feet are too big.' She had mentioned him twice and both with an unconscious glance in his direction.

'Are you and Ned…?' Because if they were that was marvellous, as it hadn't escaped his notice that Sophie had danced with her favourite human tree twice tonight already.

'Oh, good heavens, no!' Miss Isobel giggled again. 'I have my sights set on greater things than a curmudgeonly, common or garden farmer, my lord, and he disapproves of me almost as much as I disapprove of him. We've been at loggerheads since the cradle. Can you believe he thinks me flighty?' She arranged herself in his arms a tad too close, her green eyes dancing with mischief, and he could not help chuckling at her unapologetic impropriety.

'I cannot imagine why.' He slid his hand around her waist, trying not to care that Archie was doing the same to Sophie across the floor and wishing he could swap places with him. 'There is a huge difference between fun and flighty, Miss Isobel, and you are a delight.'

'That is the correct answer, my lord.' His effervescent partner beamed at him. 'I can see why Sophie likes you.'

'Does she?' She liked aspects of him rather than the whole package, and that was the main problem. She liked his body, there was no denying that. Or rather what his body could do to hers, but apart from the 'discreet comfort they took in one another's arms' when the rest of the house slept, she showed no particular partiality towards him beyond friendship. Once the deed was done and their bodies sated, she skipped off to her own room without a backwards glance. He was too proud to ask her to remain in case she rejected him, and as she had never shown any inclination to stay anyway he always bit his tongue. Outside of the Bewitching Hour as he had taken to calling it, he supposed they were friends. Usually. Which was hardly the gushing declaration of what his foolish heart increasingly wanted. 'I think tolerate would be a better word, especially given the unusual circumstances.'

She laughed at his failed nonchalance. 'Oh, my dear Lord Hockley, what a silly pair you are. Surely you must know that despite avoiding one another like the plague all evening, she watches you as much and as covetously as you watch her?' And there he was thinking he had been subtle. 'I'll wager she is watching you right now and pretending that she isn't.' She offered him a knowing grin when his eyes instantly flicked across the room. They caught Sophie's a split second before hers flicked away.

'I am right, aren't I?' Not that Isobel waited for a response. 'I have known Sophie for ten whole years, my lord, and in all that time she has never looked at any man in the way she looks at you. She looks, of course, because she is human and much too passionate in nature to be immune to their charms.' Something Rafe knew first-hand. 'But there is looking and *looking*, my lord, as you well know, and as her friend I demand to know what you intend to do about it.'

'Do?' And there was the rub, for he could do nothing. She was headed in one direction, still wedded to the imposing shadow cast by her beloved Michael, and him in another. Alone as usual, if he didn't count Archie. 'I have no plans to *do* anything, Miss Isobel, for you are mistaken. There is no *looking*. Sophie and I have called a friendly truce to hostilities, that is all.' Or at least they had up until their argument yesterday which still wasn't resolved.

Blasted woman and her blasted unwanted opinions. Thanks to her he had been second-guessing himself since yesterday. Reorganising the furniture and redecorating the mausoleum in his head. Seeing the potential of the albatross around his neck rather than the weight of it. Was he using Archie as an excuse to hide from the world? If actively avoiding the bitter sting of rejection and the blunt hammer of ignorance was hiding, then he supposed he was. Experience had taught him to always expect the worst from people but that wasn't always the case. In his army days there were men who would have died for him. Friends he had allowed himself to lose contact with since his return because…well, keeping himself separate was what he did and, despite all their loyalty, he still feared they would let him down. People wounded you less if you were detached from them. His detachment was self-preservation.

But was he holding his brother back as a result? He had been convinced tonight would be an unmitigated disaster which would prove all his ingrained fears entirely right, but watching Archie having fun and being welcomed into the fold exactly as Sophie had predicted, he wasn't sure what to think any longer.

Her again. Playing with his head as well as his emotions.

'Then you disappoint me, my lord.' Isobel released a theatrical sigh. 'For I had high hopes for you. I was convinced if anyone could turn her head away from her past then it would be you as she is as suited to a life of dull and determined spinsterhood about as much as I am. But if you are not up to the task, lack the necessary gumption to woo her and are prepared to give up so easily…' She sighed, then lent closer and gazed at him in convincing adoration. 'Indulge me for a moment. Look upon me with keen male interest even though you do not feel it, twirl me their way, and if her eyes do not shoot daggers in our direction I will acknowledge you are right and there is nothing to be done. But if they do, and *I* am right, then you really do need to do something about it, as I can promise you that that stubborn wench won't and she'll wave you a stoic goodbye without a murmur—even if it breaks her heart to do it.'

Chapter Twenty-Four

'I told you that you would enjoy yourself.' Sophie tried to sound casual after they tucked Fred and Archie in, even though her over-bright smile made her teeth ache. 'You and Isobel seemed to have got on well.' So well they had cosied up with one another, chatting for a good half an hour after the final waltz, and Rafe had to be chivvied by Archie to finish their laughing conversation and get into the carriage.

'Isobel is great fun.' Something about his wistful smile really galled. 'Her parents are lovely too. They have invited me to dinner next week.'

'Good heavens!' She had to work hard not to sound churlish. 'Doth my ears deceive me or have you made a friend in the village? Whatever next, Rafe, when you were so determined to despise them all.'

'I can't say I have any pleasant thoughts about Mrs Outhwaite. She proved to be as obnoxious tonight as she was the first time I heard her maligning me in the market square. I assume she is the one responsible for suggesting I murdered my wife under suspicious circumstances? You might have warned me that that was the egregious rumour, Sophie, as it came as quite a shock to discover that is what the Whittleston whingers all thought.'

'I had forgotten she had said that.'

'Well, you might have forgotten—but I had the devil of the job convincing some of your neighbours of the fact. I swear Mrs Harbottle, the baker's wife, is convinced I left my imaginary spouse mouldering under my floorboards in Somerset with the rest of my rattling family skeletons.' He laughed, unoffended, and shook his head. 'Some aspects of village life are interchangeable wherever you go. They are all fuelled on gossip.'

'If it is any consolation, most take everything Mrs Outhwaite says with a pinch of salt. I never believed you had shoved your imaginary wife under the floorboards.'

His feet slowed as they approached the facing doors of their bedchambers. 'Are we friends again? I feel dreadful for using your grief for Michael as a weapon. That was wrong of me and I am sorry.'

'And I feel dreadful for interfering in your affairs. You are the best brother in the world to Archie and...' For some reason, only the truth felt appropriate. 'In all honesty, I was in a foul mood before I gave you a piece of my mind. I had already lost my temper with Mrs Outhwaite and Mrs Fitzherbert and I took that out on you. Unfairly.' She stared at her hands, heartily ashamed of what the women had tried to goad her into doing.

'It doesn't matter.' His finger lifted her chin and he placed a soft kiss on her lips. 'I missed you last night.' Desire darkened his eyes. 'Lie with me.'

'About that...' As much as she wanted to lose herself in his arms, she could not do it with all the guilt on her shoulders placed there by the villagers. 'You should probably know that I lost my temper with the ladies because they implied that I should use my wiles on you to make you change your mind about selling.' She risked peeking up at him, only to see him shrug.

'That is actually not a bad plan.' He took her hand and laced his fingers through hers. 'Certainly a better one than your barricade.' He released the door with his free hand and tugged her inside. 'And one that just might work.'

She expected the usual hurry to tear off each other's clothes and tumble on the bed so they could get straight to the passion, but that did not happen. He seemed quite content to simply kiss her, something she realised they hadn't indulged in that much before. They always kissed with hunger before and after the deed was done, but they did not linger like he was now. Savouring the taste of her mouth as if it were some exotic fruit. That both thrilled her and panicked her in equal measure because it felt too intimate. A ridiculous thought when she had given him free rein over her body since that first night.

She tried to deepen the kiss and he deflected, nibbling her ear and her jaw and her neck, so she wrestled with the knot of his cravat to speed things up, only to have him catch her wrists gently in his and lower them to her sides. 'Finally, I have two working arms, so I am in charge tonight, witch.'

Her pulse ratcheted up several notches. Excitement again tinged with panic at relinquishing her control. Rafe like this was dangerous. Already every nerve ending was fizzing with anticipation. Her body melting beneath his tender ministrations. Aching. Wanting. Powerless to detach from the emotion in her heart.

He took his own sweet time undressing her while he kissed her. Peeling off every layer with reverence while teasing her with his caress. Her breathing was laboured by the time she stood before him naked, her body so desperate to join with his that her limbs were weak with anticipation. Her fingers shook as she tried to undress him and again he denied her the right. Instead, he lifted her and kissed her deeply before he laid her on the mattress, then held her gaze as he stripped himself bare.

Stood proud, naked, aroused in the lamplight, he took her breath away. Yet again, despite the obvious readiness of his body, he was still determined to take his time. He sat beside her on the mattress and traced only a single fingertip over her sensitised flesh. Face, lips, neck. Then he repeated his lazy trail with his lips.

Collarbone, upper arm, breast. Only replacing his finger with his lips when her nipples were so tight they ached. She tried to reciprocate. Tried to drag his big body down to her, but Rafe was having none of it. He sat back, his blue eyes shimmering with hunger as they raked the length of her. 'How many times do I have to tell you that I am in charge tonight, minx?' He grazed her abdomen with his dratted fingertip, watching its progress as it wandered over her navel and down into the soft curls below where they stopped short of where she needed it to be. He smiled at the involuntary arch of her hips as her body strained for release. 'The more you rebel against me, the more I will dig my heels in.' Then the timbre of the smile changed from one of smugness to one of wonder as he drank in the sight of her. 'God, you are beautiful, Sophie Gilbert. So beautiful I consider myself the luckiest man alive.'

The intensity of the blue in his eyes told her he meant it. The tenderness of his touch, the way each caress felt like a worship, told her he also cared about her. Out of nowhere, his angry parting shot from their argument yesterday whispered fragmented through her brain.

You hide your heart like a coward...

Keep the rest of mankind at arm's length...

You are scared that there is one of us here in the land of the living who might just have the gall to measure up...

Was he putting himself forward as a candidate? Jaded Rafe who preferred horses to people? Who was determined to sell this mausoleum and escape from all the human race as soon as possible? No...

No. Surely not.

'You don't have to be jealous of Isobel Cartwright.' Words she both needed to hear and wished she hadn't. 'She doesn't hold a candle to you, my darling.'

Darling? Her frightened heart stuttered at the endearment. Her head though—that wanted to run screaming for the hills.

She wanted to remind him of the parameters. Remind him that theirs was a physical relationship because it wasn't just her body he was currently seducing. It was something else. He was forcing her to feel her own emotions. Forcing her to feel his. But he had dipped his tormenting finger between her soft folds to worship her core and then she could barely think at all.

If she feared the intimacy of his kisses, his next scandalously intimate kiss sent her spiralling into the unknown. Not even Michael's mouth had tasted between her thighs before. It had never occurred to either of them to try it, but Rafe was more of a man of the world and he had clearly loved many women because he knew how to play her body like an instrument. Within seconds, she was moaning and writhing on the mattress until her climax smashed into her like a tidal wave, robbing her of both breath and thought as she sank back onto the pillows boneless with stars in her eyes.

When she surfaced from the sensual fog, he was lying on top of her, the ghost of smile on his lips and blatant affection in his intuitive eyes. 'My turn.' He swallowed her giggle in another searing kiss and refused to budge when she tried to turn him onto his back. 'And I am in charge.' Yet they both knew he would not move a muscle unless she agreed to it.

He saw her indecision. Gently kissed away her fear. 'Trust me, Sophie.'

As her head tried to comprehend the meaning and ramifications of that statement, her wanton, wayward body acted on impulse. Before she could stop it, she was nodding. Pulling his head down for another poignant, heart-rending, indulgent kiss and opening her body so his could fill it.

Which he did with aching slowness, and as he began to move and before she lost her wits all over again, his gaze locked with hers and her soul seemed to meld with his, she realised that this wasn't just a carnal joining of their bodies. A coupling driven by loneliness and desire or the scratching of a mutual itch. Or even a moment of reckless madness.

This was more significant.

This shifted all the parameters.

This—heaven help her—was making love.

Rafe awoke with an arm full of woman and his heart full to bursting. Sophie being Sophie, she had tried to creep away in the night as he dozed, and he had tugged her back and cuddled her close until she fell asleep for a change. That she was still asleep filled him with joy.

That apart from the tangled sheet gathered at her hips and his arms around her waist she was naked and bathed in daylight for the first time filled him with instant lust.

She was on her back. One arm thrown over her head. Full breasts bare and tempting. Her dark hair was a tousled riot across his pillow. Because he could not help himself, he kissed her lips and she sighed in response before she kissed him sleepily back.

'Good morning.'

Her tremulous smile was a little shy and awkward at the new intimacy of the morning, and she pulled the sheet up to cover her nudity as best she could around the cage of his arms.

'I have a proposition for you.' One he had been mulling over during the night while she slept and he had re-evaluated everything he had convinced himself was true. All the set-in-stone plans he had made before this moment smashed to smithereens and gladly because he had wielded the mallet.

Her eyebrows quirked in a knowing, sultry manner before they kissed in consternation. 'The house will be waking soon and they cannot find me here.' Then she smiled again, her eyes darkening. 'But you can ravish me again tonight.'

'I wasn't proposing another ravishing right this second, but I am always game if you are.' Oh, how he adored how she adored the physical and how she never used that passion to play coy games.

She brushed her hand down his spine to rest in the small of his back, the heat of desire already in her lovely eyes. 'Then what are you proposing?'

'I am actually proposing not being averse to the prospect of proposing.' His heart hammered against his ribs and hers at the admission, not quite believing it himself even though it felt right. 'Someday, in the distant future, so don't look so scared.' Although scared was the wrong word. Dumbstruck and frozen were better adjectives to describe her reaction. The warm, womanly body beneath his was now as stiff as a board. 'You see, the thing is...' There was panic etched in her expression now and the hand which had rested above his buttocks had fallen away. 'Against all my better judgement, it appears that I have fallen in love with you.'

The truth hurt to speak. Laying himself bare and vulnerable went against everything life had conditioned him to do. The undeniable emotion causing tight bands to wrap around his vocal chords and heart. Fear made his pulse stutter. Fear of the usual rejection. Fear of the speed, strength and depth of his feelings. Feelings he had never felt for Annabel. Feelings which made him light-headed. Raw. Hopeful. Exposed. Reckless enough to risk everything for a future he had never dared to want.

'Don't say that.' She pushed him away and rolled to sit, pulling the sheet to follow which she clutched around her chest like a shield. 'Please don't say that.' Of all the understandable resistance he had expected from her, complete abhorrence wasn't one of them. 'We barely know one another and we agreed this...' She flapped her hand between them. 'Wasn't ever going to be like that.' She groped for her chemise on the floor, anger making her movements jerky, and that anger cut Rafe like a knife.

'I knew staying here with you all night would be a mistake. Just as allowing you to be in charge was a mistake. Now it has given you fanciful ideas which are not the least bit practical, let alone possible with me staying here in Whittleston with Aunt Jemima and you leaving for the middle of nowhere!'

'Of course they are possible.'

Stay calm. Appear reasonable. Stay measured. Remain in control at all costs.

Her panic was a visceral but irrational reaction borne out of fear, grief and guilt. She didn't want her heart broken again. That made two of them, and frankly what he was proposing scared the hell out of him too. But losing her scared him more.

'I could stay here.' He stroked her arm, taking some comfort that she did not recoil from his touch. 'It occurs to me that that might not be a bad idea seeing as Archie has settled and you are right: I've been bemoaning this cluttered mausoleum for weeks when it is hardly this house's fault that my predecessor filled it to the rafters with ugly furniture. I can easily throw it all away and start afresh. *We* could start afresh together.' She still did not pull away although the furrow between her eyebrows was so deep it would hold a pencil without any bother. Maybe even two. 'Between us we could turn this place into a proper home for all four of us to live in. There's plenty of land to raise hundreds of horses, and with you by my side I could probably learn to tolerate the revolting locals so long as they abandon their placards.'

He forced a smile at the pathetic joke, hoping it wouldn't pour oil on troubled water. 'I know this seems like a big step. I also know that it is an unexpected bolt out of the blue when neither of us thought in a million years that this would happen. And I am not proposing I propose anytime soon, or even that I have any expectation that you would say yes…merely that you would consider it. That you would risk giving us a chance.'

She sucked in a ragged breath as a whole spectrum of troubling emotions danced across her features. Her dark eyes bleak, she finally shook her head. 'I can't. I won't. I'm sorry, Rafe.'

'Don't you have any feelings for me?' Because she wouldn't have been jealous of Isobel if she didn't harbour some. Or at least that is what he had convinced himself last night when he had decided to throw all caution to the wind. 'Last night I swear I saw the same feelings mirrored in your eyes.' He had seen them and felt them in her choked kisses after she had shattered in his arms. The way she had held him as if she never wanted to let him go. All different from the usual and not figments of his imagination. 'Listen to your heart, Sophie—not your head. Please.'

She did recoil then and surged to her feet, fighting her head and torso into the chemise as if it was her only way out. 'We are friends, Rafe. *Friends.*' Her head emerged for only as long as it took her to find her discarded dress and burrow inside that like a shelter. Her lush body finally covered, she scrambled around for everything else, rolling stockings, shoes and stays into a tighter bundle each time she added one to the pile. One solitary shoe sat near his feet and he bent to pick it up, only to have it snatched out of his hand. 'I do not understand why you would want to spoil that!'

Stay calm. Appear reasonable. Stay measured. Remain in control at all costs.

Control! What a joke!

As if he had ever been in control wherever she was concerned! She had led him on a merry dance, tied him up in ribbons and made him want things he had long given up any delusions of wanting. 'Because I love you, that is why!' He shot to his own feet and caught her by the elbows. 'I want more than your passion and your body, you maddening, stubborn witch. I want more than discretion or the temporary or the convenient comfort of a willing body in my bed. I want you with me all the time.'

She responded by spinning out of his grasp and marching to the door. So fast it was a miracle he was able to stop her before she disappeared through it. And even though his head cautioned him not to beg, he couldn't seem to stop. 'I am not trying to replace Michael in your affections as I know that I could never replace him. I am not even suggesting we have children if that worries you.' He hadn't realised how much he had wanted them until that moment—but he wanted her more. 'I just want you, Sophie.' He kissed her nose. Her forehead. Her lips. 'All of you.'

Her bottom lip quivered as she stared at him for an eternity, then a single tear spilled over her lashes. 'I cannot give you any more of me than I already have, Rafe. I thought you understood that.'

Chapter Twenty-Five

Irrespective of the damage it could do to his shoulder, the wretched fool galloped off in a cloud of dust that afternoon when Ned loaded the last of Sophie and Aunt Jemima's cobbled together hand-me-down belongings into his cart while Archie stood by distressed. She had not seen or heard hide nor hair of him in the week since but thought about him constantly. She didn't want to. Tried her best not to. But with tomorrow looming like the Grim Reaper, it was impossible to bottle all her tangled emotions inside like she usually did when they hurt too much.

She had never dreaded a day more. She had no clue how he would react to her by his side when they showed the clutch of potential buyers around the estate tomorrow, or even if he still wanted her to be there. He hadn't sent any word to the contrary nor had he sent any in confirmation. For the sake of the village, she had to go. For the sake of her own sanity, she would rather not, because seeing him, taking those first, painful steps towards saying a permanent goodbye to him, would be torture. Steps that signalled the beginning of the end.

Once a buyer was chosen, the papers would be drawn and signed, and then, like the sand pouring through an hourglass, she would have to count down the days to the end. A process which might take months, but could take weeks if he raced it all through. Which, knowing Rafe, he would because she had hurt him.

After that, she would never see him again. Never spar with him. Talk to him. Laugh with him. Hold him.

A stark and unpalatable reality she was nowhere near prepared for.

'Oh, good heavens above, girl, stop moping!' The thud of Mrs Fitzherbert's cane on the floor made Sophie jump. 'You've been staring at the rain for an hour.'

As she had been so lost she hadn't even noticed the sheets of rain pummelling the window, Sophie jabbed her needle in her embroidery with purpose. 'I was wool-gathering.' She forced a smile to the three ladies in Mrs Fitzherbert's warm parlour where they had relocated a fraction of the Friday Sewing Circle so that Aunt Jemima could join in. 'Thinking about the potential buyers tomorrow and what to ask them.'

'By wool-gathering, she means pining,' said Isobel beside her. 'And by thinking about potential buyers, she means that she is thinking about him incessantly. She misses her handsome lord and wants him back.'

'I do not!' Although she did. She missed everything about Rafe, from his safe, reassuring presence to his dry wit. His solid, distracting body to his soulful bright blue eyes.

'Then why are you off your food?' Mrs Fitzherbert glared. 'Why are you not sleeping? And why, pray tell, do you keep staring off into space with the most irritating winsome and tragic expression on your face? If you want the fellow as we all suspect you do, go get him, girl.' All three ladies nodded in unison with pity and frustration.

'I don't want him.'

'And I am a unicorn,' said Isobel unhelpfully. 'You pine for him just as he pines for you. Ned said he caught you crying when you left Hockley Hall. You—miss hard-hearted and no nonsense—huddled in a doorway sniffling into your handkerchief.'

'I had some dust in my eye. Hockley Hall is a factory for the stuff.'

'And now I am a unicorn too.' That came from Aunt Jemima who tossed her embroidery hoop onto the table and rolled her eyes. 'The pair of them were in despair when she rushed me out of that house. Wretched despair. She was in a blind panic and was behaving as if the sky was about to fall and he was stomping about and slamming doors and screaming at the servants.' Her aunt squeezed her hand in sympathy. 'Archie told me Rafe proposed.'

'He proposed!' Mrs Fitzherbert beamed at the news. 'Why, that is marvellous! Why didn't you say so sooner? You marrying him solves all of our problems!'

'I am not marrying him and he didn't propose!' At least not in so many words. A proposal would have been easier to deal with than his unsettling and hopeful declaration of love. She could have politely declined a proposal. Rejecting his love had been gut-wrenching. It would have been easier to cut off her own arm than it had been to walk away from him. But she couldn't listen to her heart as he had begged, no matter how much it screamed at her to succumb. What if she lost him?

What if history repeated itself? How on earth could she continue?

'Urgh!' Isobel groaned as she threw her sewing down too. 'Of course you are not marrying him. Why on earth would you want to marry a handsome, rich and besotted earl when you have the dried-out husk of spinsterhood to keep you warm?'

'I am not marrying a man I do not love.' Sophie glared at all of them. 'Not even for the sake of the village.'

'Nobody's asking you to marry a man you do not love, Sophie dear.' Aunt Jemima patted her hand again as if she were a silly child. 'We are merely baffled why you refused Rafe when it is plainly obvious to anyone with eyes that you are head over heels in love with the man.'

'I am not.' Because of course she wasn't. She would never have allowed herself to be that stupid. That was why she'd set such strict parameters. Why she'd kept the carnal and the friendship separate. Why she'd resolutely quashed every single errant thought which dared to think otherwise. She touched her chest. Conjured Michael and all the pain of her past as a reminder of what it was she was tactically avoiding. 'I have been in love—deeply in love—and cannot risk it again.'

'Why ever not?' Mrs Fitzherbert pulled a face.

'He died,' offered her aunt before Sophie could open her mouth. 'It broke her heart.'

'Poppycock.' Mrs Fitzherbert frowned as if she was mad. 'Hearts are meant to be broken and people die, yet the world still turns. Where would the human race be if we all adopted that defeatist attitude? It would come to shuddering end, that is what. The good Lord granted us the gift of life and therefore it is our duty to Him to live it to the fullest!' The cane came down like a judge's gavel. 'What is the old adage? It's better to have loved and lost than never to have loved at all.' She waved it away as if the agony of losing that love was nothing at all. 'I thought your motto was onwards and upwards? You mourn but you must move on. Exactly like I did.'

'I loved Michael dearly!' She would not be lectured by an old lady who replaced husbands like she did hats. 'He was the only one for me. The. Only. One.'

'More poppycock.' Mrs Fitzherbert slapped one wizened hand on the tablecloth. 'I loved each of my husbands with all of my heart and each time they were cruelly taken from me I swore I would never love again with the same fervour. But then fate called me a liar every time by sending me another man who filled my heart with the same purpose and the same joy. Each one vastly different, of course, as variety is the spice of life, but the feeling was the same. Just as all encompassing. Just as right. Just as passionate.' She sighed at the memories. 'It would have been easier to give up breathing than deny myself the pleasure of my husbands in my bed.'

'Shh.' Always a prude, Aunt Jemima nudged her incorrigible friend. 'There are single ladies present who may be shocked by such sentiments.'

The cane thumped the floor three times as Mrs Fitzherbert stared at all three of them in turn. 'Poppycock, poppycock and more poppycock.' The last one was for Sophie. 'You told me yourself, Jemima, that Sophie spent every single night in Lord Hockley's bed and I dare say they weren't darning by candlelight.' She narrowed her eyes at Isobel who was grinning at all the shocking scandal she was hearing as if all her Christmases had come at once. 'It would take a miracle for this one to still be intact.' Then she skewered Sophie's aunt with narrowed eyes. 'And do not get me started on the subject of you and Caleb Parker, Jemima Gilbert.'

'Caleb Parker?' Isobel was beside herself with glee. 'You had a fling with Ned's father?'

'It was more than a fling, dear.' Mrs Fitzherbert cackled as her aunt winced. 'He crept into Willow Cottage at least twice a week for twenty years!' At Sophie's widened eyes, she shrugged. 'Few of us go to heaven in a box marked unopened, and people who live in glass houses have no right to be shocked. Your aunt is a flesh-and-blood woman and women have the same needs as men.'

'He was married.' Aunt Jemima winced again as she tried to explain away the bombshell. 'Married and long separated from his horrid wife by a good hundred miles of road. But he died before she did, so we could never make things official.'

'But all that is by the by,' said Mrs Fitzherbert with an imperious flick of the wrist. 'It is Sophie's dilemma we must address, for she is the one at war with her desires. Tell us about Michael. Was he a good man?'

The abrupt change of topic and unfeeling criticism made her stiffen. 'The best.' Or one of them. Rafe certainly measured up in that.

'Was he generous in nature and kind of heart?'

Sophie nodded. 'He was wonderful in every way.'

'How lucky of you to have found a saint for they are thin on the ground.' Mrs Fitzherbert's comment made her bristle as it echoed Rafe's too much for comfort. 'But he had character too, didn't he? As a maddening, stubborn and opinionated woman like yourself would soon tire of a doormat.'

Smiling for the first time in a decade at the memory

of the man who had been taken too soon, Sophie nodded again. 'He was his own man.'

And he had been. Determined. Tenacious. So full of life nothing got him down for long. Not even her father's cruel treatment, the loss of his livelihood and his prospects dampened the fire that burned in his belly. 'Damn them all to hell,' he had said as he had left Cheapside with his head held high. 'It makes no difference,' he had assured her as he had kissed her goodbye that dreadful day. 'I am not giving you up, Sophie Gilbert, not for all the tea in China.'

And he hadn't. For two years he had moved heaven and earth to be with her and their love affair had continued undaunted. Unhindered by the many barricades fate and her father had thrown in their path. They had loved, laughed and made plans with impunity. Plans they would have carried out if fate hadn't intervened. Onwards and upwards had been his motto. Onwards and upwards and to hell with the lot of them.

'But he drove you to distraction too, didn't he? I'll bet you fought like cat and dog. Locked horns with the same frequency as you locked lips.'

Mrs Fitzherbert had that right too. She and Michael had both been leaders. Both had a stubborn streak a mile wide. She had forgotten about all the petty things they had argued about. As she felt herself frowning, the old lady cackled again. 'But it was fun making it up, wasn't it? For those flaws are what makes us human and when we love with all our hearts we embrace them as fully as we cherish the good. Did he love you, young lady?'

'To distraction.' Her tenacity and stubbornness always amused Michael. Her passion delighted him and her dreams inspired him as much as his inspired her. 'He loved me with every fibre of his being.'

'And what would he say if he could see you now?' Two wily old eyes bored into hers. 'Is this the life he would have wanted you to live? And if the tables had been turned, and you had been the one who had died and left him to face the future all alone, is this the lonely, directionless and purposeless future you would have wanted for a man you loved with all of your heart?'

The wind knocked out of her sails, Sophie gaped as she struggled to formulate an answer. Pride, guilt and stubbornness made her want to nod and kill this painful conversation stone dead, yet she couldn't. Because she knew she would have been furious at Michael if he had stood still when he deserved everything. Everything and more. And he would have owed it to the both of them to do it.

'Mrs Fitzherbert.' The maid poked her head into the parlour. 'You have a caller.'

Sophie did not realise how much she wanted it to be Rafe until Ned strode in, closely followed by a dripping Archie and an equally soggy Fred.

'Where is your brother?' Aunt Jemima asked the question she couldn't.

'Packing. Sulking.' By the defiant jut of his jaw, the youngest and the eldest Peel had had words. 'But I couldn't leave without saying goodbye no matter what Rafe says, so I crept away and I do not care if it makes him angry.'

'Goodbye? Now?' The whooshing in her head made her dizzy. 'But what about tomorrow. The buyers? The sale.'

'Mr Spiggot is going to show them all around and sell

the mossy-leem because Rafe says he's done with all of it. We are leaving this morning but...' Archie rifled in his pocket and pulled out a sodden piece of paper which he handed to her. On it was his scruffy handwriting. 'I wanted you to have our address in Cheapside so you can come and visit if you want.' The tragic hope in his bright blue eyes tore her to ribbons. 'And I shall write to you every day to tell you what we are doing and let you know the new address once we've bought our new farm so you can visit that too.' He launched himself at her and squeezed her tight. 'You will visit, won't you, Sophie? I couldn't bear it if I never see you again.'

Tears pooled in her eyes as they locked with Aunt Jemima's and her aunt shrugged. 'You are doomed to grieve him whether he leaves or dies, Sophie dearest. Either way will feel like the end of the world.'

Rafe fastened his satchel to Atlas with a decisive tug then hollered for his brother. 'Archie! We're going!' He did not care that his sibling had been inconsolable since last night when he had informed him they were off or that he, himself, had been unbearable all week until he had come to that inescapable conclusion. Nor did he care that the freezing rain was pelting down with a ferocity which guaranteed the two-hour ride would take twice as long because the roads would be a quagmire. All he cared about was putting as much distance between him and this cursed place as soon as possible. He could not face her tomorrow and pretend to be reasonable and calm on the back of her cutting rejection. And it had cut him. Deeper and wider than any rejection ever had in the past because she had mattered so much.

Yet now, in the grand scheme of people who had disappointed him, she was the biggest disappointment of them all.

Blasted witch! Oh, how he wished he had never met her. Never set foot in this godforsaken village at all when he could have sold it sight unseen and conscience unbothered from the comfort of the city.

'Archie! Get yourself down here now!' If he had to drag his brother kicking and screaming downstairs and strap him onto Alan like a blasted saddlebag, they were leaving straight away. Right this minute. Nothing whatsoever would deter him from that. 'Archie!'

'He's at Mrs Fitzherbert's.' He spun around to see a drowned rat. The most beautiful drowned rat that ever lived. Her dark hair hung in dripping strands that stuck to her cheeks. In the absence of a coat, her wool dress was plastered to her body. Water spiked her lashes as she shrugged. 'Safe and sound. He told me you were leaving.'

Because looking at her was more agony he did not need, he turned to double-check his horse's reins. 'There is little incentive to stay.'

'A wise man once told me that any decision taken in the heat of the moment should never be trusted because it is always wrong. Especially concerning matters of the heart.'

'What do you want, Sophie?' He would hand over the deeds to the whole estate if she asked him to, simply to get away from her right now.

'You. Apparently. No matter how much I try to deny it.'

He stilled but did not turn around. Did not dare in case his addled mind was hearing wrong or misinterpreting her words to soothe his misery.

'Please don't leave, Rafe. Please don't do something now that we'll both regret for ever.'

Time stilled and slowed. His heart stopped. Emotion choked him as he dared to hope again. 'Then give me one good reason to stay.' He clenched his hands into fists behind his back as he turned to face her. Needing to see the truth rather than grab the flimsy illusion of it with both hands. It had to be all or nothing.

Had to be, as nothing else would be enough.

She swallowed and closed her eyes. Steeling her slim shoulders. 'Because I love you.' She blew out a slow breath as if admitting that cost her everything. 'I wish I didn't—but I do.'

His laughter escaped like a bubble. Relief and wonder made his head spin. She loved him.

Sophie *loved* him.

She lay her palm against her heart as she edged towards him. 'It terrifies me. So much so that I tried to ignore it and when that didn't work I pushed you away. But the truth is I am miserable without you. I don't feel whole when you are not around. You made me live again, Captain Peel, and you are worth the risk. Just don't ever die on me.' She touched his cheek. Traced the shape of his features. Her expressive eyebrows a solid line of pain. 'Promise me you'll never die.'

He smoothed them with his fingers then kissed away the tension which knitted them together. 'I shall do my best. I cannot promise more than that.'

Tears mingled with the raindrops on her face as she nodded while she rearranged his dripping lapels. 'If fate is kind, I shall die first then I will never have to mourn you.'

'As I shall be the one in charge, I am afraid I cannot allow that. I have to go first. I couldn't bear it otherwise.'

'Then I am afraid we are about to have our first argument.' Even she had to laugh at the absurdness of that statement.

'Our first today, I presume, or do we brush all the placards and barricades under the carpet and pretend they didn't happen?'

'Our first as an official couple. And there will be no more barricades.' She brushed her lips over his. 'From either of us. Fate will doubtless throw more obstacles in our way as the years go by without our erecting our own nonsense to scupper us. In the spirit of compromise, I have decreed that when we are so old and wizened that the end is nigh, we shall both throw ourselves over a cliff so neither of us ever have to go through the ordeal of mourning the other. Besides, it will be cheaper for our children not to have to bury us.'

'You want children.' A lump formed in Rafe's throat.

'In for a penny, in for a pound. I am afraid I have decreed that too and will not be swayed from the decision or ever regret it if we are blessed with another treasure like Archie.' She kissed him. Long, passionate and earthy. A promise of things to come as well as an acceptance of whatever their future held. He smiled against her lips, thankful suddenly for so much, but most of all for fate sending him here. To whinging Whittleston on the blasted Water so he could finally meet his soulmate. He tore his mouth away to glare at her even though his jaded heart was bursting.

'Oh, you have decreed it, have you? I do not recall agreeing that you would be in charge of everything, minx.'

'In what army does a mere captain get to issue orders

to a general?' She quirked one vexing, maddening, beguiling dark eyebrow and pulled him by the lapels as the rain soaked them both to the skin and washed all the past away. 'So kiss me, Captain Peel. Right now, tomorrow and every day. For as long as we both shall live.'

'I am going to ignore that ridiculous order.' He grabbed her hand and tugged her to follow. 'Because I have a much better idea. Seeing as Archie is safe and sound we might as well take advantage of the peace to take advantage of each other instead.'

'But it is the middle of the morning!' She dug her heels in as those vexing brows met for a split second before her lovely eyes heated. Then she smiled the sinful, knowing smile which he would adore until they were both older and more wizened than Mrs Fitzherbert. 'Shame on you, Lord Hockley.'

* * * * *

Look out for the next book in
Virginia Heath's
A Very Village Scandal miniseries
coming soon!

And whilst you're waiting for the next book,
why not check out her other miniseries
The Talk of the Beau Monde?

The Viscount's Unconventional Lady
The Marquess Next Door
How Not to Chaperon a Lady